DEAD AND GONE

MARK L. DRESSLER

© 2017 Mark L. Dressler
All rights reserved.

ISBN: 0999062301
ISBN 13: 9780999062302

DEDICATION

This book is dedicated to my family:
Karen and Sherri
Zach, Alex, Kate, Eli, Brianna, Big Josh, Matt, Rich, Anna, and Little Josh

Especially to my loving wife Patricia whose faith, encouragement, and support made it possible for me to complete this novel.

In memory of Buster, Shiloh, and Rusty; twelve paws of enjoyment.

To my nephews Todd and Alan who were taken too soon.

ACKNOWLEDGEMENTS

Thanks to those who helped me along the way to publication.
Joellen Adai, Lew Nedell, Mary Restelli, Rick Risley
Editors Stacey Longo Harris, and Rob Smales
Cover designer Jeanine Henning

A special thanks to my cousin and best friend Marshall Dressler

PART ONE

He broke all the rules. Detective Dan Shields knew he should have followed protocol, but that just wasn't in his playbook.

Dan had been in room 317 at Hartford's Woodland Hospital, unconscious for nine hours with an IV in his arm, oxygen filling his lungs. When his eyes had finally opened he couldn't speak, and it took him a few seconds to realize where he was. His upper body was bandaged and sore from surgery that had removed a twenty-two caliber bullet from his chest. The pillow under his head hid seven stitches in his scalp.

Surviving that near-death experience, six years ago, made the hard-nosed detective keenly aware of the dangers of his job.

⋏

Dan parked his car in the nearly empty police lot, and he headed inside the dilapidated Morgan Street jail. Slated to be replaced by a modern facility, this ancient concrete structure reminded him of Rome's Colosseum; it was his place to play gladiator. The forty-four year old detective's habit of strolling through the holding tank was strangely therapeutic.

Wearing tan Chinos, a yellow button-down, and a brown jacket, he entered the noisy, foul-smelling dungeon. "Morning Dan," Sergeant Dom Denine said. "Got some new ones for you."

"Thanks Dom, can't wait to see them."

The detective began his walk through the tank, eying last night's haul of junkies, thieves, and misfits. Stopping midway down the dreary cellblock, he peered into an unlocked empty cage, opened it, and stepped inside. A mouse shot past his feet into a crack in one corner of the cold cement floor and Dan froze, feeling as if a ghost were standing beside him. Seconds later he quickly turned, exited the cell, and clanked the door shut. The detective carried his five eleven, hundred-ninety pound body up the stairs into the squad room. Grabbing a coffee from the machine in the corner, he walked silently down the center aisle, four desks on each side, and ignored the creaking wooden floor, but he couldn't shake that eerie sensation.

Flashing back to that day he was shot, Dan remembered the sharp pain of the projectile entering his body. Recalling hitting the pavement, and seeing blood gushing from the wound, gave him chills. The surreal ambulance ride was a blur, and before he'd passed out he remembered hearing EMTs' garbled words.

As Dan approached his desk, baby-faced detective Joe Scott said. "Have fun in the jungle this morning?"

Not bothering to smile, Dan replied. "Strange Scotty, real strange."

He continued to his work station. Marty Patton, sitting one desk behind, looked up from the *Harford Courant* he'd been reading, and peered at his partner. "You okay?" he asked.

Sipping coffee, Dan ran his fingers through his neatly combed hair. "I don't know—just seeing those creeps downstairs gave me the willies. It's like they're trying to tell me something."

He slouched into the squeaky swivel chair at his old gray metal desk, and stared at the clock on the wall: seven forty-nine a.m. Turning to Marty, he said. "You notice the parking lot? Not many black and whites out there."

Marty, a six-two, blond-haired rookie with a sculpted body, nodded. "I noticed, heard there's some kind of drug bust going down."

Dan finished the coffee. Looking down at the padded desk protector also serving as a calendar, he couldn't help noticing that today, May 24. 2014, was the sixth anniversary of his brush with death.

CHAPTER 2

Marty's mention of a drug bust was right. The entire Morgan Street police station was buzzing as uniforms began unloading two transport vans. Dan and Marty heard the commotion. "What's going on?" Marty said.

"Let's go downstairs and find out," Dan replied.

When the detectives got to the basement, they saw a line of undesirables being escorted into the booking area. Watching the cuffed gangster's line up for mug shots and fingerprinting, Dan's eyes focused on a familiar sight. Stumbling in at the end of the procession were Hartford gang leaders Julio Vegas, and Biggie Littlefield. Biggie's eyes met Dan's, and the thug shouted, "Whatchu you lookin at asshole?"

Dan pointed at Biggie, the bastard who had shot and nearly killed him. The detective's eyes widened. "Gained a few pounds, you giant piece of shit? I'm gonna go make sure the honeymoon suite is ready for you fuck-ups."

While the detainees were being booked, Dan and Marty headed up to see Captain Harold Syms.

Steely eyed, forty-nine-year-old Syms peered out of his glass partitioned office as the detectives approached. They entered the captain's sparsely decorated quarters through a door that was coming off its hinges. The black four-drawer metal cabinet against the back wall had a picture sitting on top; himself with Chief Hardison. The three-tiered tray in one corner of his desk was piled high with papers, and the captain's waste basket was overflowing.

Special Forces Commander Ted Willingham was seated in the corner, his hat on the short table next to him. Dan and Scotty anchored themselves in hard wooden chairs opposite the commander.

Willingham somberly slouched back. "I hate this shit. One of my guys, Jimmy Calero is dead, and I have to tell his wife she's a widow."

He paused. "Jang and Clancy are at Woodland with wounds."

Syms leaned back and looked up to the ceiling. In his raspy voice he said. "Sorry, Ted. It's never easy."

"Three thugs were taken out at the schoolyard on Brackett, where the deal was supposed to go down," Willingham said. "At least one was a Florida gang member."

"Florida?" Syms said."

"Yeah, Vinnie Martinez, whose drug empire spans the east coast, sent his boys up here to deliver a shitload of narcotics to Vegas and Biggie. We thought Martinez would be here, but he wasn't"

"What about that warehouse on Wilson? I heard shooting took place there," Syms asked.

"Vegas had a U-Haul that broke from the schoolyard and made it to the vacant storage facility. Black and whites followed it, securing the perimeter. When half my unit arrived and stormed the place, another burst of gunfire erupted inside the warehouse. The uniforms and my guys at that scene are all accounted for. I know gang members were hit, but I don't have a count of wounded or dead."

Syms and the detectives were all shaking their heads.

"What about pedestrians, residents. They must have been scared shitless. Anyone caught in the battle?" Dan asked.

"It was early enough so that not many people were around, still dark, but I think a few cars got sideswiped by the truck,"

Willingham paused. "We have a hell of a problem though. The narcotics were seized, but the money—ten million—vanished into thin air."

Syms rolled his eyes. "Ten million dollars missing?"

"We thought for sure the cash was in the U-Haul, but a search of the vehicle and the warehouse came up empty."

Dan cringed. "Jesus, I'll beat the greenbacks out of Vegas and Biggie. They'll sing their asses off by time I finish with them."

Syms gritted his teeth and stared at Dan. "Don't fuck around with those two. I don't want any of your shenanigans. I almost lost my job the last time you went rogue, and I know you have good reason to want to jamb your foot up Biggie's ass."

Dan got up. "Yes sir, I'll be a perfect gentleman. . . won't lay a finger on them..

As he turned his back to leave, Marty following, the captain yelled to Dan, "Don't you be teaching him any of your tricks."

Willingham looked at Syms. "What's his story?"

"Dan?" Syms picked up the plastic container of Advil from his desk. "See this? He's the reason I keep these here, and I may need a refill soon."

⅄

Dan's desk was on its last legs. Two of the side drawers barely opened and his wire in-basket was held in place on the uneven surface by two bookends. He placed his jacket on the back of his chair, looked at Marty and uttered. "Willingham said ten million was missing."

Marty nodded his agreement.

"How does he know how much money there was? Who tipped him?" Dan said. "I'm sure Vegas and Biggie didn't tell him."

"You think he's dirty?"

"He better not be. I'm gonna see if he's still with Syms."

Dan walked back to the captain's office and he saw the chair Willingham had occupied was empty. Syms, sorting through his paperwork, looked up and spotted the detective. Leaning on the captain's desk, Dan said. "Mind if I ask you a question?"

Syms picked up his Advil. "Doesn't matter if I mind or not; you're gonna ask it anyway."

Dan's eyes met his. "Do you know who tipped Willingham? How does he know it was ten mil, not two or three, or for that matter, a few thousand?"

Syms scratched what was left of his once curly afro. "What are you saying? You think he made off with the money?"

"It's a thought. Maybe he saw a get-rich-quick opportunity. Seems to me he should've been really glad to have gotten all those narcotics off the street, and all those gang members locked up. He didn't say anything about looking for the money; just said it mysteriously disappeared."

Syms stood, and angrily eyed Dan. "Are you crazy? You think he's dirty? Ted and I go way back. Don't forget he had casualties—He's as dirty as I am. Get your fricking behind out of here."

"All I'm saying is, we've seen stranger things."

Dan shut the door behind him and walked to Marty's desk, an old relic as well. "Something's not right, pal. I can feel it. Something's not right."

Dan glanced at the picture of Kim on Marty's desk. "Pretty, you should have great-looking kids."

"Thanks, but I don't think I want kids."

Marty heard his cell phone ding, and glanced at the text message.

Dan saw the disappointing look on his partner's face. "Everything okay?"

"It's Kim." Marty put the phone in his pocket. "Looks like I'll be stopping at Burger King again tonight. She's gotta sub for Misty at the gym. Wanna go down and rattle a few cages now?"

Rubbing his hands together, Dan pondered the adventure. "Nah, let those animals have a nice night squirming around that rat hole. I've been waiting a long time to lock Vegas and Biggie away for good. Tomorrow I'm gonna fry their asses."

Chapter 3

Dan's petite wife Phyllis, three years younger than her husband, had traded her career as a child psychologist a decade ago in order to raise their two smaller children.

The Shields family's Suffield residence, a yellow, blue shuttered, eight room colonial they'd purchased seventeen years ago, was located on a tree-lined cul-de-sac.

Dan clicked his remote and the garage door opened. He drove his black Accord inside, parking next to his wife's red SUV. Phyllis opened the mud-room door, always relieved to see her man; she wrapped her arms around him. "Still makes me breathe a sigh of relief every time I hear your car."

"Hey, back off lady," Dan said with a huge grin "I may have to arrest you for attacking a police officer."

He noticed her brunette hair had been trimmed. "I like the bangs," he said.

She kissed him on the lips. "Save the cuffs for later—you may have to haul me in for solicitation." Without missing a beat, she added. "Take your shoes off."

Dan placed his loafers next to the kids' sneakers on a mat below the coat rack. He hung his jacket in the closet, opened the custom-built side compartment, placing his holster and gun inside, then locked it. He stepped into the recently renovated kitchen: the square table and chairs had been tossed to make room for a granite topped center island. Now all meals were served in the adjoining dining room.

Mike, seventeen and a hulking six-footer, still had his baseball cap on his head, and was already seated with a slice of bread in one hand and a butter knife in the other.

"You mind waiting for us?" Dan asked. "And take that hat off."

"Sorry, but you know how hungry I am after a game."

An all-state third baseman on his high school baseball team, the teenager reluctantly put the knife down. The two small Shields children gave their dad hugs before joining their big brother at the table. Ten year-old Josh, a karate kid in his second year of lessons, already had his eyes on a black belt. Kate, nine, a budding gymnast and fashionista, undoubtedly was the family's little princess.

Dinner went smoothly until Dan looked at Mike. "Lawn needs mowing—you can do it tomorrow."

"But I have practice." The teenager testily replied. "It would be nice if you came to a game every now and then, like other dads."

Dan put his fork down. "Hey, maybe my job is more demanding than theirs, and I pay for the food you're shoving into your big mouth. Maybe you should do the lawn *tonight*. It's still light out."

"I can't, I have plans."

"Really, guess what? You have new plans now."

Mike blurted out, sarcasm in his voice. "You should buy a goat."

"Why," Dan said. "So it can live with the jackass in that chair? Maybe that's a good idea. It'd eat a lot less than you do."

Phyllis jumped into the fray. "Hold it! Knock it off, you two. Mike, go to your room. You can come back to finish your dinner when you decide to be respectful."

She looked at Josh, who was fumbling with the green beans on his plate. "I'm not eating those gross things," he muttered.

Pointing her finger at him, she warned "If you want to watch TV tonight, you'll eat them." She turned and pointed at Kate. "That goes for you too, little lady."

Dinner was nearly over when Mike reappeared. "I'm sorry for the back-talk. I'll take care of the grass. There's still some daylight. I'll start it now, and if I don't finish, I'll get it done tomorrow."

Dan placed his hands on the boy's broad shoulders." Thanks, Sit down and finish your supper."

Mike sat and buttered another slice of bread. "Dad, think you could make it to a couple of games? A lot of dads come, and when I look around the stands, I see them and wish you were there, too."

Dan lowered his head, as if Mike had shamed him. "I'd like to, but you know my job is twenty-four–seven and unpredictable. Tell you what. Put your schedule on the fridge, and I promise I'll try to catch a few."

Mike smiled. "It *is* on the fridge. Need a large print copy?"

"Okay smart ass, you've made your point. So, did you win?"

"Yeah, six to one, but I only had one hit."

"A homer?"

Mike cracked a grin. "Check swing roller I beat out, didn't exactly crush the ball today."

"Bet when I'm there you'll hit one out."

Mike gave a thumbs-up. "Thanks dad."

Later that evening after the kids had gone to bed, Phyllis shut off the TV and curled up beside Dan. "You know, you're hard on Mike."

Dan put his left arm around her shoulders, looking into her blue eyes he uttered. "I know I am. It's just that I see me when I look at him, and he's got so much more potential than I had. I don't want him to even think about becoming a cop."

"Amen. Ease up a little, and try to make a few of his games."

"I promise I'll try."

She took his hand. "Come on detective, take me to bed."

CHAPTER 4

D an checked the left pocket of his jacket before getting into his Accord. Allergic to nuts, he carried an EpiPen with him, and had and an emergency backup in the car's glove box.

The hyped up detective couldn't wait to get his hands on Vegas and that fat Biggie, whose bullet had scarred him for life. *I'm gonna grill those bastards so bad they'll have "Char-Broil" stamped across their foreheads before I'm done.*

When he pulled into the police lot, parking between two cruisers, Dan sensed something was wrong. Even the air had a stale quality. He approached the door to the holding tank where officer Tad Buckley was standing. "Can't go in this way. Have to take the elevator up, Dan."

"What's the deal?"

"You haven't heard? There was an escape last night."

Dan stopped in his tracks. "What? Don't tell me: Vegas, and Biggie?"

"Nope, some dude named Jenkins."

Dan hopped into the elevator and looked at years of graffiti written all over the back wall. He exited on the second floor, and headed straight to Syms's office.

Sitting in a chair with his arms crossed was Dom Denine. Syms eyed Dan. "Close the door."

Dan sat next to Dom and said to him. "What the hell happened? I heard someone named Jenkins escaped."

"Escaped all right," Dom replied. "Right into thin air. Armando Jenkins—and the ruse he pulled was like nothing we've ever seen."

"Who the hell is this guy?" Dan asked.

"We don't know, but he was one of Vegas's boys," the captain said. "I thought you knew them all."

Dan rolled his eyes. "Really, I thought I did too, but this guy somehow flew under the radar. So what makes him so important?'

"That's for you to figure out." Syms said as he turned to Dom. "Tell him what happened."

Dom unfolded his arms and rubbed his hands together. "I had no idea who he was. But around two a.m., we heard screams coming from his cell and went in. One of the guards saw him squirming, screaming in agony. He'd thrown up, and was curled up in a ball complaining of sharp pain in his side. A few minutes later, paramedics showed up and took him to the hospital."

"So he's in the hospital?" Dan said. "I don't understand. He escaped from there?"

Syms stood, his hands on his hips. "Nope. Never got to the hospital, and the paramedics disappeared too."

"Kidnapped? Held hostage?"

"We don't think so. They were in on it," Syms replied.

Dan turned to Dom. "Who called them?"

Dom looked into the detective's eyes. "That's just it. No one called them. They just showed up. We assumed someone had dialed 911."

"It was planned?"

Syms tapped his desk. "Looks that way, and you know the last time they had cameras down in the dungeon they were Polaroids, so we're shit out of luck for faces."

Dan rubbed his chin. "Why Jenkins? Why not Vegas, or Biggie?"

Syms sat. "Ask them not me."

Dan winced. "I want Vegas and Biggie right now."

Dom stood quickly. "I'll shake them, if they're not already awake. You want them in the interrogation room?"

"Bet your ass," Dan said. "Don't even let them take a piss."

Dom nodded and left the captain's office, heading for the dungeon.

"Officer Buckley is beside himself. Should've checked ID's," Syms said.

Dan started to leave Syms's office. "You don't think Buckley was in on it, do you?"

"All I know is that I have to get up to Hardison's office. He says the press will be all over this. You better get to work."

Dan went back to his desk and he saw Marty entering the squad room. "Follow me."

Marty popped a Tic Tac. "Where we going?"

"Interrogation room, you hear about the breakout?"

Marty shook his head. "Breakout?"

"Damn right. A thug named Jenkins escaped last night. It's time to make Vegas and Biggie sing. Those two bastards are being brought to the interrogation room right now."

⋏

Dan and Marty waited for the arrival of these scumbags, and finally the detectives heard the shuffling of feet as the cuffed hoodlums entered the room. Twenty-nine-year-old Vegas had always managed to slither away from hard time. Biggie, at thirty five, no taller than his five-ten sidekick was known to carry weapons, but he too had managed to avoid prison. Biggie's girth, gold teeth, and Mohawk amplified his nasty disposition. The cross and bones tattoos on both men's necks were the gang's trademark.

Marty sat at one end of a long rickety table, while Biggie and Vegas were forcefully plopped down across from him, onto hard chairs. Dan rubbed his hands together, and he glared at the gang leaders, as the sleepy detainees eyed him back.

The cracked plastered walls, two-way mirror, cement floor, were all this dreary room had to offer. The dull lights over the table were hanging by threads, and looked like they could fall any minute.

Dan had one foot on the ground as he propped his knee on a chair next to Biggie, and the hungry detective glared at his prey. "Nice to see you again, have a nice sleep?"

Biggie slumped back in his seat. "Fuck you, Shields," he growled.

Dan sneered. "Is that any way to start a conversation? You got me once you lump of lard. I should have called for backup then, but you're in my house now."

Biggie leaned forward. "Hey—don't talk at me til I get a shower and breakfast."

Dan loosened his shirt, rolling it up showing Biggie the scar. "Like your artwork, you fucking pig?"

Biggie tried to rise but was restrained by the two guards. He smugly stared at Dan as the detective tucked in his shirt. "Hell of a shot. Shoulda finished the job," Biggie snarled.

Dan rubbed his palms together. "As soon as you get less testy, and tell me what I want to know, you can get showered, and eat. Otherwise, my size ten shoe will be your breakfast fatso. So how about telling me what went down yesterday?"

"We was at the playground shootin hoops, and wham, here we is."

Dan gritted his teeth. "Yeah, well I guess hoops were the only things that didn't get shot, Biggie. Next time you play ball, it'll be in the prison courtyard. This time it's weapons, drugs, and murder. I don't think you'll be going home soon—or *ever*. I'm still trying to figure out how you got off last time.".

Dan leaned in. "Boys, we have a couple of mysteries here. How about at least one of you telling me where the ten million dollars went?"

Biggie slammed his cuffed hands on the table. "Ask your buddies. They got the drugs, and I bet they splittin the cash, too."

Dan had just confirmed that Willingham's number was correct: ten million had vanished. His venom kept building. "Yeah we got the goodies, but poof—no money, disappeared into thin air. What happened to it? Was it even in the U-Haul?"

"Kiss my ass! You guys is just crooks with goddamn badges. Now how bout a shower and breakfast? And where's my fuckin phone call?"

Dan got in Biggie's face, and with his harsh baritone tongue, he lashed out. "Who you gonna call, Biggie? Your mama? Won't she be proud of you?"

Biggie screamed back. "Shields, you cocksucker, get me the goddamn phone, and don't be talkin with me til I get my attorney!"

Marty took mental notes as he watched his partner berating the gang leaders.

Dan's eyes were burning as he turned to Vegas. "So. . . cat got your tongue this morning?"

"Get outta my face, motherfucker!"

Dan moved in closer to him. "Now now, no need to get an attitude. Tell me, who do you want your Mustang to go to, since you won't be driving it anymore?"

"Fuck you."

"You know, my kid always wanted a yellow 'Stang. How many miles you got on it?"

"Shut up, Shields! Get us outta here, now! Bigs is right. Where's my phone call?"

Dan sneered at his captives and threw his hands up. "Relax boys; we've just begun." He stood in front of Vegas. "Where'd the money go?"

"How the fuck do I know?"

"Tell us about Martinez, and his Florida mob."

"Nothin to tell."

Dan put his foot onto the chair next to Vegas. "So, who the hell is Jenkins, and how the hell did you manage to get him out of here?"

Vegas slumped back in his chair. "Me? The fuckin dude was sick. EMTs came and got him."

Dan was silent. He folded his arms, walking around the table. "Are you telling me you don't know that Jenkins is missing?" he said.

Vegas stared at Dan. "What the hell you talkin bout?"

Dan returned the stare. "He never made it to the hospital. He's gone, and so are the fake paramedics." Raising his voice Dan scowled. "You swear you don't know anything?"

He glanced at Biggie. "You look like you're constipated. Wanna see if my tens will fit up your ass to jar some shit loose?"

Biggie stood, slamming his cuffed hands on the table again as one of the guards stepped in to force the behemoth back down. "Cocksucker. Get us the hell out of here, now."

Dan stared at him. "You'll get out of here when I'm good and ready to let you out, and I'm not ready yet. He took one more shot at finding out about the escaped gang member. "Tell me again. Who is Jenkins, and where is he?"

Biggie was silent as he looked at Vegas. Their cold stares told Dan they weren't going to drop a dime on a gang member. Dan knew the code.

"I get it. We'll have to find out about Jenkins ourselves." Dan stood across from both thugs, pointing at Vegas. "What if I told you that we know he and the two paramedics made off with the money?" Dan paused. "Would that change your mind about ratting on him?"

A powerful seed had just been planted in the minds of the drug dealers, and Dan waited.

"Who you say you wanted to know about? Jenkins? Ferguson Jenkins? He was a pitcher for the Cubs." Biggie said.

Dan knew this interview was done. He glared at Biggie, and motioned to the guards. "Get these assholes out of here."

This had been a learning experience for the twenty- four year-old Marty, who was eight months removed from the police academy, getting his feet wet with his seasoned partner.

Marty got up and stared at Dan. "I thought you were gonna stomp those guys into the ground."

Dan patted Marty on the shoulder. "They weren't gonna tell us anything more, and the last time I kicked a thug, Syms nearly canned me."

"Too bad, I think they would have sang."

"I want those thugs gone from the streets, and if I could get them off this planet, I'd be all for that. Even though I still have a scar from Biggie's shot, I still have to do *some* things by the book."

⋏

Syms was in his office looking out of a broken window, a half-empty water bottle in his hand, he was waiting to hear how the interrogation went. Dan and Marty marched in, and the captain turned around. "How'd the grilling go?"

Dan shrugged "They were as stubborn as ever, and I don't think keeping them in this stinking place is going to motivate those thugs to talk. Besides, I'm sure their slick attorney Hancock Sasser will be trying pull strings at the arraignment."

"Maybe a couple of Big Macs will make the fat one sing," Marty said.

"I think if he ate my foot, it might help," Dan said. "Makes no sense—ten mil disappears and a mysterious gang member, Jenkins vanishes from our lockup."

"Right; so now that you've figured that out, go get him," Syms said.

Dan leaned forward. "Him? I'm thinking maybe we should get Willingham. "Who the hell else would have been capable of getting Jenkins out of here?"

Syms picked up his Advil, and he glared at Dan. "Oh no, don't go there again."

"Why not? It fits. Who else had access to an ambulance and fake paramedics?"

Syms opened the ibuprofen bottle. "Jesus H. Christ. I'm telling you, there's no way."

Dan placed his hands on Syms' desk. "I hope you're right, but I think your friend is dirty."

Swallowing two tablets, washed down by a gulp of water, the captain pointed to the door. "Out!" he commanded.

CHAPTER 5

Dan had to know more about Jenkins, so he sent Marty down to retrieve the booking file. The young detective returned, placed it on Dan's desk, and opened the folder. "Nice mug, and dreads, he looks Puerto Rican, and Black." Marty said.

"Figures," Dan replied. "No license, no known address. A real mystery dude, and watch out pal. Politically speaking, it's Hispanic and Afro-American."

Marty read further. "No priors."

"Maybe not here, we need to go national. See what you come up with."

Marty walked to a computer, and browsed the NCIC database. Dan heard the printer spitting out paper, so he knew Marty had found something. "Whatcha got?"

"A mug shot. He was arrested in Buffalo for narcotics possession, and intent to sell, as well as grand theft auto. Never did time."

Dan studied the photo. "He's bald in this one, no tat. This was four years ago. Age is thirty-two. Looks about right, nose and eyes look like a match. Come on, let's see if Syms knows anyone in Buffalo."

The detectives headed to the captain's office with the file, but when they looked in, Syms was gone. "Up for Connies?" Dan said.

"Sounds good."

◣

Connie's Place, the twenty-four-hour diner, two blocks from the police station was a landmark. Its neon light could be seen from the jailhouse. Dan opened the door and Marty followed him inside. The railroad-style diner was packed with a mix of uniforms, and local patrons. There were two vacant stools at the counter, but Dan spotted fellow detectives Bev Dancinger, and Scotty sitting in a booth, so he and Marty settled in beside them.

"Hey guys," Scotty said. "Guess we missed all the excitement last night."

"No shit," Dan said. "I don't remember the last jailbreak."

"Heard Dom's a little bummed," the very pregnant Bev said.

"Yeah. Where's the old lady? Hope she saw us," Dan said.

At that moment, Connie Castino, meshed net around her gray hair, appeared in her white apron, toting a pot of coffee. "I heard that, and for your information I'm sixty-two, my vision is twenty-twenty, and obviously ain't nothing wrong with my hearing. Now give me your cups, and don't dare ask for decaf."

She poured the black coffee, put the pot on the table, and glanced at a red-faced Dan. "Oh, yeah," Connie said. "Nice to see you again,"

She looked at Marty. "If I were you, I'd find some new friends."

Dan sipped his coffee as Connie walked away. He eyed Bev. "How much longer?"

"I'm due in three weeks. My last day is next Friday."

Dan picked up his cup and looked at Scotty. "Haven't seen any muffins lately."

Scotty sheepishly pointed at Bev's stomach "See that belly? They're all in there."

Bev laughed. "If you want muffins and a shape like this, you'd better lose that thing between your legs and get a uterus."

Scotty looked at his watch. "We better get back. You guys almost done?"

Dan finished his coffee and Marty chugged the last drop from his cup.

Dan stood, took out his wallet and placed a ten on the table. "Coffee's on me today. We should get back too."

After Bev slowly slid out of the booth, Scotty tapped Dan on the shoulder. "I need to ask you something." He looked at Bev and Marty. "You guys go ahead. I have to talk to Dan for a minute."

"What's up?"

"Marty—what's with him? It's his bloodshot eyes. Is he drinking or doing drugs?"

"What? You think he has a problem?"

"Hey, all I'm saying is you better check it out. Syms will have his ass if he is."

"I'll talk to him."

Connie, standing behind the counter waved to the detectives. "You boys stay out of the hospital. I can't be losing any more customers."

Dan waved back as he opened the door. Smiling at her he said. "Ever thought of opening a second place at Woodland?"

λ

Dan and Scotty entered the squad room a few minutes after their partners. Marty was at his desk, fishing a pack of Tic Tacs from his middle drawer. "What was that all about?" he said.

"Nothing, Scotty wanted to know if I would help him plan a baby lunch for Bev."

Dan sat at his desk and studied his partner. *He sure likes those little mints. I'll keep a close eye on him.*

CHAPTER 6

Dan arrived at the Morgan Street jail, venom running through his veins as he stepped out of his car. Determined to have another go at Vegas and Biggie, the detective entered the holding tank, but when he neared cell eight, he noticed it was empty.

You have to be shitting me. They can't be out.

But they were.

↟

Dan raced upstairs to Sym's office, bursting in as if he'd had six cups of coffee.

"Vegas, and Biggie. Where are those bastards?"

The captain held his bottle of headache medicine. "They're out. Sasser got them bail."

Dan was red with anger. "You shitting me? Those fuckers are back on the street?"

"It was Bainbridge. He set bail, and that slick lawyer Hancock Sasser posted it."

Standing in front of the captain's desk, Dan said. "I hate this fucking system. We bust our asses to get these thugs off the street, and then they're out." He angrily clenched his fists. "I didn't think Sasser would be able to get them bail this time. You better believe that sleazy lawyer has Bainbridge in his back pocket."

Syms unscrewed the pill bottle cap and took out two tablets. "No shit. Here, you need these more than me."

"I should've known," Dan said. "I should've kicked the shit out of them yesterday."

Syms waved his hands in a downward motion. "Take a deep breath. They're only out until their trial."

Dan raised his hands up in the air. "Trial? You mean circus, because that's all it'll be; might as well get Barnum and Bailey to prosecute."

Syms kicked his already dented desk. "Jesus Christ, we can only do what we can do. Go take those aspirins."

Dan took a breath, and gave the pills back to Syms.

"You got anything on Jenkins?" the captain asked.

"We know a little. Jenkins was in Buffalo, and has a short list of priors for drugs and grand theft auto, but that's it. You know anyone up there I can talk to?'

"Maybe the chief does. I'll ask him."

Dan turned to leave. "Hey," Syms said. "What's with Marty and the Tic Tac's? He have a breath problem?"

"I think he just likes the things."

Dan walked back to his desk. Marty arrived, looking a little edgy as he drank his coffee. "What's with the long face?" Dan asked.

The rookie dropped a mint into his mouth. "It's Kim. We had a little spat."

"Been there Marty, but you gotta leave that stuff at home. You heard the latest?"

"Now what?"

"Vegas and Biggie. Judge Bainbridge let them out on bail."

"What?"

"You heard me. Hang around here long enough and you'll see it all."

"I've seen a lot already."

"Listen. I just came from Syms's office and he's going to ask Hardison to get us a contact in Buffalo. Hopefully we'll know more about Jenkins soon."

Dan pulled his chair next to Marty's. "You know Vegas and Biggie are itching to get their money back, but there *is* someone else who's out ten million bucks—Vinnie Martinez. We need to talk to Willingham."

⚔

Captain Syms was on his way to the bathroom when he spotted Dan and Marty approaching. "You coming to see me again?"

"Gonna be long?" Dan asked.

"Get in my office and wait."

Dan and Marty were sitting when Syms returned to his desk.

"Can't wait to move into the new digs, those floor urinals gross me out," the captain said. "If you're not careful, you can piss on your pants."

"You speaking from experience?" Dan mused.

Syms ignored the snarky question. "So what's on your mind now?"

"Willingham, can you call him? We need to know more about Martinez."

"You know. I was actually thinking the same thing."

Syms picked up the desk phone, and called the commander.

Willingham answered on the first ring. "Captain, How's it going?"

"Let me put you on speaker. Dan and Marty are in my office. We want to know what you can tell us about Martinez."

"Like what?"

"Hi Ted," Dan said. "Why wasn't he there to collect his money? I'm sure he's pissed."

"I'm sure he's more than pissed, and he has eyes up here too," Willingham replied. "He's a slippery eel, and somehow he knew to stay away."

"One thing you should know," Dan said. "Vegas and Biggie are out on bail."

"What about the guy that escaped?"

"Jenkins? We're working on him, we may have a lead."

"What about the other thugs?"

"They're still here, they'll be transferred after arraignment, but they'd rather do time than talk to us. They know the consequences. Prison is no safe place for them."

Dan looked at Syms before continuing. "Ted. Who tipped you?"

They heard Willingham's long pause. "It was someone who had inside info."

"Like who?"

"Look. I can't tell you. All I can say is that he's a reliable informant."

Syms waved at Dan, signaling him to back off. "Thanks Ted. We've got work to do," the captain said.

As Syms hung up, Dan placed his hands on the desk and said. "Son of a bitch is hiding something. I knew it."

Syms downed two pills. "Keep digging guys."

As they were returning to their desks, Dan grabbed Marty's arm, took him into an empty conference room, and closed the door.

"I need to ask you something, and be straight with me."

Marty ruffled his brows, as Dan gave him a hard look. "I can smell alcohol on your breath. You drinking?"

Marty's eyes told it all. "What do you mean, drinking?"

"Don't fuck with me Marty. Do you have a problem?"

Marty wiped his hand across his face. "I wouldn't call it a problem. I like a few beers every now and then."

"Like, how every now and then?"

"Damn it. I stop at McHale's to have a few before going home when Kim's working late."

"How many is a few?"

"Sometimes two, three, four—depends."

"Ever have one before coming here? Is that why you're always popping mints?"

Marty didn't answer.

"God damn it, Marty. You need to quit before Syms catches on. You're a good cop—don't jeopardize your career."

"You're not the only one on my case. Kim is on me too. I know I have to stop."

Dan opened the door. "Come on. Let's do some work."

As they reached their desks Bev walked by with a muffin in her hand. "You know those things are making you fat." Dan said.

Bev rubbed her round stomach. "Bet I lose fifteen pounds before you do."

Dan headed for the coffee pot. "You want one?" he said to Marty.

"Yeah, make mine black, and grab me a muffin."

Dan returned with only the drinks. "I think Bev got the last muffin."

Marty lifted his cup and took a sip. Dan could see his partner thinking about the lecture.

"You okay?"

"Yeah, the drinking stops today," Marty whispered.

CHAPTER 7

Marty had a jealous rage inside him that flared when he thought about all the guys at the gym staring at Kim's body. He'd urged her to pursue another career. That's when things started falling apart— she loved her job, and wasn't about to quit.

Marty knew she'd be late tonight, and the words he'd said to Dan were short lived. He stopped at McHale's and sat beside a couple of regulars.

"Hey Marty, how about some darts?" good old Mack, a hard-hat construction worker said as he slurped his beer.

McHale, poured the off-duty officer a draft and Marty grabbed a handful of nuts before chugging his brew. The place began to get busier and noisier as Marty loosened his collar. "Darts? How about a game for ten million bucks?"

"Read about that," Mack said.

"Read all you want. Me and Dan are on it."

"No shit. Hey Rudy," Mack said. "You hear this?"

"Yeah," Rudy, whose long white beard often sopped up suds, said as he got off his stool, and looked at Marty. "So, you paying for the brews tonight?"

Marty drank his beer. "Shut up you old buzzard. Let's play darts."

After his fourth beer, Marty started to get a buzz and he knew it was time to leave the bar.

⋏

The Manchester apartment he shared with Kim was only a mile from the pub. Marty managed to park his car in his designated space, next to Kim's empty assigned spot, and he slowly made it up the stairs to the second floor.

Upon entering their one-bedroom apartment, he threw his shirt on a kitchen chair and opened the fridge, but it was filled with health food. Not his kind of nourishment. One can of beer remained inside the fridge door, so Marty took it, and plopped himself on the couch, flung his pants on the floor, and turned on the TV.

It wasn't quite dark when Kim pulled her Subaru into space eighteen, but she could tell Marty had been drinking because the wheels of his Mazda were on the white line, forcing her to squeeze her Subaru into her parking spot.

She braced herself and took a deep breath before opening the apartment door, hoping Marty was already out like a light. Her hopes were squashed when she walked in and saw him in on the couch in his boxers. His face was red, his eyes were glassy, and his boxers didn't hide his erection. It was nothing new, and she tensed up. She loved Marty, but hated him at times like this, and she'd begged him to quit drinking.

He leaped up, staggered a little while grabbing her around the waist, and dragging her off to the bedroom where he forcibly threw her onto the bed, stripping away her tight sweats. She knew not to fight as he violently began raping her. Kim held back her tears—she knew it would only take a minute for Marty to finish, and then he'd fall asleep. Still, when it was over she felt violated, sore, trapped, confused, and wondered how much longer she could put up with the punishment.

Kim showered, ate a small dinner, and cried herself to sleep. She woke up in the middle of the night, looked at the bruises on her arms, and saw Marty sleeping. Her mind was made up: she had to do something to stop the abuse

Kim was gone when Marty woke. She'd left him a note saying she had an early class.

⅄

It was a morning of notes for Marty. He sauntered to his desk with a copy of this morning's newspaper under his arm and a cup of coffee in his left hand. He placed the hot drink on his desk and draped his jacket over his chair before he noticed the note from Syms. Leaving the paper and coffee behind, the young detective dropped a couple of Tic Tacs into his mouth and marched into the captain's office, where he was confronted by his livid boss. "Shut the fucking door," Syms barked. "Sit your ass down Marty. What the hell is your problem? You were hired right out of the academy, number one in your class. I knew the Tic Tac's were hiding something. Drinking is one thing, but Kim is another. Explain it to me!"

Sitting in front of the irate captain, Marty began to sweat. "What do you mean?"

Syms glared at him. "You asshole, see these papers? Kim left here an hour ago, and the bruises on her arms say it all. This is a domestic complaint of rape and battery, and you need to be out of that apartment, pronto. There's a restraining order as well." Marty sat dumbfounded, his arms crossed and his head spinning, as he tried to defend himself. "I didn't rape her. It was rough sex."

Syms was fuming. "Is that what you call it? She says it's not the first time."

Marty held his head down, and swallowed the breath mints. "I can't believe it. She's my world. I wouldn't hurt her."

Syms's face grew angrier as he stood and pounded his fist onto his desk. "Oh, so now you feel sorry for yourself? This is as serious as it gets, you asshole."

"Last thing I want to do is lose Kim, please. . . help me."

"Marty, I already have. You're lucky she didn't have you arrested. You get your ass into AA and anger management right now."

Marty's eyes welled up. "I will, sir. I promise."

"You want to keep your sorry ass out of jail, you do what you're supposed to, and we'll talk later. As of now, you're suspended, so hand me your badge and gun."

Marty obliged and stormed out of the Syms's office. He stopped at his desk, picked up his jacket, and Kim's photo before rushing out of the squad room, the tepid coffee remained where he'd left it.

Dan had just arrived as Marty flew past him without saying a word. Dan had no idea what was happening, but Syms saw his veteran detective and he waved to him. Dan got the message and proceeded down to the captain's office. The detective thought he actually saw steam coming from Syms's head, as the captain reached for the Advil bottle, and opened the lid. "I suspended Marty."

"What happened? Does it have anything to do with his drinking?"

Syms downed a couple of pills. "It's a lot more serious than that. Kim was here and she filed a domestic complaint. When he's drunk, he beats and rapes her. I could've arrested Marty, but I'm cutting him some undeserved slack. He's agreed to anger management and AA."

Dan sighed. "I knew about the drinking; even spoke to him about it. He swore he was going to quit."

Dan shook his head. "I never thought he'd lay a hand on Kim."

"Well, he did and he'd better watch his sorry ass or he'll be in our lockup with all the other drunks and abusers."

CHAPTER 8

Vinnie Martinez was no stranger to Hartford, and he was certainly not a neophyte when it came to drugs and prostitution. His ties to the Colombian drug cartel gave him unlimited access to narcotics. Money was his passion, so when Vegas offered ten mil as his franchise fee, Martinez jumped on it, and sent him enough merchandise to take over New England.

The Florida drug boss also maintained a thriving business in Hartford. The Hi- Hat Club was where his hookers were routinely rotated between this strip club, and the ones he owned in New Orleans and Miami.

Martinez knew the heat was on, so he didn't travel, but he also knew he'd been robbed. He had to figure out who'd made off with the money, but he was unaware that Vegas and Biggie were out of jail. As for his own gang members, he couldn't care less about those mercenaries, but Vegas and Biggie—that was a different story.

⅄

Vegas had wondered why his U-Haul driver, Armando Jenkins, had been pried from lockup, and he didn't know who the hell those paramedics were that helped him escape.

The yellow Mustang was back on the road and Vegas drove into familiar territory. Once a prosperous, proud neighborhood, it was now a place with boarded up buildings filled with addicts, gangs, and homeless people. Even the old synagogue with its Star of David in the stained glass window above the door, now served as a crack house. Eighteen deaths by gunfire last year alone; violence contaminated these streets, and everyone knew to stay away from Vegas. . . except to buy drugs.

Word hadn't gotten around yet that he and Biggie were out, so when the easily identifiable yellow Mustang turned down Gardner Street with Latin music blaring, other cars honked, and several of Vegas's surprised customers waved to him.

He headed to Lucky's Pawn Shop on the corner of Capron and Gardner. The red neon sign in the window said "Open."

The two thugs got out of the parked Mustang and looked through Lucky's iron-barred front window. Biggie opened the door, and Brick, the muscular store guard, held onto his dog.

"What the?" Brick said.

"Yeah it's us," Biggie replied.

The eighty-pound Rottweiler sitting next to Brick recognized the men. "You're a good boy, Sharky," Vegas said.

Lucky was behind the counter, tying a tag on the Beretta he'd just taken in pawn. He wore a red bandana and his tree-like arms were covered with tattoos, a king cobra on his left arm and a black widow on the other. His earrings and goatee made him look as scary as he actually was. His real name was Renaldo, but he was known as Lucky because he should have been dead by now. He'd been shot, stabbed, and once nearly crushed by a garbage truck that had rammed his car. He gave Vegas a fist pump. "Thought they had you for keeps?"

"Sasser did us good," Vegas said.

Vegas eyed the gun case. "You dogs hear anything about Jenkins and the money?"

"Shit, man, everyone's talkin', but no one knows shit," Lucky said.

"You sure? "

"Damn sure. How come you guys didn't jump with him?"

"Why the fuck you think? He did a solo, and we gotta find his ass."

"Think he took the money?"

Biggie wandered around to the back of the counter, picking up a shotgun from the case in back of Lucky and pointing the rifle at him. "You two frickin' dudes wouldn't happen to know if any ambulances is missin, or if anyone round here plays make-believe docs?"

Brick froze. "What the fuck you thinking, bro? We couldn't even fit into an ambulance!"

"You ain't got a pawned one out back?" Biggie said, while fiddling with the shotgun and grabbing some shells. "Just screwin witch you, don't let the dog go."

Vegas had a liking for Berettas, and he eyed the one in Lucky's hand. "Gimme that thing. Is it loaded?"

"Hell, no," Lucky replied.

"Gimme some ammo, it's mine."

"Shit, it was just pawned."

"Yeah, well, it was just unpawned. We gotta get out of here. You hear anything, you got my number."

Brick opened the door, and Vegas left with Biggie, the Beretta, and the shotgun. They got into the Mustang and headed in the direction of Wilson Street.

"Where you goin'?" Biggie said.

"Warehouse, I wanna to check it out."

"You shittin me? That place was ripped."

ᛉ

Vegas had a sickening hunch as he pulled his car into the gravel driveway. Biggie was right. The building's windows were bullet riddled. Vegas stopped in front of the steel garage door, got out of the car, peeked into a shattered window, and there it was, a red and white ambulance. He tugged on the warehouse's front entrance door, and it was open.

Vegas walked back to Biggie's side of the Mustang, and the fat man rolled down the window, shotgun in his lap. "That thing loaded?" Vegas said.

"Nah, got a few shells in my pocket."

"Come on out. The doors is open, and wait 'til you see what's inside."

Biggie got out, toting the shotgun.

"That thing your new pet? Leave it here." Vegas said.

"Makes me warm, I'm keepin' it." Biggie replied.

Vegas opened the warehouse door and they went inside the musty, unlit building. The sun's rays peeking through the broken windows provided the only light. Biggie spotted the emergency vehicle. "Holy shit, the fuckin ambulance. Jenkins came here, musta had a getaway car here too." He Vegas opened the rear doors of the transport, hopping onto the stretcher.

"Get in. We gotta talk."

Biggie got in and sat on a stool.

"Let me ask you somethin," Vegas said. "Who knew 'bout the money?"

"Jenkins and us."

"Right, those suitcases was in the U-Haul." Vegas rolled his eyes at Biggie. "Who knew they was in there?

"Jenkins and us."

Vegas stared at his cohort and harshly said. "Right. Just us."

"The fuck you gettin' at?"

"Stay here for a minute. I'll be right back. I need to check somethin out."

Vegas stepped out, fetched the Beretta from his car, and loaded the gun before returning. Standing by the open ambulance doors, he looked at Biggie who was sitting under the cabinets that were full of emergency medical supplies; his hands on the shotgun.

"Ever been for a ride in one of these?" Vegas said.

"Couple times, got shot twice in New York."

"My brother died in one of these. How long you know Jenkins?"

"You know, I brought him in."

"He roomed wit you a while, right? You trusted him? Vegas frowned. "Shit, looks like that was a mistake."

Biggie clutched the rifle. "What you sayin?"

Vegas pointed the Beretta at Biggie. "I trusted you, fat man. I knew you wanted to take over, and I'm guessin' Jenkins was gonna to be your main man too. Pretty slick, havin' him escape, but where'd ya get his helpers? Those guys you been recruitin' from New York?"

Biggie raised his voice. "You crazy? You acting crazy. That's a crock. You know I wouldn't cross you. Put that fuckin Beretta away, bro."

"Where's the money, fat man?"

"You're fuckin nuts!"

"Am I? You tip the cops, or was it Jenkins?"

Biggie gave Vegas a mock smile. "You know bro. One thing I lied about." He swung the shotgun around. "This thing's loaded."

Vegas quickly fired two rounds into Biggie. Wounded and gushing blood, the gang leader's robust cohort was able to pull the shotgun's trigger and shatter Vegas's chest, sending him flying backward onto the concrete floor in his own pool of blood. Biggie's three hundred pounds of flab saved his life as he staggered out of the ambulance. He crammed himself into the Mustang, and drove to Woodland Hospital's emergency entrance, leaving the car's engine running, as he hobbled inside; a trail of blood following him through the door.

CHAPTER 9

The last time Dan had been to the high school was two years ago when he'd given a talk on drug abuse. The football, soccer fields, and track were to the right of the parking lot. Dan saw the visiting team's yellow bus stationed on the left side near the baseball diamond, and he parked his car a few spaces away. As he came around the bleachers and saw Mike at third base, Taylor Dean's father waved at the approaching detective.

"Hey, Dan, what're you doing here?"

"Hey, Jack. What's the score?"

"Three to one, we're down two. Top of the fourth."

"What's Mike done?"

"Struck out; so did Taylor. This pitcher is tough."

When the half-inning ended, Dan yelled "Mike."

The appreciative son waved to his dad. Timing couldn't have been better, because a few minutes later Mike came to the plate with two out, and runners on first and second. He hit the first pitch over the left field fence and gave his team the lead. It was a great moment for Mike and a proud one for Dan. . . but things changed quickly.

No sooner had Mike rounded the bases than Dan's cell rang: it was Syms. The captain said. "You won't believe this, but you need to get over to Woodland right now. There's been a shooting. The victim is Biggie Littlefield."

"You kidding me, where's Vegas?"

"He's missing, but I'm told his Mustang's got lots of blood inside, and it's by the ER entrance."

"I'm on my way."

Dan walked to the bench and tapped Mike on the shoulder. "Gotta go. I'll call mom. I'm gonna be late."

He got into the Accord, and with his Bluetooth connection, called Syms back. "I should be there in about fifteen. Wait for me in the ER lobby."

⋏

Dan approached the sprawling eight-story hospital, parking in the emergency lot next to Syms's Ford Taurus. He saw Vegas's Mustang bracketed by two black-and-whites. The driver's door was open, so Dan peeked into the blood-stained vehicle, spotting a white tag attached to a string sitting on the floor. He reached in, picked it up, and eyed the tag before placing it in his pocket.

Syms flagged Dan when the detective entered the ER through the sliding glass doors.

"Where is he?"

"Room 317."

Dan shook his head. "I know that one. Spent a few days there. Remember?"

Syms nodded, and Dan showed him the tag. "Found this in the Mustang. It's from Lucky's Pawn."

They followed the yellow line on the floor to the elevator. When the door opened, a couple of nurses got out before the captain, and Dan got in.

Syms pressed three, and when they got out, Dan turned left. "Follow me."

They walked past a nurses' station, took a left, and saw two uniforms standing outside the door of room 317.

Dan peeked inside. "He awake?"

"Oh yeah—already asking for food," a uniform said.

Biggie was hooked up to monitors, and he had an IV stuck in his left arm. He rubbed his huge belly, as if proud that it'd had two bullets removed a couple of hours ago. He was slightly propped and full of pain meds, and he blinked at Dan and Syms who were standing by the bed.

"Remember me?" Dan snidely barked.

"Don't make me puke. Just get outta here."

Dan sat in the chair beside the bed, pointing to the IV bag dripping pain meds. "Want me to pull this now, or would you like to tell us what happened?"

"Motherfucker, you wouldn't do that."

"You see any witnesses? I know my captain is nearly blind. Wanna hear something that should amuse you? This is the same room I was in when you put me here with a bullet in my chest. How's that for laughs?"

Biggie groaned. "Very funny."

"Funny enough for you to start talking?"

"Vegas shot me."

"Where is he?"

"The fuckin asshole's dead. I blew his head off with a shotgun after he shot me."

"Where?"

"The warehouse."

"Holy shit." Syms reached for his phone. "I'm calling Dixon. Gotta get a team down there as soon as possible."

"So what happened?" Dan asked the beleaguered patient.

"Motherfucker's head was all fucked up. He thought Jenkins and me was hidin' the money. Thought I was in on it. Shoulda seen him. He was crazy nuts, pulled his Beretta and got off a couple of shots before I blew his ass away."

"Why did he suspect you?"

"Dumb ass thought we was takin' over."

"We?"

"Me and Jenkins. I brought the dude in from New York. I think when Vegas saw the ambulance in the warehouse, he freaked."

Dan leaned in close to Biggie. "So where is he? Does Jenkins have the money?"

"Get back," Biggie said. "I told you. Don't know."

Dan looked at Syms. "The getaway ambulance, we have to get to the warehouse."

As Syms and Dan got up, the detective felt the tag in his pocket. He pulled it out and showed it to Biggie. "You recognize this?"

"Shit, that was on the gun Vegas took from Lucky."

"Biggie, it's been nice talkin'. I'll see they get you a steak before I come back. Better sleep with one eye open. Sometimes patients mistakenly end up in the freezer downstairs."

Dan and Syms rushed out of the room. As they passed the nurses' station, Dan eyed the big white board on the wall, and in blue marker letters he spotted the names Jang and Clancy—Room 309. Dan knew he'd be back as soon as possible, but he didn't want to tell Syms what he'd noticed.

They exited the hospital heading for their cars. "I'll be right behind you," Syms said.

Dan's head was spinning as he thought about Jang and Clancy. He wondered what these men could tell him about Willingham.

⅄

By the time Syms and Dan arrived at the warehouse, three cruisers, a fire truck, and paramedics were on the premises. The warehouse door was wide open, and several uniforms were surveying the murder scene. The power had been shut off inside, and the air still held the smell of bloodshed from the big shootout, as well as the fresh body fluid.

The ambulance was in the middle of the warehouse floor, and lights had been spread out by the firemen. Vegas's ripped apart body had been flung about fifteen feet back from the vehicle and hadn't been covered. The sight made Dan queasy. "Jesus Christ, I may lose my lunch."

A paramedic threw a cover over Vegas. "He's all yours— better call the coroner to come and get him."

Dan and Syms looked inside the ambulance, taking in the sight of Biggie's blood and the shotgun on the floor. "Look at this thing—it could kill an elephant."

Dan walked around the otherwise empty warehouse and saw another set of tire tracks to the right of the ambulance. He knelt down. "Captain, look at these. They must have had a getaway car in here and left after ditching the ambulance."

"Here's CSI now." Syms waved to the team of examiners who were entering the building. "Over here Higashi."

The captain pointed to the tire tracks. "Get some photos of these."

"Will do," Higashi said as he slipped on rubber gloves, "but I'm pretty sure these were from the U-Haul that we shot last time."

"That reminds me: I have to get a tow down here to impound the ambulance," Syms said.

"Make that two," Dan uttered. "Send one to Woodland to tow the Mustang. That impound lot must be getting pretty crowded."

Chapter 10

Phyllis had been nervously awaiting Dan. She heard his car and saw the head-lights pulling into the driveway. Relief was written all over her face when her husband walked in.

"Where were you? Mike said you showed up at his game, but had to leave."

He put his arms around her. "I'm sorry. I said I'd call you, but I forgot. Syms and I had to rush over to Woodland. Who won?"

"Let's put it this way: a happy camper he isn't. They lost seven to six."

"He get any hits beside the homer?"

"One. He *got* hit. He has a nice bruise on his thigh. You want some coffee?"

"Would love some."

Dan took off his jacket, and locked his gun up, before he headed upstairs. "I need to get out of these clothes. I'm going to change."

Kate and Josh were sleeping, but Mike's door was open. "Hey heard you caught one." Dan said.

Mike removed his headphones and rolled down his pants. "Like it?"

The purple thigh bruise was the size of a grapefruit. "You ice it?"

"Twice. We lost anyway."

"I heard. See you in the morning."

Dan changed and went back downstairs where Phyllis had poured him a fresh cup of coffee. He sat on a stool at the center island; a box of Girl

Scout cookies next to his cup. "Kate must've done a good job this year," he remarked.

"I think we helped her out quite a bit. There are four more boxes in the cabinet," Phyllis replied.

"How many chocolate mints?"

"Three."

"I need to relax and watch some TV."

"Ok. That's decaf, so it shouldn't bother you."

"Thanks babe. I love you. Go get your beauty sleep."

Phyllis rolled her eyes. "What's that supposed to mean? You thought I was pretty enough the other night."

"Go to bed, Cinderella, before *I* seduce *you*."

"Really? Is that a threat or an offer?"

"You devil. I'm going to take a shower, and I better find you naked under the covers."

"Or what? You going to arrest me?"

⅄

When his alarm went off at six-fifteen, Dan rolled over. Phyllis was already in the kitchen fixing breakfast and preparing lunch for the kids to take to school. He smelled bacon, and hoped there was still some for him.

The lucky detective found scrambled eggs, toast, and two slices of bacon on his plate when he entered the kitchen. "Thanks babe."

Phyllis smiled. "You earned it last night."

"Kids gone?"

"Just left for the bus. Mike's still here. I think he's being picked up by Taylor."

Mike saw Taylor's Corolla and headed for the door. "You okay?" Dan said. "You look a little gimpy."

"I'm okay. I'm going to practice later. See you."

Dan finished his breakfast. "Gotta go. See you later hon."

Chapter 11

Syms's chair was turned around, and he was gazing out the back window when he heard Dan's footsteps. The captain swiveled to see his detective who was standing at the office door. "Where the hell were you this morning? I thought you'd be here at the crack of dawn, like me. I couldn't sleep after seeing Vegas's guts splattered on the warehouse floor."

"Don't remind me."

"What do you make of Biggie's story?" Syms asked, as his detective took two steps and sat on a wobbly chair.

"I think he didn't have anything to do with Jenkins, or the money," Dan replied. "I think he's told us what he's going to tell us. With Vegas out, he's the boss. Something else. That ambulance. I noticed it was an Emergency Services Company vehicle. I wanna know if it was reported stolen."

"Go see Dixon."

Syms pointed to his aspirin bottle. "I'm running low."

Dan knew that was the captain's subtle way of telling him to ante up for a new supply. The detective got up and turned to leave. "See you later, boss."

"Not so fast, Dick Tracy. What was that bullshit you pulled at the hospital? So now I'm nearly blind, and you would've cut the IV drip?"

"You know I probably wouldn't have done it."

Syms stood and pointed his finger at Dan. "Probably? That's the kind of crap that almost got us both fired the last time you pulled one of your shenanigans."

"You referring to the one where I had that Nun pick out Daltan Gemmison in a line-up?"

"Nun? My ass. She was a homeless person you put a habit on, and instructed her to pick him. I don't want to know what you paid her. What exactly would you have done if she was called to testify in court?"

"Hey, he was guilty as could be. I couldn't let him walk—I would've found another Nun. They all dress the same. Nobody would've known the difference."

Syms shook his head, laughing lightly he pointed to the door. "Out."

Dan returned to his desk, looking across to Marty's empty seat. Kim's picture was gone, and he looked at his own pictures of Phyllis and the kids. He smiled. *What a lucky man I am.*

λ

Coffee: a good cup of coffee was what he needed, so Dan headed to Connie's, and as before, Scotty and Bev were there in the same booth.

Dan glanced at Bev. "Still with the twins, I see."

"Very good—you sure have a keen eye."

Connie greeted Dan. "How about a muffin with your coffee?"

"Whatever you say. Nothing with nuts."

"Heard from Marty?" Scotty asked.

Dan bowed his head. "Listen, I know you tipped me about his drinking. I did confront him and he fessed up, but obviously he didn't tell me everything. Haven't heard from him." Dan paused as Connie brought over a blueberry muffin. "Thanks, sweetie," he said with a smile. He lifted his hot cup. "Syms went light on him with the suspension. I still can't believe he'd beat Kim."

"Booze can really screw with you," Scotty said.

"Dan finished his muffin and coffee. "By the way, how is it you guys are *always* here?"

Scotty looked at Bev. "Because she's feeding three people."

"I'm heading back. Have lots to do, and now I'm solo."

"Go ahead," Scotty said as he reached for his wallet. "My treat today."

As Dan began walking, he thought about Willingham's wounded warriors. *I think it's time to pay them a visit.*

⋏

Officer Jang was in room 309. Sitting in a chair, he was wearing a neck brace, and he had bandages wrapped around his left shoulder.

Dan entered the room. "Jang?"

Jang looked at Dan, and inquisitively asked. "Are you a lawyer?"

"I'm Detective Dan Shields." He pulled his badge from his jacket. "How's Clancy?

"He was released this morning. I'll probably go later today after they check my wound."

"Glad he's okay, and you are, too."

Jang reached for the glass of ginger ale on the table next to his chair, and took a sip. "So what's on your mind?"

"I need to ask you a few questions."

"About the raid?"

"Kind of. More specifically, about Willingham."

Jang put the ginger ale back on the table. "Ted?"

"How long have you worked with him?"

"Three plus. He knows what he's doing."

"I'm sure he does. Do you know who tipped him?"

"No. All I know is we got orders."

"When?"

"About a week before the drug bust. It had to be planned so that we could take control quickly and minimize casualties. Obviously, that didn't happen."

"Did he ever tell you how much money was involved?'

"He never said, but we knew it was more than measly chump change. I did read it was ten million. You got any idea where it went?"

"Where was Willingham during the shootout?"

"On the bugle horn, shouting directions."

"He could see all the action?"

"I guess so. What're you getting at?"

"Bear with me."

"You and Clancy. What happened?"

"We were on the front line. Neither of us saw any shooters. We got close to the U-Haul and then we took hits. Both lucky shots because they struck us where the Kevlar wasn't."

Dan paused. "What do you know about Willingham's personal life?"

Jang shook his head. "He's getting a divorce. Maggie's trying to take him for everything."

Jackpot, he needs cash, Dan thought. "You ever met her?"

"Once. Willingham threw a barbecue at his place last year."

"You know what she does? Or where she works?"

Jang paused. "I know she's a manicurist. Can't remember the name of the place, but it's at Brookland Mall."

Dan had heard enough. He stood and shook Jang's free hand. "Thanks. Hope you go home later."

Chapter 12

Dan wasn't sure what to do with his new information about Willingham, but he did know Syms wouldn't want to hear it, so he filed it away for later.

Lieutenant Dixon's office was one floor below the squad room, in the same spot as Syms's. Dixon looked surprised to see Dan standing at his door. "What brings you down here, Shields?"

Dan looked at the empty chair beside Dixon's desk. "May I?"

"Come in."

"You just impounded an ambulance, correct?"

"Bloody mess, but we have it. Belongs to ESCO."

"Do you know if they ever reported it stolen?"

"Funny you should mention that. It was. But not right away. They reported it a couple of days later."

"Who called it in?"

"The dispatcher. His name is Wiley."

"What exactly did he say?"

Dixon hit his computer. "Wiley claimed the vehicle had been taken to the garage for maintenance, and it was stolen from there."

"What's Wiley's number?" Dan asked.

Dixon looked over his glasses at the detective. "911."

"Never mind, I wrote down the number that was on the side of the ambulance. I'll try that one. Thanks for your help."

⅄

Scotty and Bev were coming from the direction of Syms's office when Dan walked by. "That guy's off the wall today," Scotty said.

"He's tired. We both had a late one last night."

Bev started to sweat. "I need to sit. Holy Jesus, my water broke! I'm in labor."

Scotty looked at Dan. "We need to get her to the hospital."

"Bev, can you walk?" a frenzied Scotty asked.

"Get an ambulance," she yelled.

Every detective in the squad room heard the commotion and gathered around the soon-to-be mother as Dan called 911. Syms came out of his office and saw the puddle of liquid. "She gonna have her kids here?

"EMTs are on the way."

"Good God, I thought she wasn't due yet!" Syms said..

Dan looked at his fellow detectives, and held Bev's hand as she sat on a chair. "Come on, guys, step back and let her breathe."

Scotty held the door as the EMTs, wheeling a gurney entered the room. "She's having twins," he said.

"Oh my," the female EMT said. "She sure is. The paramedic pointed to the gurney and said to her male partner. "Get those blankets on the floor and grab the pillow. The babies are coming. We need to deliver here."

"You shitting me?" the nervous captain said.

"Afraid not," The female EMT said as she placed Bev on the blanket and urged her to push. Bev gritted her teeth, face tightening with every surge of pain. She pushed and screamed.

"I can't give you anything—keep pushing," the EMT said. "We're almost there."

One more push and a baby girl came out. A couple of pushes later, her brother arrived.

Scotty squeezed Bev's hand as she and the babies were about to be taken to the ambulance. "Call my husband. Tell him to meet us at the hospital," Bev said as the newborns were being wrapped in towels. "Let's go," The male EMT said.

"Wow. That was certainly something we don't see every day." Dan said.

"No kidding," Scotty replied. "I have to call Vince and tell him the news."

Syms headed back to his office. "Scotty. After you call her husband, call the cleaning crew to sanitize the room."

⋏

Dan followed the captain. "How about that," Syms said. "Babies, right here. Twins. Think she'll name the boy Harold?"

"I know she isn't gonna name the girl Harold."

Syms tapped his desk. "So, what did you find out? And where the hell are my Advil?"

"I forgot. Besides, if you get a headache, I can call 911 again."

"Funny. So do tell."

"The ambulance was reported stolen, but get this, not until a couple of days later. Could be a while before we know if we have any useable DNA from the vehicle." Dan said. He shook his head. "Somehow, I got a feeling it was wiped clean by the fake paramedics, or someone else."

"What are you getting at?"

Dan looked Syms in the eye. "I keep coming back to Willingham."

Syms had fire in his eyes. "Get off him. I told you to knock it off."

Dan stared back at the captain. "Think about it. That warehouse is in Vegas's territory, and Jenkins would have known where to ditch the ambulance. If Jenkin's had tipped Willingham, then he would have known where the ambulance was. And your friend, the commander, would know where Jenkins and the money went."

Syms got up. "Damn you. I'm gonna take a crap and then I'm out of here. Been a long couple of days."

"You scram too—and you better stop at CVS before I see your ass again."

CHAPTER 13

Syms had given Dan a subtle order, so the detective heeded the captain's demand.

Walking down the aisle of pain relievers, Dan stopped and took a large box of Advil from the top shelf. Not finding the extra- strength package, he brought the medicine to the pharmacist.

"Excuse me," he said. "Do you have any stronger Advil's? I didn't see any on the shelf."

The pharmacist eyed the box. "They're on order, should have them to-morrow. Try our store brand. They're just as good, and less expensive."

Dan returned to the pain med aisle and placed the box back on the shelf. He spotted the store brand and took a package, before heading to the register to purchase the pills.

ᛉ

Mike was getting out of Phyllis's SUV, as Dan's Accord entered the driveway. Two pizza boxes were in his son's hands. "Good timing dad."

"Guess so. I can smell the pepperoni. These from Gianni's?"

Dan opened the front door and the two Shields men walked into the kitchen, the aroma of hot pizza accompanying them. Mike placed the medi-um-sized boxes on the center island.

"How about that," Phyllis said. "A two-fer, both of my guys landing to-gether. Kate and Josh are in the dining room. They'd heard the word '*pizza*' and scurried to the table a half hour ago."

She looked at Mike. "Did you forget something?"

Mike grinned and took the change from his pocket. "Here."

Phyllis placed the hot cardboard food containers in the center of the table and they all dug in. When the pizza fest was over, three slices remained.

"I'm taking these to school tomorrow," Mike said.

⋏

Phyllis followed Dan into the den, and before he picked up the remote and sat on the couch, she opened the bottom left-hand drawer of the desk next to the TV. She pulled out a red rectangular hard-bound portfolio with white letters on the front, and set it next to her husband. "You know what this is?"

He picked it up. "Yeah. It's your degree from North Carolina State. Haven't seen it in years."

"Well it's been here gathering dust, just like me."

"Hey, babe, I like your dust."

She turned to the computer and clicked on a web site. "See this?"

"The Psychology Clinic?"

"They're in Enfield. I spoke with Doctor Brant Englander. They have an opening for a child psychologist and he said I could start as soon as I want. I've been itching to go back to work, but never could find the right time to discuss it with you."

Dan placed the degree in her hands. "Hon, I'd never stop you from going back."

Phyllis sat beside him and he looked into her sexy eyes. "What about Josh and Kate after school?"

She smiled. "Have it all worked out. Nana Rosa is on board."

Dan gave Phyllis a blank stare. "My mother?"

"What's wrong with Nana Rosa? She's retired, lives ten minutes away."

Dan sat back. "If this is what you want, go for it." He saw the smile on her face. "We could use another paycheck."

Phyllis stared at him and frowned. "Is that all you care about? The money?"

Dan kissed her on the lips. "Of course not; I care about you being happy. Besides I don't think your soliciting job is working out too well. You only have one customer, and he's real cheap."

She grabbed his crotch. "Later, Grinch, and this time, leave your wallet under my pillow." The happy wife whispered in his ear. "I like all this activity lately, but you know I can still get pregnant. Think about a vasectomy. You'll get more bang for your buck afterward."

"Nice. I like it when you talk dirty to me."

She got up and took a pamphlet out of the desk drawer.

"Good. I brought this home from Dr. Reinberg. You need to read it."

"I will. I want to watch the Yankee game."

"Promise you'll look at this," Phyllis said as she handed it to him.

"Sure thing hon."

⅄

Later that night when Dan went up to the bedroom Phyllis was in bed with a book in her hand. "Can we talk? Dan asked.

Phyllis closed the book and placed her reading glasses on the table. "Is this about the vasectomy?"

"Good guess."

He opened the pamphlet. "This says that even after the procedure, there's a period of time I could still get you pregnant. It says we should use condoms for a while until he checks my sperm count."

"I saw that. We've been lucky so far, and to be safe, if you don't want to use them, we shouldn't have sex for a while."

Dan jerked his head back. "Jesus. Maybe I can borrow some rubbers from Mike."

Phyllis closed her eyes for a moment. "That's a comforting thought."

"Well, he's almost eighteen and popular. I'm sure he's screwing his girl-friend Lanie, or some other girl in his class." Dan looked at Phyllis's belea-guered face. "What? Like we were virgins when we graduated high school?" he uttered.

"Do you have to say that?"

"Hey, I'm just being real here."

Phyllis closed the pamphlet and placed it next to her glasses.

"By the way, your pre-op visit is tomorrow, four p.m."

A cold sweat poured over the stunned detective. "What?"

"Okay cowboy. Stop perspiring. There's a box of condoms in your night-stand drawer. I already emptied your wallet, so you might as well put one on and get your money's worth."

Chapter 14

Two blueberry muffins were sitting on Dan's desk, and he looked back at Scotty. "No nuts, right?"

"Right—and I'd put these up against Connie's any day."

Dan took a bite. "Good. Darn good. I need a coffee. Keep watch on these."

Dan walked over and poured himself some caffeine. He stopped at Scotty's desk and placed his hot cup on it. "Heard from Bev?"

"Yeah, I stopped to see her and the twins. They're doing well."

"Names?"

"Amy and Andrew. Good names."

Scotty had been divorced a few years ago and the single dad retained liberal visitation of his eight-year old son Eli. Dan looked at the boy's picture that was on Scotty's desk. "How's he doing?"

"Great. Smart little shit. He's into karate."

"Really? So is Josh. Someday they'll beat the crap out of us."

Dan took his cup from the desk. "Mind if I give the other muffin to Syms?"

"No prob."

Stepping into the captain's office, before saying a word, the brash detective placed the muffin on Syms's desk.

"Nice to see you, too," Syms said. "Thanks, but didn't you forget something?"

Dan reached into his pocket and placed an aspirin box next to the muffin.

"What's this shit? This isn't Advil!"

"It's the same thing. They were all out of the extra-strength ones, and the pharmacist said these were just as good."

"Horse crap. Take 'em back and get the real stuff."

"Come on, be reasonable. Try them."

"If they don't work, you're replacing them."

Dan sat.

"Did I tell you to sit?"

"I thought I heard sit."

"You heard wrong. I said shit. So, what's on your mind?"

"A couple of things. Buffalo for one. You heard from Hardison yet?"

"Been too crazy around here, still have a sticky on my desk. I'll give him a buzz and get back to you."

"Okay. How about this one? I need to visit Lucky's Pawn. Biggie and Vegas were there, and I want to see what I can find out about that place."

"You know where that shop is? That's the most dangerous part of the city. Black-and-whites hate going there."

"I gotta go. It's another loose end."

"Your end might be loose if you go."

Dan stood and leaned on the desk. "Relax and eat your muffin. I'll be back in a flash."

Syms opened the bottle of ibuprofen. "Damn it. You be careful. Hey, how about taking Scotty with you?"

"You read my mind. I was thinking the same thing."

Dan returned to the squad room and found Scotty. "Hey. I got Syms's permission to take you on a scouting mission. He loved the muffin, too."

"Where are we going?"

"Come with me. I'll tell you while I'm driving."

Scotty got up and started walking with Dan. When they got into the Accord, Dan started driving toward a section of town known as *Hell Town.* "Your gun loaded?" he asked his companion.

"What? Yeah. It's always loaded," Scotty replied.

"Good. We're going to Lucky's Pawn."

"You crazy? There were two murders right outside that place last week."

"That was last week. I have a few questions for Lucky; you can stay in the car. Call for backup if we need it, but I'm just planning to talk with him."

"Ever met him?"

"Nope, but he's never met me either."

⅄

Dan drove down Gardner and stopped at the corner of Capron. He was sure they'd already been pegged as cops by the people they had passed on the streets. Dan's exterior remained calm, but inside he had some turbulence. *Phyllis would be going through the roof if she knew what I was doing.*

He parked across the street from the shop so Scotty had a good view. As Dan got out, a dark cloud appeared, obscuring the sun. He nervously crossed the street, but felt as out of place as Santa Claus at a bar mitzvah. Two teenagers in black hoodies approached him as he neared Lucky's door. He kept his head down and stepped into the pawn shop.

Standing inside the door was Brick and his dog Sharkey.

Dan stopped.

"You a cop? 'Cause white dudes ain't come here," said the strong man, whose sleeveless tee showed his muscles.

"Yeah, I'm a cop. "Are you Lucky?" Dan asked.

"I'm real lucky," the big goon replied. "You feel lucky today? I'm Brick." He pumped his muscles. "Lucky's in back."

Dan was uneasy, ignoring the distinct odor of marijuana permeating the shop as Lucky appeared.

"That's Lucky. He ain't as nice as me, Brick said."

Wearing his red bandana and earrings, Lucky put his elbows on the counter and he focused his untrusting eyes on Dan. "Speak, cause I'm busy. You got five minutes, and the clock started tickin when you came in."

Dan approached the counter, noticing the man's tattoos, and he placed the white tag he'd taken from the Mustang on the glass top. "This was found in Julio Vegas's car, and I want to know how he got it."

"You fuckin serious? Stupid motherfucker took that Beretta right out of my hands. Didn't know he was gonna shoot Biggie. Fuckin Biggie stole the shotgun he used to take that mother out too."

The Rottweiler was sitting near Dan's feet. "How about moving the dog back?" he said.

Brick looked at Dan. "It's a big floor, how about moving your ass over: I'd do it real slow if I was you."

Dan stood his ground and leaned into Lucky. "Why did they come here? What can you tell me about them?"

"They was always here. Assholes thought they owned the place."

"You paying for protection?"

"Bastards tried to burn this place down; even lit my car once."

"So you're not too unhappy Vegas is gone and Biggie's laid up?"

"Got that right—so's a lot of others."

Dan reached down to pet the dog. "Good boy."

The big guard pulled the menacing canine back. "You done?" Brick said. "Cause like the man said, we got shit to do."

"I'm done. Thanks."

Dan turned around and headed toward the door before looking back. "Can I ask you one more question? Was Armando Jenkins ever here?"

"Dude liked bling. . . bought shit all the time."

"So what was his job? Was he a cutter, seller, money man?"

Lucky looked at his Rolex. "Time's up. You gotta go. And in case you can't count, that was too many questions."

Dan left, sprinting to his car where Scotty was sunken in his seat. "How'd it go?" he asked.

"Piece of cake, but I think our allotted time in this hood is up. Do I smell like weed? That place reeked of it."

Scotty gave a whiff. "Jesus. You do. They give you a joint?"

The Accord sped out of the area as if it was leaving Dodge City being chased by Jessie James's horses.

Dan shook his head, mumbling to himself as they drove back to the police station.

"What's the problem? You look a little frazzled, Scotty said."

"It's Willingham. He and Syms are old friends, and the captain is turning a deaf ear to my suspicions. I still think Willingham's dirty. I talked to one of his guys named Jang in the hospital, and he says Willingham is being taken to the cleaners by his soon-to-be ex."

"What're you getting at?"

"I think he conspired with Jenkins and the fake paramedics. Willingham's hurting for money because of a messy divorce, and splitting ten mil puts a lot of bread in his basket."

Chapter 15

Ted Willingham's Special Forces unit had prepared for quashing the drug deal, and they had known things might not go down as planned.

The last time there had been a casualty was four years ago. Bart Chollie, a hostage negotiator, had been killed when he tried to talk a crazed gunman into releasing two captives. Ironically the incident ended when Jimmy Calero took down the bad guy with a shot from a hundred feet away. Now Jimmy was gone too.

Willingham, however, had personal problems. As Dan had learned from Jang, the commander was in the middle of a nasty divorce.

Dan had smelled a rat from the beginning. He couldn't let Willingham go, especially after chatting with Jang. The detective was determined to speak with the commander's soon-to-be ex. It was clear that Syms didn't want to hear anything negative about his friend, so Dan had to go behind his bosses back to dig up whatever he could to convince the captain to listen to reason.

Maggie Willingham: Dan knew where to find her so he proceeded to the mall and four doors down from the center entrance, on the first floor, was the Nail Palace.

Peering into the open store he saw two rows of work stations, six on each side, nearly all occupied by manicurist's and customers.

He approached a tiny young Asian woman who was standing behind the front desk, her purple and yellow floral smock covering her body. "Is Maggie Willingham here?" Dan asked.

"Yes, third station on the right," she replied.

"Can you tell her I'd like to speak with her?"

"Is she expecting you?"

"No. I need to ask her a couple of questions."

The receptionist walked over and interrupted Maggie. "There's a man in front who wants to talk to you."

Maggie looked at Dan. "Did he say who he is?"

"No, He only said he wants to ask you something."

"Tell him to wait about ten minutes. I'll be done with Mrs. Petersen."

Dan sat waiting for Maggie. He thumbed through a pile of magazines that were stacked on a table. The woman sitting next to him clutched her purse as if he was some kind of mugger or pervert.

Dan got up when he saw Maggie approaching. She appeared to be in her late forties, with streaks of white in her mid-length auburn hair. "I'm detective Dan Shields. Is there someplace we can talk in private?"

"What's this about?"

"Your husband, I want to talk about him."

"Ted?"

"Yes."

"Come with me."

They walked to the back of the salon, into a break room that also appeared to serve as a kitchen, and sat at a round table.

"What can you tell me about him?" Dan asked.

Dan could see the hatred in her eyes. "He's a cheating bastard who I decided to throw out after nine years."

"I take it he's not living with you?"

"He's got a small apartment—my lawyer made sure he moved out."

"Look, I know divorces are sometimes wars. You said he was cheating on you?"

She shook her head. "More than once, but when I learned one of his whores had a six year-old daughter that was his I decided to end it. The lousy hooker's taking him for back child support, and I'm taking him for the rest. He deserves what he's getting."

"What about you? Are you all right?"

"Happier than I've been in years. My lawyer is on top of things, and Ted knows he doesn't want to go before a judge. We're close to settling. He can have his truck and his clothes."

The detective had heard what he needed to hear. He'd, confirmed Willingham was in dire straits and needed money. Dan extended his hand to Maggie, thanked her, and left the salon.

Chapter 16

Phyllis was happy as a lark, having dusted off her college degree and accepted the job with Doctor Englander. Her office was small, but had the usual couch, chairs, desk, computer, filing cabinets, and a few other things, like Kleenex. The walls were painted a calming shade of blue.

She was proudest of the nameplate on her door. *Dr. Phyllis Shields, Psy. D.*

As a child psychologist, she made sure a few friendly stuffed animals were in the room. The one thing apparent to Phyllis was her lack of appropriate attire, only one pantsuit in her closet, so she took action to remedy her sparse array of working outfits.

Dan saw Phyllis's SUV, so he knew she was home. He stopped to take the mail from the box at the end of the driveway, and then parked beside her vehicle. When he entered the foyer and passed by the living room, he noticed shopping bags from Macy's on the couch. "Hi babe, how's it going?"

She smiled. "Great. Dinner will be up shortly."

Hearing his loafers she said. "Shoes?"

"Here's the mail. I'll be right back."

"How about rounding up the troops?" Phyllis said.

"Dinner!" he shouted."

Phyllis groaned. "Thanks. I could have done that."

"You been shopping? I see bags from Macy's."

"I'll show you later; get the kids."

He sifted through the mail and noticed an envelope from Arizona State University addressed to Michael Shields. "Look at this."

"That's one of the schools he applied to. Let him open it."

They all gathered at the table and Dan held the envelope out to Mike. His son's eyes lit up as he took the mail from his father and ripped it open. He pulled out the letter and silently read it. "I'm in!" he yelled. "Full athletic scholarship!"

"Really? Let me see that." Dan said. He got up patted his boy on the shoulders. "This is great. I'm proud of you."

Tears were in Phyllis's eyes. "I'm so happy for you."

"This is unreal," Mike said. "With all that money you're saving you can get me a Vette."

Dan smiled. "You mean vet, as in dog doctor. Nice try. How about graduating college first?"

Mike tore away from the table. "Can't eat, I have to call Taylor. Hope he got in too!"

The rest of the family continued eating. As soon as the table was cleared and the dishes stacked into the dishwasher, Phyllis retrieved her purchases, three new pantsuits and blouses.

"So how much is your new job costing us?"

"Hey, these are deductible. If you're lucky, I'll show you what else I bought later."

"Is it red and lacy?"

She whispered. "Purple, and just think... you won't have to use a condom much longer."

Dan cringed. "Hope that doctor knows what he's doing."

CHAPTER 17

S cotty was at his desk with an arrest warrant in his hand.

"How's it going?" Dan asked.

He saw the paper Scotty was holding. "That a warrant?"

"You got it. This is Landry's, but he's out with the flu. Syms wants me and a couple of uniforms to go snatch a guy right out of his office. Son of a bitch drove his Jeep over an old lady on Rosedale a couple of days ago and sped away. The owner of the vehicle is Grayson Garrett, and there were witnesses."

"Grayson Garrett? As in Garrett Lumber?"

"That's him, and I confirmed he's at work, and so is the Jeep." Gotta go; the uni's are waiting. See you later."

"Hey. What about the victim?"

"She's alive. Both legs broken, and a displaced hip. I'm sure she's got lawyers pounding on her hospital door."

⚓

Dan entered the captain's office and took a seat. "Nice to see you," Syms said. He picked up his sticky note. "I have something for you. It's a name. Hardison said to give Captain Wally Bates in Buffalo a call. Here's his number."

Dan turned to walk out. "Thanks. Maybe this guy can give me the low-down on Armando Jenkins."

⚓

Back at his desk, Dan's hopes were up as he opened Jenkin's file and called the number on the sticky note.

The captain answered. "Bates."

"Hello, this is detective Dan Shields from Hartford. Chief Hardison passed your number along to me because I have some questions about a gang member who has a prior up your way."

"What's the name?"

"Armando Jenkins. His rap sheet says he was arrested for narcotics and grand theft auto. I need to know more about him."

"Name doesn't ring a bell. Any aliases?"

"Not that I know of."

"What's the deal?"

"He was arrested here a few days ago, and he escaped. He may have connections in your area."

"Let me see." Dan heard the clicking of fingers on a keyboard. "What did you say his name was?"

"Jenkins, Armando Jenkins."

"He's not in our system, and I know most of the thugs up here—but like I said, never heard of him."

"Are you sure?"

"Very sure."

Dan sat back, silent for a second. "I don't understand. We accessed the NCIC and he came right up. Buffalo, New York arrest records, and mug shot."

"How long ago?"

"Four years."

Four? Damn. I've been here thirteen and I was on the drug team then. I would have known that name. You sure?"

Dan couldn't believe what he was told. "What the hell is going on?"

"Beats me," Bates said.

"Thanks captain. Something's not kosher."

Dan hung up and raced to see Syms. "You won't believe it. They have no re-cord of Jenkins in Buffalo. This mug shot and rap sheet on NCIC clearly say Buffalo. Could this be bogus for some reason?"

Syms scratched his head. "Fake? Who the hell fakes raps sheets and mug shots?"

Dan had an idea, but kept it to himself. "Beats me. I'm going to do some digging." He picked up the aspirin bottle from Sym's desk. "These working for you?"

"Lucky for you, they are, but I have to take twice as many. Hand me the bottle and go to work."

CHAPTER 18

Dan didn't sleep well: his appointment with Doctor Reinberg kept him tossing and turning all night. The pre-op visit was one thing, but the actual procedure was another. Dan showered, and did something he never thought he'd ever have to do. He shaved his scrotum.

Phyllis handed him a pair of sweats to wear. "Honey. Thank you for doing this."

"Let's backtrack a step." Dan said. "I think this is what you would call sexual blackmail."

"No, I think this is what you call securing our nest egg. No more kids."

"By the way, exactly where did you tell them we were going this morning?"

"To join the gym. Mike's got practice, so we have to drop Kate and Josh off at Nana's"

"Good one dear. You tell her we're going to the gym too?"

Phyllis tossed him his Yankees cap. "Let's go, Yogi."

⋏

Dan pulled into the medical building lot, parked the car and handed Phyllis the keys. "We have a will, don't we?" he said.

"That's it. I want everything, now, can't wait until you croak."

Dan opened the door to Reinberg's office, checked in with the receptionist, and signed the consent papers.

"Doctor will be right with you, Mr. Shields."

A nurse in a green gown saw Dan. "We're ready for you, Mr. Shields."

Dan looked back at Phyllis. "Are we sure about this?"

"Go ahead. I'll admire the work afterward."

"See you in a bit."

He followed the nurse to the procedure room where the doctor was waiting. Dan saw the bright lights and snipping instruments on the counter.

"Morning, Mr. Shields. Did you read the instructions that I gave you after your pre-op visit?"

Dan shook his head. "I did, and so did my wife."

What did you eat for breakfast?"

"One egg, and a piece of toast."

"Perfect. Is there anything else you'd like to know before we begin?"

"Will my voice change?"

The doctor looked at his patient and smiled. "Not unless your vocal cords are in your scrotum."

Doctor Reinberg, who appeared to be about fifty, was wearing a white gown, and he adjusted the small light that was strapped to his cap. "Hop up on the table and we can start—should take twenty minutes or so."

Dan looked at the female assistant who was still in the room. "Is she staying?"

"I'm sorry. You haven't met my wife Sarah. She's my partner. She did my vasectomy."

Sarah smiled, and she picked up a syringe. "Drop the sweats. I'll give you a little medication, and you won't feel anything, except a little prick," she said.

Dan eyed her. "Funny, I bet you tell all your victims that."

Dr. Reinberg slipped on a pair of disposable gloves.

"How many of these have you done?" Dan asked.

"One, I saw a video on YouTube. Piece of cake - snip snip."

The doctor began the procedure, and twenty-two minutes later, Dan had been snipped, and had his post-op instructions. He came out and winked at Phyllis. "All done, you get my ice cream yet?"

"A half-gallon of chocolate fudge is waiting for you."

He took her hand. "That's my girl. Take me home."

CHAPTER 19

Captain Syms liked the early morning peace and quiet of his office, but it was usually short lived. Arriving at six a.m. allotted him time to relax and gear up for the normally chaotic day.

His hot coffee and daily newspaper were on his desk. He hadn't turned a page yet when his phone rang; a sure sign of trouble. As soon as he picked up the receiver, he knew this day was going to be bad. The voice on the other end was Sergeant Streeter of the Manchester Police Department.

"Captain Syms. We have a detective named Marty Patton in custody; He says he's one of yours." The captain braced himself for bad news. "Sort of, he's under suspension. What's he done?"

"He's in Eastside Hospital. There was a domestic last night, and his wife got the best of the fight."

Syms leapt out of his chair. "What? Is she hurt?"

"She's down here filing a complaint. She's okay, a little shaken. I understand this isn't the first episode."

Syms's blood was boiling. "God damn it. There's a restraining order. How the hell did this happen? Jesus Christ, keep Kim there until I get there. I'm going to the hospital first to have a few words with Marty."

"He'll be coming here when he gets out of the hospital. There are uniforms with him."

"I'll see you in bit."

Syms slammed the phone down, rushing out of his office. He raced down to his car, and with the siren blaring and flashing lights running, he sped to the hospital. His eyes were lit with fire and his fists were ready to pummel Marty.

⋏

Syms rushed inside to Eastside's registration desk and presented his badge. "Marty Patton, what room is he in?"

The clerk looked him up. "He's in 221, second floor."

The captain brushed past a nurse and sprinted to the elevator. As soon as he got off, he saw a uniform standing outside room 221, and he headed toward the officer. "I'm Captain Syms. This idiot is one of mine."

"He's laid up pretty good. His wife kicked him in the balls. Bullseye. I hear his nuts are the size of softballs."

Syms burst into Marty's room, staring at the wounded, motionless detective. "Marty! How they hangin'?" he angrily uttered.

Patton's eyes shied away from Syms. "You look at me," Syms said. "You're in deep shit. This is going before the board. I'm sure you'll be fired soon. Son of a bitch, I should've had you arrested the first time, but I'm too nice of a guy. God help you, because you'll need a good lawyer, and you know what? Judges don't think too highly of domestic abuse and people who violate restraining orders, especially when it's a fucking cop."

Syms didn't skip a breath as he continued his scolding. "Guess you're going to leave here with your balls in a sling. Don't call me, Marty; I'll let the Manchester police keep you for a while."

Marty took the lambasting without uttering a sound.

Syms glared at him. "Can you talk or what? I see pissing is a problem."

Marty mumbled, "I didn't mean it. I love Kim."

Syms got closer to him, eyes blazing. "Shut up, you asshole. I don't want to hear that shit. You still have booze on your breath. So much for AA. You're going straight to jail from here without passing go. Don't look for a 'get out of jail free' card, either. You so much as *look* at Kim again and I'll have you castrated."

Syms stormed out of the room. The uniform's eyebrows shot up. "Haven't heard a tongue lashing like that since my mother caught me stealing comic books, straightened my ass out real quick."

"Keep an eye on him, and tell the nurses to go easy on the pain meds. Let him suffer."

The irate captain briskly strode back to his car, and headed straight to the Manchester police station.

⅄

He entered the building, showed his ID and was directed to Streeter who looked up from his desk and saw the beleaguered captain storming down the corridor. "I'm Syms. Is Kim Patton still here?"

Streeter put his pen down and held up a piece of paper. "Yes. I told her you were coming. I'll take you back. One of my guys is still with her."

Streeter and Syms entered the small interrogation room, and the uniformed officer left. The captain stared at Kim in a fatherly way. Although she'd been crying, Syms was silently relieved to see her unharmed. He put his arms around her. "I just saw Marty and read him the riot act. How are you?"

"I'm fine," she said, tears in her eyes. "But I don't know what to do with Marty. He's so messed up and needs help, but I have to keep him away until he's better."

"What happened?"

"Marty was drunk and he came to the apartment. I still care about him and didn't want him driving home, so I told him he could sleep it off on the couch. He grabbed me and tried to rape me again, but I was able to kick him, and call for help."

"Some kick. I think you could get a job with the Giants. Was this the first time he's tried to see you?"

"No; he's been to Silver's a few times, and I always tell him to go away, and he does."

Syms responded. "Marty knows he shouldn't be going there, or anywhere near you. Do you know if he's been to AA or anger management classes?"

"He quit AA, and I don't think he ever started anger management."

"Where has he been living?"

"He had no choice. He's been staying with his parents."

"Are they aware of his problem?"

"I don't know. His father is an alcoholic too. I guess that's where he gets it from."

Syms sighed. "Well, at least Marty won't be able to harm you anymore. He'll be booked when he gets out of the hospital."

Kim started to cry, and Syms handed her a tissue. He took out his card and wrote his cell number on it. Here's my personal phone number, so call me if you need anything."

"Thank you for coming."

Syms looked at Streeter. "Is she done here?"

"Yeah, we were waiting to take her home."

"Don't bother." Syms helped Kim up. "Come on, I'll take you home."

⋏

Back at headquarters, there was a full squad room. Dan noticed the captain's empty office. "Wonder where Syms is?"

Scotty pointed to fellow detective Joe Gendreau. "Joe had just gotten to his desk and he saw Syms bolt out of here like a bat out of hell. You're a little gimpy today. Have a good weekend?"

"Think I pulled a muscle, and these new briefs are a little snug."

"Snug? You look like you need a cane," Scotty said.

"Come on smart ass. Let's go to Connie's"

"We walking, or you need a cab?"

⋏

The sparring detectives made it to the diner and sat in the booth that Scotty and Bev usually occupied. Connie greeted them.

"What'll it be, boys?"

"The usual," Dan replied.

Connie obliged and filled two cups with black coffee. "I'll be back with a muffin."

"Not today," Dan said. Coffee is fine."

Scotty stirred sugar into his cup. "Did you talk to Willingham's wife?"

Dan rubbed his chin. "That's what I need to see Syms about. I talked with her, and she said a mouthful. Willingham is so hard up for money he may need a second job. What about you? You arrest the lumber guy?"

"No problem. He came quietly."

"So what's the deal?" Scotty said. "You're walking like you rode a horse all day yesterday."

Dan picked up his cup and grinned. He whispered. "Okay, smart ass. I had a vasectomy, you happy now?"

Scotty smiled. "Yeah, I didn't know you and Phyllis still did it?"

"Funny. Guess what? It gets better with age. Finish up. Let's get back."

⅄

The short break was over and the detectives were at their desks.

Dan looked into Syms's office—still empty.

Then they heard loud stomping footsteps: Syms zipped past his entire crew without saying a word, although Dan heard the captain muttering under his breath. As he turned for his office Syms yelled out, "Don't anyone bother me! Stay away."

He immediately grabbed the Advil and swallowed a few with a chug of water.

Dan and Scotty looked at each other. "What the hell is eating him?" Scotty said.

"Beats the shit out of me, but I'm going to find out," Dan said.

"Better not, he'll blast the shit out of you."

Dan saw the two day old muffin on Scotty's desk. "Give me that."

"Come on, Dan. What are you doing?"

"Been nice knowing you: I'm going in."

"But that's stale, should be in the basket."

Dan grabbed the brick anyway and he marched down the hall. Syms was staring out a window with his back to the office door when the brave detective went in and stood in front of the gray desk until the captain turned around. "Jesus. What the hell are you doing in here? You deaf or something?"

Dan placed the muffin on the desk. "Thought you might like this."

"What the fuck do you think I am?" He tossed the hard muffin in the basket. "I told you to get out and leave me alone."

Dan shut the door and stood face to face with Syms. "Okay. I'll leave, but you want me to call an ambulance? What the hell is going on with you?"

Syms sat with his hands on his head. "Sit down, dipshit." The captain took a deep breath. "It's Marty—it's that fucking asshole. He's at Eastside" Syms snickered. "Should see him. His balls are hanging in a sling."

Dan cringed, knowing his own testicles had recently been tampered with. Then he broke an inquisitive laugh. "His jewels?"

"Yeah, last night he showed up at their apartment, drunk as a skunk. He tried to rape Kim again and she kicked him so hard in his nuts, he couldn't move."

"Kim okay?"

"Yeah, I drove her home from the police station. This time he's been arrested." Syms was more relaxed and reached into the wastebasket. "Think this muffin is still edible?"

"Any rats in the bucket?"

"No."

"Then enjoy it."

Dan got back into detective mode." Listen, I have to tell you some stuff, but you may not like it, so bear with me."

"Okay. I'm ready."

"It's Willingham. I spoke to one of his guys—Jang—and he told me Ted's in the process of divorce, and his wife Maggie is taking him to the cleaners."

"Here we go again," Syms uttered as he bit into the muffin, and spit it out. "What the fuck is this thing. I almost broke a tooth," he said as he tossed the muffin back into the basket.

Dan shook his head. "I'll have to talk to Scotty about that," he said. "Listen. I spoke with Maggie. Turns out she isn't the only one emptying his wallet. He had a mistress who's suing him for child support. They have a six-year-old daughter."

Syms bowed his head and reached for pill bottle "Already took a few of these babies. Damn it, he better not be dirty. Keep digging, and I'll keep my eyes closed until you can prove something. Now get out of here."

Dan was about to leave. "Hey," Syms said. "Thanks. And what's with the funny walk?"

"Long story," Dan said, then he slowly strolled back to his desk where he noticed the ESCO ambulance company phone number that he'd written on his desktop pad. He picked up his phone, and called, hoping to speak with Wiley.

Dan was in luck as Wiley answered. "This is detective Dan Shields. I have a few questions about an ambulance that you reported stolen."

"Like what? I reported it."

"I know you did, but why did it take you so long?"

Dan heard Wiley take a breath. "That ambulance had been dropped off at the garage for maintenance, along with two others. We have a fleet of twenty-four, and have them all serviced twice a year. I got a call from the garage saying they had paperwork for three ambulances, but only two were in their lot. It was stolen from the garage."

"Where is this garage?"

"It's on Plimpton, Bagwell's. You can talk to Buzzy if you want."

"Do you have his number handy?"

Wiley read it to Dan. "Thanks. I'll give him a call."

The detective wasted no time and called Buzzy. The garage owner echoed the same story as Wiley.

Dan asked. "How is it that no one noticed the vehicle was missing?"

"This is a busy place. It wasn't until we went to work on the third vehicle, we couldn't find it, so I called Wiley and he swore it was dropped off. That's when we realized it was gone."

"So no one saw or heard anything suspicious?"

"No. That's all I can tell you."

"How about videos? You have cameras in the lot?"

"No. Been thinking about it."

Dan wasn't pleased with these conversations, but he had no choice and accepted Wiley's, and Buzzy's explanations.

CHAPTER 20

Commander Willingham had dispatched half of his highly skilled men to a training exercise. The other half had gone through the rigorous routine yesterday. Although he still had Jimmy Calero's funeral to attend, Willingham was mildly comforted knowing Jang and Clancy would be back to work soon.

His office in the back room of a barracks-style building displayed a large American flag hung on a wooden stand, beside the window to the rear of his desk. The picture on the wall to his left was Governor Bushnell, and next to the pictures were FBI, DEA, and ATF commendations.

The commander's door opened and Jang walked in, his left arm in a sling.

Willingham stood and shook his soldier's free hand. "When's that thing coming off?"

"I'm going to the doctor as soon as I leave here, and then I start rehab. Could be back in two to three weeks."

"Nice. Have a seat. Seen Clancy?"

"Talked to him yesterday, he's coming along fine."

"I have to call him. You were on my list, too. I saw Jimmy's family, and of course they're a wreck."

"When's the funeral?"

"There's a wake tomorrow night, and he'll be buried the following morning. A bunch of us are going to the funeral home and the church. We'll have a presence at the cemetery as well."

"Count us in. Clancy and I will be there, but there's something I want to tell you."

Willingham furled his eyebrows. "Shoot."

"When I was in the hospital, a detective Shields came in and was asking a lot of questions about you."

"Me?"

"Yeah. Kind of recreating the raid and where you were the whole time?"

"What was he getting at?" Willingham paused. "Did he ask about Jenkins or the jail break?"

Jang shook his head. "No. he asked about personal stuff, you and your wife."

Willingham sat back and rolled his eyes. "What did you tell him?"

"Only thing I said was that you and Maggie are getting divorced."

"That son of a bitch. I'll have to talk to Syms, and he can straighten his detective out. If he contacts you again, let me know."

Jang got up. "Roger. I have to go get this sling off. See you at the wake."

"Sure thing, thanks."

Willingham wondered if Dan had tried to talk to Maggie, so he picked his phone and called her.

Maggie answered. "What do you want? You have my lawyer's number."

"Come on Maggie. I only want to know one thing. Did a detective come to see you?"

"What if he did?"

"Come on. I need to know what he said."

"All right. I told him what a scumbag you are. He knew about the divorce, but he didn't know about your kid, and mistress."

"You told him about that shit?"

"Sorry, but the truth always hurts, doesn't it?"

"Damn it Maggie, I wish you'd keep your mouth shut."

"It is now. Call my lawyer."

As soon as he hung up, Willingham grabbed his hat and headed out to see Captain Syms.

⋏

Willingham's truck rolled into the Hartford jail's parking lot. He got out and his hat nearly blew off his head as a gust of wind hit him before he entered the building. The commander felt several sets of eyes on him as he stalked to Syms's office and barged in, slamming the door.

"What the hell is bothering you? Syms asked.

Willingham placed his hat on the captain's desk and he leaned in. "Shields. It's him. Are you dogging me, too?'

"What're you talking about? Sit down and be civil."

"Don't pretend, Harold. Dan's been slumming around, asking questions. Talked to Jang and Maggie about me. What's he up to?"

"Why are you so edgy, Ted?"

"Hey, I lost a guy, remember? And I have a funeral to go to."

"Hold it. We both know our jobs are dangerous and we both know what comes with the territory, but you're a little off the wall."

"Am I? I also have a bloody divorce with a bitchy, soon to be ex to deal with."

"What about the mistress, and the kid?"

"Jesus, Dan told you about that, too?'

"Yeah. Regardless of what you think, he's a good cop."

"What's he really after?"

"I'll let you think about that."

"I want Shields to back off, or I'll go to Hardison and have him suspended."

Syms stood, leaning closer to Ted's face. "Really? You'll have to get me suspended, too. What is it you're hiding?"

Willingham pulled back. "It's the money. He thinks I stole it, doesn't he?"

"It's a hell of a theory. Did you?'

Willingham had rage in his eyes. "Do you think I made off with it? And what about that ambulance and Jenkins—you think I was in on that, too?"

Syms glared, eye to eye with him. "Like I said, hell of a theory, Ted. All we know is that your money is drying up, and you could use the cash."

Willingham angrily stood, placing his hands on the desk. "God damn it. How long have we known each other, Harold? You think I'd pull shit like this?"

"Ten million is a great motivator, and you better not be dirty."

"I'm getting out of here—and if I did stash the money somewhere, you think I'd tell you?" The commander picked up his hat, storming out of the police station.

Dan rushed into the captain's office after he saw the fleeting commander crash through the front door. "Shut the door and sit down." Syms said. "Look, as much as you aggravate the shit out of me, you may be onto something. Ted was all over you about talking with Jang and Maggie. Wants to rip your badge from your body." Syms popped a couple of tablets. "He crossed a line with me. I told him you were a good cop. He was really uneasy, like you struck a nerve."

Dan grinned. "You stuck up for me?"

"You know, you have a lot of nerve, but yes, you're a damn good detective."

"I'll keep shaking him down."

"Okay, but that's one tall tree, so better bring a rake to catch all the leaves when he falls."

Chapter 21

Dan saw Nana Rosa's white Lincoln alongside Phyllis's car and knew there'd be a dinner guest. He parked the Accord in back of his wife's SUV and went inside. He had to admit his mother's homemade pasta sauce was the best, and the smell of garlic and fresh basil hit him as soon as he went into the kitchen. He sidled up to his mother and gave her a kiss on the cheek. She handed him a ladle. "Taste."

"Terrific,—you gonna bottle this someday?"

The five foot, white haired, pear-shaped chef opened the oven door. "Stand back. Garlic bread is done."

Phyllis stayed out of her mother-in-law's way, so she set the table and wisely let the old woman work. Noticing her husband's gimpy walk, Phyllis said. "Still a little sore?"

Dan grinned. "I'm fine."

Nana heard the exchange. "What's the matter, you get kicked by some crazy hoodlum?"

"No. I got out of bed the wrong way and twisted something. It's nothing."

All three children were politely behaved for their grandmother. As soon as the family gathered around the table, Dan said grace and they all dug in.

"So, what's this I hear about my big grandson moving to Arizona?" Nana said.

"I'm not moving Nana. It's just college," Mike said.

"So, you couldn't get into UConn, Yale, or anyplace else around here?"

Dan smiled at his mother. "It's about baseball. Arizona has a top level program. He'll be fine, and you can send him some sauce."

Nana looked at Josh. "And what about this one? You going to send him to Japan because he's good at karate?"

Dan grinned. "That's what I like about you mom; you always can see the future."

Nana looked at Kate's pretty little face. "And there's Miss America. I suppose she's going to modeling school in California."

Dan's mother was a piece of work, full of guilt trips and unsolicited advice, and at times he was too glad to see her go home. This was one of those nights: when Nana left, the whole house breathed a sigh of relief.

Later, Dan sidled up next to Phyllis in bed. "Any interesting patients? Anyone else's mother screw them up?"

"I haven't had any yet that I could recommend sending to a mental institution, but they all have issues, and I have to respect each patient's privacy. I'll let you know if I get a serial killer, though. Your boys really okay?"

"They're a little tender. That reminds me. I should apply a little ice. Wanna get me a pack?"

Phyllis got up. "That's the least I can do for you. You'll pay me back in a week or so."

⅄

Dan rolled over when his alarm went off at five-thirty a.m.

Phyllis had gotten the kids up, and the Shield house's daily routine was underway. By the time Dan came downstairs, Mike, Josh, and Kate had already walked to the school bus stop, and coffee was waiting for him. He watched Phyllis pour a cup and place it on the island.

"Thanks, hon. Is that one of the new outfits?"

"Like it?"

"Real nice, love you in blue, matches your eyes."

Phyllis picked up her purse and took out her car keys. "Have an early one. See you later."

Dan finished his coffee, locked up and got into his car.

There wasn't a cloud in the sky, but he had no idea a storm was brewing at police headquarters.

⋏

Dan pulled in and saw the unmistakable rear fins of Scotty's 1957 Chevy. Scotty also had a five-year-old Camaro, but he'd mentioned it was in the shop, getting new brakes. Dan parked next to the Chevy, admiring the vehicle as he made his way to the back door of the headquarters. He felt the need to step down into the dungeon.

"Thought you swore this place off," Dom said.

"I did, but we should be moving into the new building soon, and let's face it: this is a zoo that can't be replaced. I only hope we get a better class of animals in the new tank."

"Go ahead, get a whiff of these sweat hogs."

Dan went in and slowly perused the crowd. He recognized a couple of street criminals who were no strangers to this lockup. As he got to the end of the floor, he was struck with another eerie feeling that sent shivers through his body. Maybe it was just the chill of the dank dungeon. . . or maybe it was something else. He walked up the stairs into the squad room. The floor creaked as he approached his desk.

"Brought you a present," Scotty said.

"If it's the Chevy, I'll take it."

Scotty pointed straight ahead to Dan's desk. "Close."

"Jeez, biggest muffin I've ever seen. No nuts, right?"

"Only the one standing next to me."

Dan peeked down the hall and saw Hardison sitting in Syms's office.

"What's the old man doing down here? Hope he's not handing out pink slips."

"If he is, I'm sure ours are right on top. He's been in there awhile."

"Guess I'll grab a brew and eat the muffin before I find out what's happening."

Minutes later Syms's door opened and Hardison left. The captain got up and headed to the bathroom. Dan decided to follow him in. Syms didn't smile when he saw Dan standing next to him at a urinal. "Great minds think alike don't they?" Dan said.

"Get in my office when you're done, and no peeking."

Syms flushed, washed his hands and went back to his office. Dan followed suit.

The captain waited, closed the door behind Dan, and they both sat.

"See this smile?" Syms said.

"What smile? You look like you ate something other than a few ibuprofen."

"God damn right. I just ate a pile of shit. You see the man leave here?"

"Yeah, so what's up?"

"Up? You're up. I'm up, the entire jig is up."

"What the hell are you talking about?"

"Willingham, I'm talking about my friend Ted. He wants you off his ass. He told Hardison to put a dart in your behind and ground you."

"Can he do that?"

"No. He can't, but a judge can."

"What're you saying?"

"That bastard had Judge Zimmerman talk to Hardison? She put a leash on him, and she's tied our hands behind our backs?"

Syms stood and eyed his detective. "We've been ordered to drop the case, everything. Willingham, the money, Jenkins, Biggie. Everything."

Dan put his hands on the desk, leaning forward. "I told you your buddy was hiding something."

"Maybe he is, but it may not be what we think. According to Hardison, this case is bigger than us, and we need to back out."

"How's that?"

"He didn't say, but if I had to guess, it has something to do with Martinez, and Willingham has information he can't or doesn't want to tell us."

Looming large was Vinnie Martinez, a fish the commander thought he would reel in during the daring raid. The lure of all that money was sure to nab the Florida gangster, but things didn't turn out that way, and the big time drug lord was still free.

Martinez's thriving Hi-Hat club operated with a bevy of dancers/hookers. The man in charge of the place was Cecil Flores, who stayed away from the deadly gang life, but was heavily into drugs. Cecil knew people, and he was the one who informed his boss that Biggie had shot and killed Vegas. Cecil was no stranger to the local courts, and reported seeing Jenkins in the club several times with Vegas and Biggie.

Cecil was Martinez's ears, and he'd knocked on several doors trying to get a hint of what had happened to the money and Jenkins, but hit a dead end. Even Lucky couldn't help him.

Whether Willingham was dirty or not, he'd thrown a dagger at Dan and Syms.

Dan moved to open the door to leave Syms's office. "Willingham may have given us all a bath, but I still think there's dirty water in his tub," the detective said as he departed.

PART TWO

CHAPTER 22

Ten Months Later

State trooper Elijah Rawls had stationed his cruiser along I-84 in Tolland when he received a call. Turning on his flashers, and windshield wipers, he sped three miles to forty-seven North Anchorage Road. The log cabin home, barely visible from the street, sat on five acres of wooded land. A marker next to the driveway and a black mailbox were the only indicators that anyone lived on this property. Branches strewn on both sides of the winding, tree-lined entrance, and the mucky terrain made it difficult for Rawls to maneuver his vehicle up to the house.

Will and Amanda Merline, both in their late thirties, stood on the sheltered front porch along with their children: Zach, twelve, Alex, ten, and their muddy-pawed English setter, Buster.

Several days of heavy rain had left the ground a slushy quagmire.

Rawls got out of his cruiser. The six-two trooper, wearing rain gear over his gray uniform, approached Will, who directed him to a swampy hole about a hundred yards from the rear of the house. Rawls trudged his way up the hill, raindrops falling from his hat, and he saw a black male, face down in a watery grave. The dead man's clothes were soaked, and from the corpse's position it was impossible to tell if he'd been shot, stabbed, or beaten. He appeared to be about five-nine or ten. Rawls sloshed through the area before the mobile crime unit and his boss, Major Rich Carroll, arrived. Other emergency vehicles responded, but there was nothing the fire crew, or paramedics could do.

Carroll, several inches shorter than Rawls, but nearly twice the twenty-five year old trooper's age, eyed the crime scene. Both officers made their way down to the house, removing their wet rainwear and boots, placing them on a bench in the back hall. They joined Will, Amanda, their boys, and Buster, who were gathered inside the cozy family room. A pile of wood and a set of andirons sat next to a lit fireplace that took the chill out of the air.

Carroll took out a pad and pen as he looked around. He couldn't miss the moose head hanging above the fireplace, or the framed hundred-dollar bill displayed on the mantle.

He looked at Will. "You shoot that moose?"

Will grinned. "No such luck. That was here when we bought the place."

Zack and Alex sat on the floor with Buster between them. The dog got up and placed his head in Rawls's lap while the boys eyed the officer's holstered weapons.

The major got down to the business at hand. "So tell us what happened."

Amanda pulled her dark hair back, tying it in ponytail. She looked at her sons and softly said. "You boys go to your room. We need to talk with these policemen."

As soon as Zack and Alex were out of sight, Will, still unshaven, clad in Levi's and long-sleeved, checkered shirt began talking. "I'd let Buster out this morning as I usually do, but he didn't come back right away. Then I heard him barking so I looked out the back window and saw him. He wouldn't come when I called, so I went to get him. When I got closer I saw the body, grabbed Buster by the collar, came back inside, and I called 911."

"You never saw or heard anything before the dog alerted you?" Carroll asked.

Will shook his head. "No. We were in Maine until late last night, and it was raining pretty heavily."

"How long were you gone?"

"Just the weekend, we left Friday."

"So you didn't notice anything unusual before you left?"

Will pointed to his dog. "No. He would have sniffed out the body, if it had been there."

Carroll looked at Buster, as the pet nestled up to him. "You're right. I've had setters, and they can smell a dead animal a mile away."

Rawls looked at Will. "Anyone know you'd be gone this weekend?"

"Not that I'm aware of."

"Neighbors?"

"I can't say that we know many of them. As you can see, we're pretty isolated here. There's a few places with a lot of land nearby. It could just as well have happened on any of the other properties."

"True, but it didn't. It happened here, and we'll probably get no discernable footprints with all the mud." Rawls added. "It certainly doesn't appear that a vehicle could have made it up there."

Rawls reached over and petted Buster.

"We need to go check with the lab crew." the major said. "We should be done soon."

Carroll and Rawls got up, gathered their outerwear, and went outside where Chief Medical Examiner Max Arnstein stood over the victim. The troopers got a better look at the body that had been rolled out of the muddy pit. "I don't see any bullet holes or stab marks. Do you?" Carroll said to Rawls.

"No. Shirt's not ripped and there don't appear to be blood stains anywhere."

"We'll see what the autopsy reveals," Arnstein said.

The body was bagged and readied for transport to the University Medical Center.

$$\curlywedge$$

At the morgue Arnstein, a board certified pathologist, approached the corpse that had been laid on a steel examining table. Bright lights illuminated the now cleaned up naked dead man. The Medical Examiner had begun the autopsy when the lab's phone rang. A female associate inside the office, answered the call.

She got the chief's attention. "It's for you—this guy says it's important, can't wait."

"Who is it?" Arnstein replied.

"He won't say. He says it's urgent."

The white gowned pathologist slipped off his mask, and removed his latex gloves, tossing the hand protectors into a medical waste container as he entered the office. He took the phone and listened to the caller. Arnstein's head jerked back.

"What did he do?"

That question went unanswered, and the caller said one more thing.

Arnstein paused before responding. "I'll be here, alone waiting for you."

The conversation abruptly ended. Arnstein was befuddled, but he had his orders. He donned fresh gloves, put the mask back on, and continued his examination of the corpse. Upon completing the autopsy, he wrote a name on a tag, and told Brendan, the associate who had washed the body, to attach the stringed ID to the right toe of the victim.

The name written on the tag was Cosby Davis.

CHAPTER 23

Captain Harold Syms stood in his new office looking through a window, watching the morning traffic: like all the law enforcement officers, he was glad to be out of the torn down Morgan Street jail. The new police headquarters sat on a piece of land once owned by Samuel Colt, and had easy access to the highways and city neighborhoods.

Syms's phone rang; he picked it up and heard the voice of an old friend.

"Harold. This is Rich Carroll."

"Hey, how's life out in the sticks, Major?"

"Great. How are you big city boys doing?"

"We're having a good old time here."

"Have you heard about the body we found in Tolland a couple of days ago?"

"Yes, I'm aware of it."

"Well, the corpse is at the morgue, and I spoke with Arnstein. He said they came up with a positive. The vic lived in Hartford, and his name was Cosby Davis."

Syms jerked back in his chair. "You sure about that? How old was this guy?"

"I have the pathology report," Carroll replied "Says: Cosby Davis, black male, thirty years old, cause of death— undetermined."

Syms's jaw dropped. "What the hell is going on? Something's not right here. That guy committed suicide a few months ago. A name like his, you don't forget."

"Sure it's the same guy?"

Syms chewed on his pencil. "We sure as hell have to find out, because if it is, some gravedigger is on the loose. Hold on a sec. I'm bringing up Davis's obit."

Syms began reading. "Unless he had an identical twin with the same name, it can't be him." Syms read aloud. "He was thirty, says here there was a graveside service, so he was buried. How did Arnstein know his corpse's age? Did he have and ID, or was he counting rings around the corpses trunk?"

"He claims a wallet was inside the man's back pocket." Carroll paused. "Let me drop by the new place in the morning and see if we can piece this together. I'll bring what I've got. I'm interested in taking a look at the new headquarters anyway."

Syms tried to absorb the news as he walked into the squad room; the walls still smelled of fresh paint. Dan and Scotty were in adjoining cubicles, each with an undented gray metal desk, computer, and printer, plus a table, two chairs, and a coat rack. Name tags affixed to the outside of the partitioned workplaces identified their spaces. The creaking floors were gone, and lots of windows and plenty of overhead lights brightened the room.

Dan had already toured the new booking area and holding tank on the ground level. His only negative thought was that criminals didn't deserve cells as nice as those. The sprawling new four-floor campus was easily three times the size of the old jail. A welcomed addition was the cafeteria, although it could never replace Connie's Place.

Syms rapped on Dan's wall. "Let's go to my office. Grab Scotty."

They entered Syms's corner office where his desk shined, the chairs had no broken legs, and the door wasn't coming off its hinges. Sitting in the middle of his desk was a familiar sight. . . a giant-sized bottle of Advil.

Dan and Joe sat as Syms rubbed his hands over his eyes. "Got a good one for you two. Remember my old buddy, Major Carroll?"

"The state trooper?" Dan said.

"He just called. You heard about that body they found in Tolland?"

Dan and Scotty nodded.

"Got a little problem," Syms said, twirling the Advil in his hand. "Coroner says the vic's name is Cosby Davis."

Dan and Scotty looked blankly at each other. "Can't be two guys with the name Cosby Davis." Dan said.

"Could be if one's a junior," Scotty replied.

Syms rubbed his hands across his face. "Not likely. Their ages are the same, and I doubt that twins would have the same name. Carroll is coming down here in the morning to fill us in on what he's got. This could get interesting."

"Interesting?" Dan said. "If I remember right, Davis and his girlfriend committed suicide sometime last year. How the hell does his body wind up in a muddy grave? What about the girl? What was her name?"

"Gomes. Yolanda Gomes," Scotty said. "Wasn't that one Gendreau's?"

"Yeah, it was his last case before he retired. Carbon monoxide poisoning, they were in a car inside a garage and a neighbor reported it."

Dan shook his head. "Gendreau, 'Sloppy Joe' Gendreau. Maybe it wasn't so cut and dried. You know him: if he could close the book easy, then he'd close it. His only commitment was to retirement and his pension."

"Yeah, but he wasn't a bad detective," Syms said, fumbling the Advil bottle.

Dan started out the door, then turned back. "Heard anything about Marty?"

"Funny you should ask. He's getting out in couple of days. He'll be on probation, and he has to continue anger management and AA. He'll still have to stay away from Kim."

"What if he straightens out? He's young; any chance of reinstating him?"

"I've thought about it, but it's unlikely, not after what he did to Kim. Besides, I don't think the board would be willing to give him a second chance."

Syms pointed at Scotty. "You seen Bev?"

"Spoke with her the other day. She's doing fine. Not catching much sleep, but she's down to her old weight."

"She's about up on maternity leave," the captain said. "Unless we open a daycare, I don't expect her back anytime soon." Syms pointed to the door. "See what you guys can dig up before Carroll gets here."

⋏

The detectives went back to Dan's cubicle, and the senior detective got on the computer.

"What're you looking up?" Scotty asked.

"The Davis/Gomes closed case number," Dan stated. "I want to pull the hard file and have it handy when Carroll gets here. Let's head downstairs to fetch it."

Dan and Scotty took the stairs down to the file room, commonly known as the library, where the desk sergeant allowed them access. They found the file, signed it out, and brought it back upstairs. Scotty looked over Dan's shoulder as they browsed the paperwork. "Here's the incident report. There's a few pics, too," Dan said, flipping to Gendreau's notes. "There's more here than I expected to see from Sloppy Joe. Coroner's report is here, too." He nudged Scotty. "You got any muffins today?"

Scotty laughed. "Out of luck, wanna hit Connie's?"

Dan opened the autopsy file. "Official cause of death was carbon monoxide poisoning." He paused. "This is interesting. Both Davis and Gomes had chloral hydrate in their systems as well as alcohol."

"Mickeys?"

"Leave it to Sloppy Joe to let this slip. Hope he's enjoying retirement."

Dan closed the file. "Let's go to Connie's."

⋏

The unfortunate thing about Connie's Place was its location a block from the old jail. That entire corner of the city had been targeted for demolition, while the new jail erected four blocks away was in prime territory. Connie looked up as Dan and Scotty entered the diner, the detectives complaining about the long walk.

"Hey strangers, good to see your legs still work."

Scotty looked to his left, saw a few patrons, and the detectives headed for their favorite booth. Connie followed with her coffee pot, and poured them each a cup.

"Guess you've taken it hard since we moved?" Scotty said.

"Move over," she said, squeezing into the booth beside Scotty. "Truth is, I could've sold the diner and retired a while ago. Now I have to vacate because the city's taking this place. I'll be out by the end of the month." Connie sighed. "Lots of good memories here, I'm gonna have to find a hobby."

"Maybe you and Scotty can go into business making muffins."

Connie grinned. "I don't think so. A little birdie told me his are better than mine?"

Scotty looked at Dan. "You told her?"

Connie smiled. "I don't think so, not unless *he's* nursing twins."

"We're gonna miss the place too," Dan said.

Connie gave him a curious look.

"We'll miss you too granny, he said."

She and the detectives got up. They gave her a big hug and kiss, and headed for the door. She winked at them. "You boys try to stay out of the hospital."

CHAPTER 24

A Fed-X box was sitting on the front porch and Dan picked it up before entering the house. He carried it into the kitchen where he saw Phyllis pacing the floor. Kate greeted her dad as he placed the box on the island. "Josh was fighting," the little girl said.

Dan turned and he noticed the angst in Phyllis's eyes. "He got sent home from school, he's in his room."

"What? What happened?"

Dan kissed Phyllis and picked Kate up to give her a hug.

"He hit a boy," Kate said.

Dan put her down.

"I had to visit the principal," Phyllis said. "Josh is fine, but the other boy has a loose tooth."

"Why were they fighting?"

"Josh says it wasn't his fault. He says the other boy hit him first. The other boy and the principal see it differently. They say Josh threw the first punch."

Dan shrugged. "Oh great, I'll go talk to him."

"He's probably scared. I told him you'd be up to see him."

"Let me hang up my coat, and I'll take care of it. Looks like this package is from Mike."

"Dinner will be ready in about ten, so bring Josh down with you."

The boy's bedroom door was closed, but Dan knew Josh could hear his footsteps. Dan opened the door. "So little man, what happened at school?"

Sitting on his Spiderman bedspread, and staring blankly at the blue walls covered with Bruce Lee posters, Josh whimpered. "He pushed me and I hit him."

"He pushed you. Who pushed you?"

"He did."

"Who did?"

"Jamie. He's always pushing kids."

"So you hit him?"

Josh pouted. He said I was a wimp, and didn't know anything about Karate. He shoved me and I gave him a chop right in the mouth."

Dan held back a grin and put his arm around his young son. "You know you shouldn't fight over things people say, right? Karate is for self-defense only if you really need it."

Josh looked up at Dan. "Okay, but I got him good."

"And you're going to apologize to him and the principal. Come on downstairs, dinners almost ready. There's a package from Mike, can't wait to see what he sent."

They left the room and headed downstairs.

$$\curlywedge$$

"Dinner's on the table," Phyllis said. "You two have a nice chat?"

Dan smiled at Josh. "Sure did, everything's okay. Josh is going to apologize tomorrow." Dan looked at Josh. "Right buddy?"

Josh smiled. "Yes."

"Good, let's eat."

"I wanna open the box," Kate said.

"It can wait until were done, so if you eat fast we can see what's inside sooner," Phyllis said.

It didn't take long for the food to be gone and Dan placed the box on the table. He pulled at the tape, opened the box, and removed the contents. "They're ASU baseball caps: pink for you girls, and regular ones for me and Josh. See, I knew he missed us."

Phyllis opened the note inside, and handed it to Dan. "Think again, hon."

Hi, thought you would like these. Love Mike.

P.S. They cost eighty bucks. Think you can send me some cash?

"He misses us all right, but he misses my wallet more." Dan laughed. "At least he still knows where we live. I'll send him some money."

"I think it's sweet of him. I miss Mike."

"He'll be back. He's a good kid, and he sure knows how get cash from me."

Josh and Kate disappeared with their caps on.

"So what did the principal say?" Dan asked Phyllis as she was clearing the table.

"I don't really know, a couple of kids saw the punch and said Josh started it."

"He's not that kind of kid, He said this Jaimie kid shoved him first, but I told Josh he was wrong for punching him. Does he need a note or anything?"

"I have to bring him to school and get back with the principal. Jamie and his mother will be there, so we can put this behind us."

Dan shook his head and laughed. "At least I know, if anyone messes with Kate, Josh will beat the crap out of him."

Phyllis rolled her eyes. "You call yourself men, but you're all still little boys aren't you?"

Chapter 25

D an's morning drive was a time of solitude, but this day the name Cosby Davis kept reverberating in his head. *Hard to forget that name. Can't wait to see what Carroll has.*

There was plenty of parking at the new headquarters. He saw Scotty's Camaro and parked beside it. Before strolling to his desk, Dan had an urge to visit this building's lock-up area. Once a daily habit, he'd only been to the new holding tank a few times.

He looked around the sparsely filled room and realized it must have been a slow night in the city. As he neared the end of the cells, he saw a familiar face. If there was a town drunk, it was Paxton who always managed to get into some kind of altercation. Dan saw the seventy year-old boozer clinging to the iron cell bars. "Paxton, what the heck did you do this time?"

Staggering a little, the red-eyed man slurred "Don't remember." Still reeking of alcohol, he mumbled. "Gotta piss."

"Damn it Paxton, judging by your wet smelly pants. I'd say you already did. Where the hell were you last night?"

"Don't remember, but I think I was with Bubba."

Dan looked to the cell to his right, and there he was snoring like a train, Bubba Johanson.

"Go sleep it off Pax." Dan said. "I'm sure you'll be out of here later."

⅄

When he got to his cube, Dan picked up the file he'd left on his desk. He turned to Scotty. "Hey, How about looking at Gendreau's notes again?"

"Be right over. Let me get a fresh cup of coffee."

Scotty returned and sat next to Dan. "You smell like booze."

Dan rubbed his eyes. "I was down below. Paxton and Bubba are there."

Dan opened the file. The crime report gave the location, description of the scene, witnesses: the usual stuff. They looked at a half dozen pictures of Davis's and Gomes's bodies hunched over inside the car. Dan couldn't know for sure if Gendreau had botched this case and merely written it off as suicide for selfish reasons, but there was one name on the witness list that raised a red flag in his mind. And the Mickeys were bothersome.

↙

Syms popped out of his office and told his detectives to join him while they waited for Carroll. Dan held onto the file as they marched to their boss's quarters. The captain swirled around in his chair. "Love this place. Nice view and modern stuff. How about that bathroom? Nice urinals, don't even need to flush."

The state trooper's hat gave Carroll away as he neared Syms's office. He shook the captain's hand. "Good to see you again," Carroll said.

"You too stranger." Syms replied. "This is Dan Shields and Joe Scott— we call him Scotty. Have a seat."

"Nice to meet you guys." Carroll said as he sat next to Dan. He placed his hat on the corner of the captain's desk and took a folder from the soft briefcase in his left hand. "So, the name Cosby Davis is familiar to you?"

Dan held up the Davis file. "Sure is. We've read it, double suicide that was open and shut quickly. I'm not so sure there isn't still some meat on the bone here."

Carroll opened his incident report. "Here's what I can tell you. We were called to a house in Tolland, where the owners found Davis's body in a swampy grave. There's several acres of land, and the corpse was discovered about a hundred yards from the house. It was a quagmire, and still raining. Carroll took out pictures. "All we have is a body, face down and a muddy mess. No shoeprints, and there's no way a vehicle could have made it up that hill. We went back out there, but couldn't even find any broken branches or anything that we could use."

"What about the owners?" Dan asked.

"Will and Amanda Merline have two kids and a dog. The dog discovered the body, and Will called 911."

"They heard nothing?" Dan said.

"They think the body was placed there over the weekend. They were away, and first thing Monday morning the dog went out, and found the body. That's it. So what's Davis's story?"

Dan read from the report. "Cosby Davis and Yolanda Gomes were found in her garage at Landon Place, early in the morning. The car was running, and they died of carbon monoxide poisoning." Dan paused. "But the victims were slipped Mickeys. You sure Arnstein identified the right guy?"

"Arnstein's the best; can't see him making a mistake. He was positive."

"How is he so positive so quick?"

"I talked with him last night. He was able to get a DNA match, and he had Davis's wallet to boot."

Dan scratched his head. "He still have the body on ice?"

"Yeah, but Arnstein and I agreed, for now Cosby Davis is John Doe."

Dan shook his head. "I like that. We don't want the press all over it, and I don't want to alarm the Davis family until we know more." Dan paused. "But there's something else here that bothers me. Davis and Gomes were found by a neighbor who was apparently walking his dog and noticed the garage door closed with the car running." Dan looked at Syms. "His name is Cecil Flores."

Syms leaned forward. "You kidding me ? That scum ball."

Carroll looked puzzled. "What's his M.O?"

"Drugs and pimping?" Syms said.

"So how does any of this make sense?" Carroll asked.

"It doesn't," Dan said. "We need to get to the bottom of this." He looked at the file Carroll was holding. "Mind if we look at that? I'd like to talk to the Merlines, and check out the place."

"You can have it. Damn governor's cutting my budget, and I have to let go of two troopers. That's why I was going to ask you guys to take the case."

Carroll stood, picked up his hat, and opened the door. "Let me know what you come up with." He motioned to Syms. "You going to show me around now?'

"Right," Syms said as he stood, and pointed at his detectives. "You guys put a reopen status on the Davis-Gomes case, and figure out what the hell is going on. I'm going to show my friend the digs."

ⴵ

Dan spread both files on his desk. "According to this, Cosby's mother's name is Martha."

He turned to Scotty. "They must've had a funeral. If he was buried in a cemetery, how the hell does his already-dead body wind up in Tolland?"

"Hold that thought," Scotty said, moving to the computer. "I should be able to find his obit."

A few seconds later: there it was. The detectives studied the notice in more detail than Syms had. "Davis was thirty," Dan said. "Has a brother named Barrett, and Cosby was buried at City Cemetery. Samuel Funeral Parlor took care of it. Says Davis was an airport employee. What about Gomes? Her obit there?"

Scotty browsed the site. "Can't find her, seems odd."

"Check for the newspaper story. It might help us."

Scotty found the *Courant* piece about the suicides. "It says what we already know, but it also says she was twenty-six and a TSA agent at Bradley." Scotty paused. "Wait, it also says Davis was a supervisor in the baggage department."

"Good. That's a start. We have to find Flores too. How about pulling up his rap sheet?"

Scotty played magic with the keyboard again. "Here he is, five-seven, scrawny little thug. Last booked two years ago— selling drugs. Two priors, nabbed in a raid at the Hi-Hat, arrested for pimping, and there's a traffic-stop possession charge. Looks like all he does is pay fines, although he did get slapped on the hand with three months for the intent to sell charge."

"Print it."

Dan began reading the file Carroll had left them. "We need to set up something with the Davis family, and get out there as soon as possible. I know I said we should wait to find out more before talking to them, but if Cosby Davis's name leaks out, Martha may have a heart attack. I think we should make a visit."

"How are we going to ease into *that* conversation?"

"Gently, her number is here, so I'll give her a call."

CHAPTER 26

M artha Davis was in the kitchen peeking into her hot oven while banana bread was baking when the phone rang. Barrett, who was sitting on the front porch, his two pit bulls chained to the fence, heard the ring and he ran inside to answer the call.

"Is this Barrett Davis?" Dan asked.

"Yes. Who's this?"

"Barrett. This is Detective Dan Shields with the Hartford PD. I was wondering if my partner and I could come over to chat with you and your mother about Cosby."

"Cosby? You know he's dead, right?"

"I do know that, but I want to know some details about his death and funeral. It's just routine in order to close the case file that's been sitting on my captain's desk. Can we stop over to see you? Is one good??"

"Yes. I'll tell her you're coming."

"You still at 421 Killingworth?"

"Yes."

"See you later."

Dan turned to Scotty. "All set. We'll see them around one."

"How about getting out of here? Ever been to Freddy's?" Scotty said.

"Great burgers, I'm up for that. You driving?" Dan replied.

"Sure."

⅄

Freddy's Memory Lane, a throwback institution for anyone who grew up in the fifties and sixties had old Seeburg juke boxes and forty-five rpm records were stuck on the black and white subway tiles. Howdy Doody posters enchanted the little kids, and employees wore *American Bandstand* tees. The decorations were a draw, but the burgers were the real stars.

After getting their juicy all-beef patties on toasted buns, they took their sandwiches, cokes, and fries to a table near a jukebox; the cloth they placed their meals on was a replica of an Elvis album. "Blue Hawaii"

I saw the movie," Dan said.

"You're old, "Scotty said with a grin."

"So how's the bachelor life?" Dan asked.

"Not very exciting, I've never adjusted to the dating scene. It's awkward, even after three years, so I don't go out a lot. I've had fix-ups, but man, that's a bad deal from the get-go. Easy to lose friends, because they think they've found a match. The only good thing is that some of these women are really horny. I spend as much time with Eli as I can, take him to Red Sox games at Fenway."

Dan rolled his eyes. "Should have known you're a Boston fan."

Scotty took a bite of his burger. "Really? You're a Yankee?"

"New York all the way. Someday Mike's gonna be playing at Yankee Stadium."

The detectives finished eating and Scotty drove to the Davis's house.

⋏

When they arrived at the small fenced-in ranch-style home, two pit bulls and Barrett, were waiting for the detectives.

Dan noticed the twenty-eight year old's prosthetic left leg. The man's shorts were khaki, and his tee was army green. The cap he wore said it all: 33RD INFANTRY DIVISION.

"I'm Barrett. Don't worry, my two pals, Hide and Seek won't bite."

"Nice to meet you. I'm Dan Shields."

Scotty stuck out his hand and shook Barrett's. "I'm Joe Scott."

"Come on in and sit down while I get mama," Barrett said. "Don't mind the leg, I'll tell you about that later."

Dan looked around the cozy, beige-walled living room, and the detectives sat on the tan four-cushioned sofa in the middle of the room.

The fireplace looked like it hadn't been used in years, and two chairs that matched the sofa were on each side of a glass top coffee table. A mirror above an old upright had a small crack, while the piano was missing a few ivory keys.

The detectives rose as Martha entered the room. Her well-worn apron looked like it had been through many kitchen sessions.

Barrett introduced the detectives to his mother. Martha sat in one of the chairs and Barrett occupied the other one, as the detectives returned to their positions on the couch. Dan was careful not to hastily jump into the disturbing conversation they were about to have. "I see you're a baker, smells terrific in here."

The plumpish woman of sixty-eight-years smiled. "Took out a banana bread from the oven a little while ago. It's cooling. You can have a piece soon."

Barrett sat forward. "Bet you're wondering about the leg?"

"My guess is Iraq," Dan said.

"Got that right, got shelled near Mosul. Worst part was, it was friendly fire. How's that for fate? Maimed by a friend. Three of my buddies died. I was the lucky one."

"I can't imagine that. Sorry to hear about it," Scotty said.

"I call myself lucky to be left with one leg and PTSD. You should see some of the guys at the VA. Anyhow, I'm not bitter."

He looked at his mother. "She raised me and Cosby right."

Martha started to get the banana bread.

"Can we ask a few questions first?" Dan said as the little baker sat back down.

"We're sorry about Cosby, but could you tell us a little about him? Our files don't say much."

"He was a good boy. Went to church and had a good job at the airport," Martha said. Her aging eyes began to well up, and Barrett handed her a tissue. "I can't believe he and that girl were crazy enough to leave that car running in the garage."

"Did you know much about Yolanda?"

"Met her a couple of times. Pretty little thing, Cosby was head over heels for her, and I can't understand why they had to die."

"Did you go to the morgue to identify Cosby's body?"

Barrett closed his eyes. "I went with my buddy, Chaz. Mama stayed here. She was too upset."

"That's understandable. So you positively identified Cosby?"

"I did."

"Tell us about the funeral?"

"Not much to tell," Barret said. "Samuel Funeral Home took care of it. They buried Cosby at City Cemetery."

Dan was trying to get his head around the fact that the body was positively identified and had been buried at the cemetery. "Was there a wake, an open casket?"

"No. Mama didn't want an open casket. I don't want one either, when I go."

That raised one question in Dan's mind. *How the hell would anyone have known if Cosby's body was inside that casket?*

Dan paused: the hard part was coming. He looked at Barrett, and then Martha. "Listen. What I'm about to tell you will be very disturbing, but please hear me out." He leaned forward. "A few days ago, a body was found in a muddy hole on private property in Tolland." Dan paused again "Now, it's hard to believe this, but the coroner identified that corpse as Cosby, and as far as we can tell it's him."

Martha and Barrett looked dazed. "How can that be?" she said.

"That's what we have to find out. It's complicated, so we're reopening Cosby and Yolanda's case."

Dan leaned back. "I said this would sound crazy. We don't have the answers right now, but we wanted to give you a heads-up, because this information could be released to the press any day now."

Barrett went to get the shaking Martha a glass of water and some aspirin. She still trembled, and spoke softly. "What are you saying? Someone stole his body?"

Dan took her hand. "We don't know for sure. His grave is going to have to be opened."

Martha regained her composure and got up. "Would you boys like that banana bread and coffee now?"

"Thank you. We'd love some," Scotty said.

Martha went off to the kitchen. Barrett shook his head. "Are you saying that you don't think Cosby committed suicide?"

"It's too early to say, but obviously something isn't right,"

Dan replied. "Did your brother live here?"

"He had an apartment on Framingham Ave. 2912. The landlord's name is Jasper Olden."

"What about friends?"

"Cosby was a loner, but a hell of a nice guy."

"How long did he know Yolanda?"

"They'd been friends awhile."

"We couldn't find an obit in the paper for her. Do you know if she had a funeral?"

Barrett sat back. "She was from New Orleans, and near as I can remember the police contacted her family."

Scotty looked at Dan. "That would explain the missing obit."

Martha returned, holding a tray with coffee and slightly warm banana bread. Dan grabbed a napkin and a piece. He sipped his coffee, and then took a couple of bites. Immediately his lips began to swell, and he felt his tongue growing too large for his mouth. He reached into his coat pocket, but it was empty; he'd left his EpiPen in another jacket at home. Dan, gasping for air, pointed at Scotty. "Get my EpiPen., it's in the glove box."

"Not in my car, it isn't!"

Dan lay back on the sofa. "Call 911."

I hope it's not a heart attack," Martha said.

"I think it's the banana bread," Scotty said. "Must be nuts in it."

"Martha's face was filled with fear. "Oh my lord," she said. There's walnuts in the bread."

Scotty took out his cell and made the emergency call. "We need an ambulance. 421 Killingworth. male, forty-five, with an allergic reaction to nuts." Dan heard Scotty yell into his phone. "No, he doesn't have an EpiPen, hurry."

Barrett went outside to watch for the ambulance, and the pit bulls reacted to the siren as the emergency vehicle stopped in front of the house. He took the dogs, tied them to the fence, and they barked as the EMTs rushed into the living room where they saw Dan straining for air. "Check his airway," one EMT said.

"It's closing. Inject him fast."

The needle was poked into Dan, and an oxygen mask was quickly strapped around his head with air flowing through his nostrils. Within a few seconds he began to react positively. He sat up, still wearing the oxygen mask.

"We're checking your vitals. Keep breathing the oxygen," an EMT said. She looked at her assistant. "Let's get him to Woodland."

Dan shook his head.

"Are you saying you don't want to go to the hospital?" she asked.

Dan nodded.

"Are you sure? It's standard procedure."

The EMTs waited, and several minutes passed; his vitals were good, and the oxygen mask was removed.

"Give him some water and he should be okay."

The EMTs packed up, but made Dan sign the rejection of a ride to the hospital.

Martha was beside herself. "Not your fault. I should have known better," Dan said. He picked up the glass of water she had gotten for him and drank it. "That was a close one. Mind if I sit for a while?"

About an hour later, Dan felt well enough to leave, but before going he had one request. "When the media learns Cosby's identity, they'll be hounding you to talk with them. Please don't speak to the press. Simply state that the Hartford Police Department is investigating. No matter how much they pressure you, don't tell them anything. Our work will go a lot smoother without their interference."

Barrett looked outside and pointed at Hide and Seek. "I think they can handle the press."

Chapter 27

Dan had some story to tell when he got home. He considered how he'd tell Phyllis about his stupidity. The good news was he hadn't gotten shot by a gun. The shot he'd taken was from a syringe.

Dan eased his car into the driveway, avoiding Josh's bike and Nana's Lincoln. Double trouble: he had to tell what happened to both women. The harsh scolding was likely to come from his mother.

He opened the front door, hung his jacket in the closet, locking his weapon in its special compartment, and kicked off his shoes. Dan strolled into the kitchen and he pecked his mom on the cheek as she dropped a pinch of salt into a pot of pasta sauce. "Smells good,"

"You look a little frazzled, tough day?" Phyllis said.

He hesitated. "I sort of had an accident."

"The car?"

"Not exactly, the husband."

"Excuse me?"

"Well, it's like this. I had a nut reaction and the paramedics had to come and give me a shot."

Nana turned, pointing a ladle at him. "How many times have I told you to check your food?"

"You okay?" Phyllis asked. "I knew one of these days something would happen. So where was your EpiPen?"

"I'm okay. I had a pen in the car, but Scotty drove, and I didn't have my other one with me; it's in my tan jacket."

Phyllis sighed. "So I guess I have to make sure one is stuffed into your pocket every day."

"Lighten up ladies. I'll be more careful. Anyway, we were at a house in Hartford. The nice woman we were talking with had made a banana bread and she offered us some. I took a bite before realizing it had nuts. Scotty called 911 and the EMT's gave me a shot of epinephrine."

Nana looked at him. "Sit down—you look a little flushed, and you shouldn't have driven home by yourself. You could've called. Next time we'll find you in some hospital. I'll make some chicken soup."

Dan had no choice but to listen to his mother's words of wisdom. "I'm fine. I don't need soup. I'll go to bed early and I'll remember my EpiPen." He grabbed a pencil and sticky note. "See? I'm putting a reminder on the fridge."

Nana poured pasta into a strainer. "You need to put it on your forehead."

$$\lambda$$

The next morning Dan checked his coat pocket before leaving home, and the EpiPen was there. Phyllis wasn't about to let him make the same mistake again.

He strolled into the squad room and saw Scotty sitting in Syms office, so he joined them. "Good to see you alive and well," Syms said. "Heard about you almost dying."

"Dying? That part didn't almost happen until I went home and told Phyllis and Nana the story. Talk about a tongue lashing."

Dan reached into his pocket and held up his EpiPen. "It won't happen again."

"Scotty told me about the Davises."

Dan sat. "We've got some leg work to do. We're gonna have to check with the funeral home, and we'll have to get a court order to exhume Cosby Davis's grave at City Cemetery."

"I don't remember any reports of vandalism at the cemetery recently," Syms said.

"You know, the interesting thing is that Martha Davis doesn't believe in open casket wakes, so Cosby's body was never viewed. Barrett ID'd it at the morgue, and they saw the casket entering the ground, but maybe someone else was in it?" Dan said.

"Sounds like a good TV show, doesn't it?" Syms said. "How the hell does a funeral home make a mistake like that, and why?"

"I don't know. And if the body was switched, where the hell was Cosby's until last week? I want to visit the crime scene, and talk to the Merlines. We may as well start at the beginning and see where it goes."

"Can't wait 'til I hear what you find out," Syms said.

⚔

The detectives went to Dan's cubicle, where he picked up the phone and dialed the Merline's number.

Will answered. "Hello?"

"Mr. Merline?" Dan said.

"Yes."

"Hello, sir, I'm Detective Dan Shields. I'm calling about the unfortunate incident that occurred on your property."

"What do you want to know?"

"We've read the report, and the state police asked us to follow it up. Can Detective Scott and I come out to see you and your wife?"

"Is it necessary? We've already talked to the troopers."

"I understand, sir, but since we've been handed the case, my partner and I would like to view the crime scene and chat with you."

"I guess that would be okay."

"Can we stop by this afternoon? It shouldn't take long."

"Amanda's working today, and I have a few things to do. Can you come tomorrow morning, before noon?"

"How's nine-fifteen?"

"That's fine."

Dan hung up. "All set, nine-fifteen," he said to Scotty." Let's leave here at eight- thirty; we could hit traffic. Ever been to Landon Place?"

Scotty shook his head. "Nope, but I hear it's nice."

"How about taking a ride? I'm driving," Dan said. "According to the file, the suicides occurred inside the garage of number seventeen. That was Yolanda Gomes's unit. Maybe it hasn't been re-rented yet."

"What if it has?"

"Let's give it a shot."

Arriving at Landon Place, located on the fringe of West Hartford, Dan drove inside the gated entrance and stopped at the small guard house. "Hi," he said. "I'm looking for the management office."

The gray-uniformed guard pointed to his left. "The office is four units down. You can't miss the sign."

Dan parked in front of the red and white Management Office sign that was planted on the neatly manicured lawn. The license plate on the white Beemer next to Dan's car read *GALSAL*. Dan opened the office door, and he saw a tall woman standing at a file cabinet. Her long red hair flowed down the back of her mid-length yellow dress. She turned when she heard the detectives enter. "Hi, gentlemen, I'm Sally Grennon. How can I help you?"

Dan introduced himself, and Scotty, whose face had taken on a glazed look of awe as he studied the sexy young lady, held out a hand. "I'm Joe Scott, but everyone calls me Scotty. It's nice to meet you."

"Ms. Grennon," Dan said. "This is a beautiful complex."

"Our landscaper does a great job, but I take care of the flowers outside this office. We have a few vacancies."

"Looks expensive, "Scotty said.

"They range. There's a hundred-sixty units, all freestanding, some one level, some two."

"Ballpark?" Scotty said.

"They range from eighteen-hundred to twenty-four. Were you interested in one?"

Dan noticed Scotty's eyes fixed on her green eyes and juicy red lips.

"Actually, we're not here to rent," Dan interjected. "We're here to ask about an event that happened a while back."

"You must be referring to the double suicide. I heard about it. I've only been here three months."

Sally reached inside her desk drawer, and she handed her bosses card to Dan. "I'm sure Jessie Colton could tell you more than I can."

"Thank you. We'll definitely call him. Does Cecil Flores still live here?" Dan asked.

"Yes, number fifteen; why?"

"Just curious, do you know much about him?"

Sally rolled her eyes. "He's a little creepy, luckily, most of the time I'm gone before he comes home, but he's been in the office, usually smelling of alcohol, and he tries to hit on me. We've had complaints about his dog—or I should say about him not picking up his poop."

Scotty took a deep breath. "His poop, or the dog's?"

Sally smiled. "Guess."

"Do you have a file on Flores?" Dan asked.

She turned to the cabinet in back of the desk and retrieved a manila folder. "Here it is. Cecil Flores." She placed it on her desk and opened the file. "All I have is a reference sheet and photo ID. He's been here three and a half years. He's employed by HHC of Hartford, and his dog's name is Corky. Drives a Lexus."

"The dog drives a car?" Scotty said with a grin.

Sally laughed. "Yeah, the dog, he's quite talented."

"We're familiar with Flores's employer," Dan said. "We may be going over there after we leave here."

"What exactly does he do?" Sally asked.

Dan didn't want to come right out and say Flores was a pimp and drug dealer. "Let's just say he manages a bar that pays well. Mind if we get a copy of his file?"

"I'll make a copy. Mr. Colton would have a complete file."

"Wait," Dan said. "What about Yolanda Gomes? Have a file on her?"

"I'll take a look."

Dan noticed Scotty watching Sally closely as she turned to the cabinet again and pulled out a folder. "She lived at seventeen, next door to Flores. It's been rented."

"Is there a picture?" Dan said.

Sally grinned "Of the unit, or Yolanda?"

That sassy remark made Scotty smile.

Dan looked at the file. "Attractive young lady," he said. "We know she worked at the airport."

Sally took a few steps to the copy machine and made copies of the two information sheets, handing them to Dan.

"Do you have any idea what time Flores gets home from work?"

"Not exactly, like I said, I'm usually out of here by the time he comes home, so sometime after five."

"One more question. Do you keep master keys in case of emergencies?"

"I do, but like you said, they're only for emergency use."

"Mind if I take one of your cards?"

"Sure."

Dan pocketed one from the card holder on her desk. "Thanks for your time."

He looked at Scotty who appeared to still be distracted. "I'm sure we'll be back."

As soon as they got into the car, Dan shook his head. "Pretty obvious what you were paying attention to. Did you hear anything we said?"

"Hey, I heard you. Like you didn't notice how gorgeous she is? Great smile and sense of humor as well."

Bet your ass I noticed, but Phyllis has me trained ignore stuff like that."

"Think she's single? I didn't notice a ring."

"Is that why it took you so long to release her hand after you shook it?"

"Hey, I'm just saying."

"You better act more detective-like if we go back there. Try not to get a hard-on."

Chapter 28

As Dan drove down I-91 toward home his phone rang, and he accessed the Bluetooth connection. "Hi hon, I'm on my way home."

"Good. Nana's cooking and she needs you to stop at the market to pick up a couple of things."

"How many is a couple?"

"She needs some Parmigiano-Reggiano, and we need milk."

Dan heard his mother in the background. "Not the cheap stuff."

Phyllis added. "And pick up some bananas."

"Ok. See you in a bit."

Dan had his orders and knew if he brought home the wrong cheese, he'd be in trouble with his mother. He entered the market and picked up a hand basket. *Why the hell is it always ten below zero in here?* The milk was at the rear of the store, so the cold walk was prolonged. He approached the bananas. *Better grab a big bunch—you'd think I was raising little monkeys.*

He got to the back of the store, reached into the refrigeration unit, and removed a large milk container. He held it as he leaned into the cheese case, eyeing the abundance of sealed packages before he spotted the right stuff. He shook his head. *Nineteen bucks for ten ounces.*

Orders were orders, and he'd learned not to disobey Nana a long time ago, so he placed a pie shaped slab into the basket and headed to the ten-items-or less checkout lane. Three people were ahead of him, and the line moved quickly until the woman in front of him swiped her credit card and it was rejected. Her debit card was no better, even though she swore she'd used it an hour ago.

Dan waited patiently. *Why am I always in the wrong line?*

It took a few minutes for the manager to straighten things out, and the woman left with her items. Finally it was his turn, but before the cashier scanned his items she asked, "Do you have a loyalty card?"

"No, just ring the items up, please." *Another pain in the butt. You have to carry cards for every store to get the special prices. What a crock.*

At last a haggard Dan was in the car and only five minutes from home. With a sigh of relief he entered the house, smelled the pasta sauce, and headed straight to the kitchen. Phyllis took the milk and bananas as Nana held out her hand. Dan gave her the cheese and she pecked him on the cheek. "Good boy; now give your wife a kiss."

He obliged, and minutes later they were all at the table.

"Still seems a little funny without Mike around." Dan said.

"I hope that boy is eating right at school," Nana remarked.

"I'm sure he's fine. We send him money," Phyllis said.

Dan laughed. "Yeah, but if I know him he's eating at McDonald's and pocketing our change."

Kate and Josh finished their meals and waited for dessert. Nana's brownies with ice cream were always a treat.

While Nana cleaned up. Phyllis took Dan into the den. "I was thinking about Scotty," she said. "I think he'd like Terry. She's been divorced a few years, and her kids are out of the house."

Dan sat back on the couch. "Terry? I don't think she's his type."

"Do tell, what exactly is his type? Terry's attractive and has a good personality. She's a good baker, and you told me that he is too."

"Oh no, I don't want to get involved. I like Terry, but she's got a little baggage, and I don't think these fix-up things work out very well."

Phyllis rolled her eyes. "Like he doesn't? We all have baggage."

"It's not a good idea. Besides, he's kinda got a new girl."

"Really? So, what's she like?"

"Let's just say she's attractive."

"How attractive?"

Dan paused, and came up with the perfect answer to that trick question. "Almost as pretty as you hon."

Phyllis smiled. "And just how is it that you've met her? You two double dating at the office?"

"Funny," Dan said. "Okay, here's the scoop. We're working on a case and we interviewed her. Scotty's eyes froze over like he'd seen heaven."

"What does she look like?"

"She's a tall redhead, drop-dead gorgeous."

"Think if I had red hair, I'd be as gorgeous?"

Dan was trapped again, but he didn't hesitate. "I think you're drop-dead gorgeous, just as you are."

She laughed and snuggled up to him. "Nice save, dear, I'll drop the Terry thing."

CHAPTER 29

Listening to the radio on his way to work, Dan heard the bad news of the day. The Red Sox had beaten the Yankees, and he knew Scotty would be rubbing it in.

Scotty was silent as his partner walked by, but the open sports page sitting in the middle of Dan's desk was punishment enough. "Funny, pal. It's a long season. The war isn't over yet."

Scotty threw a muffin. "Here grouchy."

Dan caught it. "Bet there's nuts in this one."

"Nice catch."

"Speaking of catches, I told Phyllis about Sally, but only after she tried to set you up with her friend Terry."

"What did you say, and who's Terry. Is she a fox?'

"She's a neighbor, nice enough, but no Sally for sure. I remembered what you said about fix-ups and I talked Phyllis out of the idea."

"You tell her how drop-dead gorgeous Sally is?"

Dan took a bite of his muffin. "Jesus. The more I talked about Sally and her red hair, the deeper my foot kept getting in my mouth. I had to convince Phyllis she's prettier than her."

"How'd that go?"

Dan smiled and chomped on the muffin. "I guess I did a good job, she took me up to bed."

The detectives heard a strange noise coming down the corridor. Looking back they saw Bev, a stroller, and two sleeping babies. "Hey, look who's here!" Scotty said.

All the detectives surrounded Bev to get a look at the little ones. Dan peeked in and touched their tiny fingers. "Precious, Bev. It's been a while since my kids were that young."

"How are you doing?" Scotty said. "Thanks for coming in."

"We're all fine. This new place is a whole lot different than the old one."

"So, are you coming back?"

"That's what I need to talk to Syms about. You probably guessed I'm not."

"We did," Scotty said. "How could you leave these little angels?"

"Is Syms in his office?"

"If he's not there, he's in the bathroom. Those are his two hangouts," Scotty said.

Bev aimed the stroller down the hall. "It's time to see the captain."

⋏

The new mother rolled the stroller into Syms's office, and he stood. "Hey, how's the little family?"

Bev smiled. "We're great. How are you doing?"

Syms peeked into the stroller. "Cute." He eyed Bev. "So are you coming back soon?"

Bev opened her purse. "I think you know that answer." She handed the captain her badge, and gun. "These little ones are my new career."

Syms accepted the badge and handgun. "I don't blame you Bev. I'll get the paperwork going, but you should stop by HR. Promise you'll stop by every now and then."

She hugged the captain and proceeded back to the squad room. Before leaving she gave Dan and Scotty hugs. "You guys stay out of harm's way."

"Wait, Bev." Scotty handed her a cranberry muffin. "Take care, mom."

Dan looked at his watch. It was a few minutes past eight thirty.

"Hey we gotta go to Tolland."

⋏

Dan parked next to a white Dodge pickup. Off to the side was a silver SUV. A man looking to be about six feet tall was standing on the front porch. He appeared to be in his mid-thirties, with dark hair. Dressed in khaki's and a long-sleeved striped shirt, he greeted his visitors. "I'm Will. Come on in."

Thanks. It's nice to meet you. I'm Dan Shields, and this is Joe Scott."

A brown and white setter wagging his tail sidled up to the detectives. "This is Buster."

They entered the family room where Amanda Merline introduced herself. The boys had already been shuttled off to school. She offered the detectives coffee as they sat on the couch. Dan was ready for his second cup of the day, but Scotty decided to skip his.

Buster sat on the braided area rug beside the detectives.

While he waited for his coffee, Dan looked around the room and spotted the moose head.

"Do you hunt?"

"No. That was here when we bought the place."

Dan noticed the framed hundred dollar bill on the mantle. "Was that here too?"

Will walked over and picked up the frame. "Doesn't everyone keep the first dollar they ever made? Mine happened to be a hundred."

Dan snickered. "Mine was a nickel from my paper route, but I never thought of framing it."

Amanda, had shoulder length auburn hair, and her blue rimmed glasses matched the color of her eyes. She returned and placed the coffee on the table, as Will put the frame back on the mantle.

Dan picked up his cup and took a sip before speaking. "We've read the report from Major Carroll, and we'd like to take a look at the area where the body was." He took another sip while Buster nestled up next to Scotty. "Tell us about yourselves."

"We have two great boys," Amanda said. "They love it here."

Dan noticed photos of the boys that were on the table next to Amanda. "Nice looking boys. He paused. "So how long have you been here?"

"Less than a year," Amanda replied. "We're from Baltimore, and moved up here because Will had an opportunity to take over his dying uncle's printing business."

"You have a shop in town?" Dan asked.

"It's a small business," Will replied. "Totally online, my workshop is downstairs."

Dan noticed Amanda wore what appeared to be lavender scrubs outfit. "Are you a nurse?" he asked.

She smiled. "Not quite, I work at the medical center diagnostics lab, drawing blood."

Scotty cringed. "I'm not too good with that stuff. I can go to a messy crime scene, but hate that needle stuck in my arm."

Dan looked at Will. "Do you mind telling us who the previous owner was?"

"Actually, we only know his name, Manuel Vinton. The house was vacant. We dealt with a realtor named Jessie Colton."

Dan and Scotty exchanged glances. "That's interesting. His name popped up yesterday on another issue. We're planning to see him about that," Dan said as he stood. "Would you mind showing us to the spot where the dead man was found?"

Will took the detectives through the kitchen to the back of the house, and he pointed to the yellow crime scene tape that had been placed around a cluster of trees. "It was quite a quagmire when the troopers were here," Will said. "It's pretty dry now."

Scotty and Dan slowly made their way up the hill and took a few pictures with their phones. "Wish we'd seen the corpse," Dan said. "Guess this will have to do. According to the file, the body was lying face down. This hole isn't that deep. What do you make of it?"

Scotty walked around it and stood looking back toward the house. "Strange; it's almost like someone *wanted* the body to be found. No tracks, not even any broken branches, so how the hell did it get up here?"

"Beats me. According to the report the family went to Maine, and when they came back the body was there," Dan said. "Who the hell else would even know about this property?"

"The real estate agent," Scotty said.

The detectives hiked back to the house. "That's quite a healthy walk," Dan said.

"The uphill is a lot worse than the downhill." Will replied. "So who's the dead guy?"

Dan wasn't about to tell him. "The body is still at the morgue, and because of the decomposition they haven't made a positive ID. As of now he's John Doe."

"Was he shot or stabbed?"

"All we know is he was black and dead."

Amanda had her purse in her hand. "I have to go, but it was nice to meet you." She exited and the detectives sat back down with Will and Buster.

"Would you mind telling us again about what you saw, starting from when you got home from your trip the night before?" Dan asked.

Will wiped his hand across his face. "It was about eleven p.m. and raining. Amanda and the kids rushed into the house while I retrieved the bags and kept an eye on Buster."

"Did you notice anything unusual?"

"No, everything seemed fine. After Buster came in, we all went to bed. I let him out to do his thing in the morning, and that was it. He was barking up a storm and I went to fetch him. That's when I saw the body."

Dan continued looking at his notes. "I know it was rainy and muddy, but you didn't see any tire tracks or evidence that someone had been on the property?"

"No. With all that rain, even my vehicles had a tough time navigating the driveway."

Dan studied Will. "Thanks. We'll be on our way, but we could be back after we talk to Jessie Colton. Have a nice day."

The detectives got into Dan's car, exiting the winding driveway.

"What do you think?" Scotty said.

"I don't have the warm fuzzies. Something's not right here. All those trees, and all that hard-to-get-to wooded land. No vehicle could've gotten up there. Somehow the timing was perfect because of the weather. Planting a body and walking away without the ability to trace footprints. That's all too convenient, and whoever did it also had to be familiar with the property. That brings us to Colton."

CHAPTER 30

Jessie Colton's name had come up twice in the past twenty-four hours. Dan kept one hand on the steering wheel as he pulled out his wallet, handing the leather money holder to Scotty. "Colton's card is on top."

Scotty took it. "Want me to call him?"

"Use the Bluetooth and punch the numbers in."

Scotty did so, and Colton's receptionist answered. "Colton Realty."

"Hi, my name is Detective Dan Shields. I was wondering if I could speak with Mr. Colton."

"He's in a meeting. Is this urgent?"

"Do you know when he'll be available?"

"It's a staff meeting and should be over soon."

"Would you mind telling him that I'll be there soon with my partner."

"Can I tell him what it's about?"

"It's about some property he sold."

"I'll give him the message."

"Thanks, I appreciate it." Dan disconnected the call.

⅄

Colton's office was on Oak Hill Road; part of the Windsor Hotel complex, comprised of three detached office buildings, the hotel, a small lake with a picnic area, and a walking trail.

It was easy to spot the three story building where Colton maintained his business quarters. The tall red and white COLTON PROPERTY MANAGEMENT and REAL ESTATE sign gave it away.

The detectives entered the building and on the first floor to their left was a set of French doors with Colton's name etched into the glass. Dan opened the door and they approached a dark-haired receptionist at the marbled counter. The middle-aged woman dressed in a gray suit greeted them. "Hi Gentleman, can I help you?"

"Hi. I'm Dan Shields. I believe I just spoke with you."

"Oh, yes, I'll let Jessie know you're here."

She disappeared down the corridor to her left, then returned after alerting her boss. "Go ahead. His office is at the end of the hall."

Dan noticed fresh plants in the reception area as well as pictures on the walls of what appeared to be large estates. They passed the bathrooms, a conference room, and a couple of empty offices, with name plates on the open doors.

The sharply dressed businessman shook the detectives' hands as they introduced themselves. His tanned face and slick black hair made him look younger than his thirty-nine years. The gold ring on Jessie's left hand and Rolex on his wrist signaled that he had expensive taste.

His ebony desk faced a large window overlooking the pond. Dan and Scotty took seats on matching leather chairs as the businessman sat behind his desk in his high-backed chair.

Dan noticed a mini-bar on the credenza behind Colton, along with a mountain of brochures, and a trophy for his "Realtor of the Year" designation.

"You said you wanted to talk about some property I sold."

"Correct," Dan said. "The Merline house in Tolland. We spoke with Will and Amanda. They told us that you sold them the property."

"Yes, I did, nice piece of real estate."

"Would you mind telling us about the previous owner? I believe his name was Vinton. The Merlines said they never met him."

"True, Manuel Vinton moved to Florida, and I managed the property in his absence."

"Tell us about him. Was he the original owner?"

"He was. He bought the land and had the house built about five years ago."

"How long was the house vacant?"

"Several months. There were tenants for a while, but they moved out of state too."

Dan took out his notepad and pen. "So Vinton rented the place out?"

"Only once to a couple of UConn professors."

"What happened to them?"

"The Prescott's moved up academically. They both took professorships at Notre Dame and moved to Indiana."

"What about Vinton? He built the place and didn't stay that long. What's his story?"

"He's an investor, single, and he wanted a private place to have parties. He had a lucrative opportunity come up and moved."

"How come he didn't sell the property?"

Colton sat forward and clasped his hands. "Money, the market had dropped and no one wanted to buy a place with that much land. His next-best option was to rent it out. Fortunately for him and us, the market rebounded, and we listed it. He was able to walk away with a nice profit after selling to the Merlines."

"How'd that sale happen? Amanda said they came from Baltimore."

"Internet. We have listings. They saw it and contacted me."

"Just curious," Dan said. "How much did it go for?"

"Seven-fifty. They paid cash."

"Cash? You mean no mortgage?"

"You got it. Simple title search, wire transfer, and deed filing."

Dan shook his head. "Interesting story. Mind if we switch subjects? We spoke with Sally Grennon at Landon Place about the Cosby Davis and Yolanda Gomes suicides."

Colton shuddered. "Sounds like dead people follow me around, doesn't it? The suicides were terrible, but Sally wasn't there then."

"Who was?"

"Jenny Hampton was the office manager, but she took a job in New York City with one of the big guys."

"What can you tell us about Cecil Flores and Yolanda Gomes? As we understand it, they were neighbors."

"I know Cecil found the bodies in the garage."

"We've read the reports and there's a few loose ends. The case was never closed, and we're taking another look at it."

"You think Flores had something to do with it? You don't think it was suicide?"

Dan held up his hands. "Whoa. Let's not make that leap. All I said is that we're trying to put closure on the case. What else can you tell us about Flores? Sally copied his file and Gomes's file for us. Do you have more detailed information, like earnings, family, other personal info?"

Colton stood. "I'll be right back. I'll have my secretary get them."

The business man returned and they waited until his secretary entered the room empty-handed. "I couldn't find them," she said. "They must be misplaced. I bet they were among the files we lost when we relocated."

Colton rocked back in his chair, looking at Dan. "Unfortunately, a few boxes were lost when we moved here. With our new computer system, we were planning to create a comprehensive database, but obviously we're missing data."

Dan was miffed by the casualness and almost scripted answer from Colton. "You met them both, didn't you?"

"Once, I signed their lease contracts."

"You must have thought they could easily swing the rent payments. Do you remember what they earned?"

"I'm not sure, but I wasn't worried about their making the monthly payments."

"Do you know if they paid by check or cash?"

"I'm not sure about Gomes, but Flores always paid cash."

Dan squinted at Colton. "Didn't you find that a little odd?"

Colton squirmed in his chair. "Okay, so you and I both know what Flores does for a living. The Hi-Hat is a cash business."

"You a customer?"

Colton stood. "Jesus no, I'm a happily married man." He pointed to the picture on his desk of his wife, a former Miss America contestant. "That's my angel. She's Colombian, her name's Lily."

"Pretty," Dan said.

Colton took his seat again.

"What about Gomes?" Dan asked. "We know she worked at the airport."

"From what I could tell, she was a TSA agent. Her references checked out."

"You know anything about Cosby Davis?"

"Only what I read. He was her boyfriend."

Dan looked at Scotty and they got up. "Thanks for your help," Dan said. "We may be back."

The detectives got into Dan's car and headed back to Hartford.

"What's the likelihood he lost those files?" Scotty said. "It's almost like he expected to be asked about Flores and Gomes, and rehearsed his response."

"I still can't get over the Merlines coming up with that much cash."

Chapter 31

Cosby Davis, Yolanda Gomes, Cecil Flores. Was it a coincidence that Cecil Flores lived next door to Yolanda, and that her body, along with Cosby's, was discovered by Flores?

Dan placed the information Sally had given him inside the suicide case file. He turned to the M.E. report, and couldn't figure out why Gendreau had missed the Mickey laced alcohol in both victims systems. One thing Dan knew was that Flores drank heavily, and certainly had access to all the drugs he wanted. It would've been unrealistic to believe Gomes and Cosby didn't know Flores. For that matter, they may have been drinking with him. *Was that it? Were they drinking together and Flores slipped them the Mickeys. Could he have placed their bodies inside that car and faked the carbon monoxide poisoning?* It was enough to fill the detective's head with suspicion.

Dan heard Scotty, who had placed a Tupperware container on his partner's desk. "Muffins, I take it?"

"You sure are sharp today," Scotty said. "Orange cranberry."

"What's the extra container for?"

Scotty smiled. "I was kinda thinking we should drop in on Sally."

"Nice try, but we have police work to do. Try a dating service."

"Maybe I should hide the muffins from you."

"Sure. Listen, I was browsing the suicide file again and I don't like the whole Flores thing. Let's go see Syms—and bring a muffin."

⅄

The detectives strolled into the captain's office. "Hey muffin man, and it's nice to see you too, Dan."

Scotty handed Syms a muffin.

"Okay. Have seat boys."

He eyed Scotty who was wearing a blue buttoned-down shirt, tan Chino's and a blue blazer. "And what the hell are you all spiffed up for?"

"I wanted to look a little more professional?"

"My ass," Syms said. "Where you guys off to?"

"Not sure yet," Dan said. "There are a lot of pieces we need to put together. It seems odd that Jessie Colton claims to have lost his master files on Yolanda Gomes and Cecil Flores, and that Flores lived next to Gomes."

Dan scratched his head. "The purchase of the Merlines' house is bothersome, and so is their alibi."

Syms bit into the muffin. "Damned good."

"We have to revisit Landon Place, too," Scotty said with a smile.

"I want to drop in at the Hi-Hat to talk to Flores," Dan uttered.

"Whoa," Syms said. "Be careful, you've already been in that neighborhood once."

Scotty nodded. "Lot of shootings down there."

"They don't hunt cops. They shoot themselves," Dan said.

Syms took another bite of the muffin. "Make sure you're not the first ones. By the way, I put in that request for exhuming the grave that supposedly contains Cosby Davis's body, but haven't got an order yet. You checked out the funeral home?"

"That's on our plate." Dan replied. "Just think: if we go to the Hi-Hat first, we may end up at Samuel anyway."

Syms pointed to the door, and as Dan walked out, the captain shouted. "You want a pine box, or something sturdier?"

Ⱥ

They returned to their desks and Dan saw Scotty about to make a phone call.

"Who you calling?"

"Here goes. Hope Sally's at work."

"Hold it, Romeo. We're not going there yet."

"We have to. The muffins are fresh. I'll tell her we have a few more questions."

Dan couldn't keep a straight face. "You know, you have a way about you. Give her a jingle and make it fast."

Scotty picked up the phone and it was done.

"Wipe the smile off your face," Dan said.

"Remind me to be professional when we get there."

Sally was outside, knelt beside a flower bush with a watering can in her hand when Dan's car stopped next to hers. She placed the tin can on the ground as they approached, and she opened the office door. Scotty carried the container of muffins in and placed them on her desk. "It's nice to see you again. I brought you a treat," he said.

She opened the plastic box and smelled the muffins. "These look very good. Did you make them?"

Dan stood in the background and listened to them carry on.

Scotty gawked at her green floral print dress, his eyes wandering up and down those long legs. "I have coffee brewing. Would either of you care for a cup?" Sally asked.

Dan declined.

"Only if you're having one," Scotty replied.

She poured two cups and took a muffin out of the box. "Want one?"

"No thanks, they're all for you."

She winked. "Trying to fatten me up?"

"God forbid."

She eyed his jacket. "You look nice today, I love blazers."

"Thanks, you look great too."

Dan felt invisible as they sweet-talked each other. He waved his hand in the air at Sally. "Has Jessie Colton spoken to you?"

She wiped her face with a napkin. "Briefly, he said you spoke with him about Flores and Yolanda Gomes."

"Did he say anything about our conversation?"

"Not really, but he thought you might come back here."

"We need to get into Flores's place. You said you have a master key."

Sally balked. "I'm sorry. I also said I can't let you in unless it's an emergency. Why don't you call him?"

Dan thought Scotty was having too much fun. "Hey, lets' go see Flores at the Hi-Hat."

Scotty eyed Dan. "You serious?'

"You a detective? Let's go."

Dan turned to Sally. "It was nice to see you again."

She put a hand on Scotty's arm as he was leaving. "If I can do anything else for you, please don't hesitate."

"We'll be back," Scotty said as Sally pointed to the empty vase on her desk.

The detectives got into the Accord. "She's a pistol, pal," Dan said. "I think she told you to bring her flowers. You better save up, and don't get her crappy grocery store ones."

"Deal, you see those legs?"

"I saw them last time, they haven't changed."

"Some piece of ass. Where we going?"

"I told you, the Hi-Hat to see Flores."

"You serious?"

"Not really. The funeral home is on the way back. We're going to visit Samuel."

⅄

A wake was in progress at the Samuel Funeral Parlor. Dan and Scotty walked past a hearse and entered the single-story white building where an attendant held the door open for them. Dan whispered to the employee "Where can we find Mr. Samuel?"

"Last door on the right."

"Thanks," Dan said.

The detectives walked down the corridor passing two empty rooms. The third was filled with mourners.

Dan and Scotty entered Grayson Samuel's office. Wearing a dark suit, the middle-aged, white-haired, mortician raised his head from his desk. "Gentlemen, can I help you?"

Dan showed his badge to the funeral director, and Samuel cordially invited the detectives to sit. "Mr. Samuel," Dan said. "I hope you don't mind if we ask you a few questions about Cosby Davis's funeral."

"Mr. Davis?"

"We understand he had no wake, so the family never saw his body inside the casket before he was buried."

"That's not unusual."

"It might be in this case. We're obtaining a court order to exhume Cosby Davis's body."

"Why, what's going on?"

Dan realized Cosby Davis's name hadn't been made public yet. "I can't get into details, but we have reason to believe someone else was in that casket."

Samuel arched back in his chair and raised his brows. "Say that again?"

"Cosby Davis may not be in that casket. Did you see his body? Did you positively identify it before burying him?"

"That's not or job. I thought the Davises identified him at the morgue. Someone had to. The corpse was released to us at the Davises request. They, and the coroner had to sign the death certificate. We embalmed the body and dressed him in a suit Barrett Davis brought here."

Samuel stared at Dan. "Who do you think we buried, if not Cosby Davis?"

"That's what we need to find out. You'll be notified when we exhume the body."

"True. By law we'll have to be there. I can't believe this."

"Thanks for your time, Mr. Samuel." Dan handed the man his card, eying the portraits on the wall behind the desk. "Is that your brother? You two look alike."

"Everyone says that. Clifton was two years older. Unfortunately; cancer took him a few years ago."

"Sorry for your loss," Dan said. "We'll let you know when we get the go ahead on the exhumation."

"I'll be waiting. Have a nice day." Samuel said.

Mourners were exiting the parlor, and the funeral procession was lining up as the detectives headed for Dan's car.

"Let's get going before the hearse pulls out," Dan said.

CHAPTER 32

Dan and Scotty entered Sym's office. The captain always had his hands full, but now he actually seemed flustered as he glanced up at the detectives. "It's shit," he said. "The press knows Cosby Davis's name, and they're going to go public with it! Who the hell leaked it? They'll be all over us. Hardison's on his way down. What do you two want?"

"Calm down," Dan said. "We've got some stuff to tell you."

"Not now. You guys want to deal with the media instead of me? Get the hell out, here comes the chief."

⅄

The detectives retreated to the squad room and Dan pulled out his phone. "We need to tell the Davises the press will be hounding them. Barrett thinks he can handle it, but I want to warn him to be on the lookout."

Dan made the call to Barrett, who had assured him he'd handle the press.

Scotty, standing beside his partner said. "Know what? We better tell the Merlines, too"

"Right, I want to take another ride out there anyway because there are a few questions we need to get answered".

Dan dialed Merline's number, and after two rings heard Will's voice. "Hello, detective."

"Morning, Will. Something's come up and Scotty and I need to see you as soon as possible. We can come now, if it's okay. It won't take long, but it's important."

"That's fine, Amanda will still be here."

"Thanks, we'll be there in a little while." Dan ended the call and looked up at Scotty. "Let's go, pal. The Merlines are waiting for us."

Dan checked his coat pocket.

"What are you looking for?" Scotty said.

"My EpiPen. People don't leave home without American Express. Now Phyllis makes sure I don't leave home without an EpiPen. It's here. Let's roll. I'm curious to see Will's reaction when he hears the name Cosby Davis. And I want to know more about the cash purchase."

⅄

Thirty-five minutes later Will opened the door, Buster wagging his tail, as Dan petted the dog. The detectives entered the family room with Will. Amanda, already dressed in her lab coat, was sitting on the couch.

"You have something important to discuss?" Will said.

"Mind if we sit?" Dan asked.

"Wouldn't be very hospitable if we said no, would it?" Amanda said.

Will sat in a chair opposite them. "What's so important?'

"It's the corpse. They've identified it and the press knows his name."

Dan looked into Will's eyes and anxiously awaited the man's reaction. "The victim's name is Cosby Davis, and he was from Hartford."

Dan noticed that Will's eyes didn't flinch. It was as if he already knew what the detective was going to say. "Who was he? Was he shot?" Will asked.

"All we have is his name, and he wasn't shot. We've notified his family and need to find out more about the man, but we're sure the press has your names too, so be careful and don't say anything to them. Simply tell them the police are investigating."

"Okay," Will said. "That's it?"

"Not quite. We spoke with Jessie Colton, and he told us one unusual detail about the purchase of this property. It was a cash deal: no bank, no attorneys."

"It was the only way Mr. Vinton would sell the place," Amanda said. "We were just as surprised as you."

That was a piece Colton had left out, and Dan wondered why the real estate agent had omitted that fact. "Really, do you know why he insisted on cash?"

"Jessie Colton told us the man would settle for less money if we gave him cash."

"So let me get this straight. You shelled out seven- hundred fifty grand cash, which was less than the asking price?"

Will jumped in. "It was on the market for eight- twenty, but we offered seven- fifty, and he took it. His only condition was no bank. No loan. No attorneys. Just cash. Colton said he'd use all of his resources to handle the transaction. We never even met Mr. Vinton."

Dan looked at Scotty, who had his hands full with Buster's head in his lap.

"What about the cash? That's a pile. Did you sell a huge house in Baltimore?"

Amanda sighed. "No. If you must know, my father died a year ago and left me a nice sum of money, so we could afford to put up cash."

Dan looked at Will. "Mind if I ask you one more question?"

"What's that?"

"Can you give us the name of the place you stayed in Maine?"

Amanda went to the kitchen, returned with a piece of paper torn from a pad, and handed it to Dan. The header on the preprinted page read PINE STATE Vacation CABINS. The address, phone number, and email address were below the name. "Thank you," Dan said.

The detectives left the residence and Dan made a right turn onto the main road. About a hundred feet down he spotted a black mailbox and drive- way similar to the Merlines'. He stopped the car. "Wonder who lives here?"

⅄

Dan drove up the driveway and saw a slim man in blue jean overalls with an axe in his hand, and he appeared to be chopping wood. The man put the dangerous instrument down when the black sedan neared him. Dan stopped the car and rolled down his window. He could see the wrinkled-faced man was well above retirement age.

"You boys got the right place?" the older man said in a scratchy voice.

Dan displayed his badge.

"You're cops?"

"Yes sir," Dan said. "Can we ask you a couple of questions?"

"I'm Preacher Fergusson."

At that moment Preacher's wife came out of the house and joined her husband at the car. "This is Emma, my bride of fifty-seven years." He took her hand. "These boys are police."

"Can we get out?" Dan asked.

"Sure," Ferguson said as he took off his hat and wiped his forehead. "There's some nice rockers on the porch if you want to sit and chat."

They proceeded to sit in the rockers. "So what did you want to talk about?" Preacher asked.

Dan smiled at him. "Is that your real name?"

"Preacher? Naw. It's Earl. I used to be on the town council. The other councilmen were a bunch of worms, and I took to preaching common sense whenever they'd make a ridiculous motion, or try to put something in play that wasn't in the town's best interests. People started calling me Preacher. Guess it stuck."

"Interesting story," Dan said. "Can you tell me about your neighbors?"

Preacher pointed to his left. "You mean the ones over there?"

"Yes, the Merlines."

"You boys want some cold lemonade? Got a whole pitcher inside," Emma said.

Dan knew better than to refuse the offer. "That's very nice of you."

"I'll be back."

Emma returned with the pitcher and four glasses on a tray. She poured the drinks and handed the detectives their lemonades.

Preacher continued talking about his neighbor. "Don't know a rat's ass about them. Only know they bought the place a while back, have two boys and a nuisance of a dog."

"Buster? We've met Buster. Seems like a nice dog."

"Maybe so," Preacher said as he pointed to his right. "See those chickens?"

Dan and Scotty both looked. "They lay eggs?" Scotty asked.

"Those ain't hens. Ask them about the dog."

"Are you saying Buster comes up here and bothers them?" Dan asked.

"That's a fact. See the wood I'm choppin'? That's for a new fence around the coop to keep the dog out. Heard about the ruckus though. Found some dead person on their property."

"That's what I want to talk with you about," Dan said. "Did you hear or see anything unusual the night before or the morning Buster found the body?'

"Heard the chicks, and figured Buster must've been around."

Dan looked at Scotty, and turned back to Preacher. "Do you have coyotes up here?"

"You bet."

"How do you know Buster was here, and not the coyotes?"

"Ever heard them howl? Different than a dog's bark, Buster was here. Them coyotes don't come out until later."

"Later? What time did you hear Buster?"

"Must have been soon after dark, cause a short while after came the monsoon."

"You sure it was the night before all the commotion? The Merlines were in Maine and didn't get home until around eleven. You sure Buster was here?"

Preacher scratched his head. "Can't say for sure. I didn't see him, but sounded like him."

"Did you see any lights, or vehicles, or hear voices?"

"Can't really see the place that well through the trees, and we wouldn't hear anything unless they was shouting. Besides the downpour rattled my roof and we could hardly hear us talking."

"What about that vehicle that poked its headlights into our driveway?" Emma said.

"There *was* a truck or something that turned in and went back out quick," Preacher said.

"Sure it wasn't a car?"

"Mighta been. Can't say for sure."

The detectives made sure to finish their refreshing lemonade.

Dan rose from his rocker. "You've been very helpful.. Thank you, and that lemonade was really good."

Scotty stopped rocking and stood. "Have a good day, folks."

Dan backed the car down the driveway onto the main road."I don't like it. I don't like the whole story," Dan said. "Merline's timeline is off. He said they got back from Maine late, and I saw the look in his eyes when I mentioned Cosby's name. He didn't even flinch. And that whole purchase stinks."

"So does Colton," Scotty said. "What's the link between him, Flores, Gomes and Vinton?"

"We need to check out the Maine story, but I bet you dollars to donuts the place will verify the Merlines' visit." Dan paused. "But I might not buy it."

"Make that dollars to muffins, I don't make donuts."

"Right," Dan said as he turned onto the highway.

. "Where we going?" Scotty asked.

"Your choice, The Hi-Hat or home base."

"Home James."

CHAPTER 33

Scotty's was prepared to see Sally again. Flowers were in his car.

He entered the squad room and tapped Dan's shoulder. "What time are we going to Sally's place?" he said.

"Jesus. I think she's all you think about. You better get your detective head straight. You sleep late today. I was beginning to worry about you."

"Don't worry. I'm cool. I was thinking about Flores and we may have to sweeten the ante for Sally to help us. I had something to do before coming in. There's a basket of mums in my car."

Dan smiled. "You sly dog."

"She should be there, it's after nine."

Dan lifted his coffee mug, and chugged the remaining caffeine. "Let's take a ride. Have to admit, I wouldn't mind seeing Sally again."

⅄

Sally's surprise was in Scotty's hands as the detectives approached her office. Dan opened the door and he let his partner precede him, flowers leading. "Are those for me?" Sally said, as Scotty handed them to her. "They're beautiful. I need to put them in a vase with water. I'll be right back."

The detectives watched her head to the bathroom as Scotty wiped his brow.

She returned and smiled. "Thank you! How'd you know I like mums?"

"A little birdie told me."

"Did he mention I like Tiffany too?" she said with a wide grin.

Her teal dress was cut lower than the ones she'd worn before, and Scotty took notice.

Once again Dan stood back and watched these two engage in playful small talk.

"Could have fooled me," Scotty said. "I don't see any rings."

"I keep the good stuff in my safe at home. Only wear them on special occasions."

Dan interrupted. "I'll be back in five minutes. I forgot something in the car."

He walked out and waited, having served notice that the lovefest needed to end soon. Five minutes later, Dan reentered the office and addressed Sally. "So, did Scotty tell you why we're here?"

"Not really."

"I'd like to meet Cecil Flores at his place, but I don't want him to know we're coming."

Sally gave Dan an inquisitive grin. "What are you asking me to do?"

Dan thought for a second. "How about leaving a message on his machine that you'd like to come to his unit to drop off a package that was delivered to the office."

Sally brushed her hand through her long red hair and thought about that proposition. "Okay, but I'm not delivering it. When do you want to do this?"

Dan placed his hands together. "I was thinking you could make the call now and we could deliver the package in the morning":

Sally paused and looked at Scotty. "You two are delivering the imaginary package, right?"

"We'll do it, all we need is for you to walk ahead of us and ring his bell. We won't be far behind." Dan said.

"What do you want me to say?"

"Say you'll be out this afternoon, and you'd like to deliver a package to him that was dropped off here by UPS. Tell him you'll bring it over first thing in the morning."

Sally pulled Flore's file and found his home phone number. She picked up the office phone and left a message on his machine. "Done, but you guys better be here before me. I get in at nine."

"We'll be here around eight-thirty." Scotty said.

Dan winked at Sally and he grabbed Scotty's arm. "Say goodbye."

"See you tomorrow," Scotty said.

"Bye. Thanks again for the flowers."

The detectives left Landon Place. Dan eyed Scotty. "So, what's the scoop?"

"She lives in Rocky Hill. I'm meeting her at the park Sunday. Might do a picnic, or eat at the Duck Pond Café. I have to call her later."

"Nice job, lover boy. Next time keep your eyes above her tits."

"Think she notice me staring?"

"I did, so I'm sure she did."

Scotty smiled. "Nice, aren't they?"

CHAPTER 34

The black Caddy that pulled up in front of the Hi-Hat club belonged to Vinnie Martinez, and a bewildered Cecil Flores jumped to his feet when he saw Martinez's two henchmen entering the club. Mo Harris and his sidekick Frankie Cruz made quite the sight wherever they went: both dressed in Calvin Klein suits, Mo in his ever present fedora, he towered a full eight inches over Frankie's five-seven frame.

Boozer B. was behind the bar pouring drinks for customers. Not many people knew the lanky bartender's name, DeCarlos Blanks. He was always Boozer, whose dreads hung down below his shoulders.

Flores had taken over managing the club two years ago, and he hadn't seen Mo and Frankie since then. He ushered Martinez's heavies into the back room, away from the crowd, and the topless dancers.

Mo stared at the performers, and Frankie lifted his sunglasses to take a long gaping look at the girls before following his intimidating partner into the room.

"What's shakin'?" Flores said.

"Looks like a couple of fine asses," Mo replied.

The old pool table standing on broken legs shifted as Mo leaned against it. Flores sat on a stool while Frankie took a cue stick from the rack on the wall.

"Vinnie ain't heard from you in a while," Mo said.

"Been busy, this place is hoppin'."

"That's one of the problems."

Frankie, a toothpick hanging from his lips, shut the door and stood beside Mo.

"Vinnie thinks you're shortchanging him. Profits are down," Mo said. "You pimpin some of these whores on the side?"

Flores hopped off the stool. "Hell no! you think I'm crazy?"

"Maybe, so sit back down. You know he let you off easy asshole. Vinnie was pretty pissed when his prized piece ended up dead."

"Yeah, but he didn't understand. That bitch only worked weekends here. He let her keep that airport job to bring in high paying customers. She decided to freelance and keep a few regulars to herself, but Vinnie never believed she did that. He was blind to her."

"Yeah, but that's only half the deal. He wants his money, and he's getting a little impatient, and you ain't found out shit. Or have you?"

Frankie, who had a short fuse, snapped the pool cue in half and Flores hopped off his stool again. "That's a whole 'nother story," he said. "This is my job. I ain't had nothing to do with the drug deal."

"Well, now you do, dog. You seen Biggie?"

"He's hangin' at Lucky's again. Dude has nine lives and a shit- kicking mouthpiece. Sasser got him off on self-defense and had the charges dropped on the gang shootout."

"You better get with the fat man and figure out where the money is, or you'll be seeing a few of Vinnie's guys who ain't as nice as us. Know what I mean? We're just the messengers. And you better answer your phone from now on, and check in with the man a little more often. Now, how 'bout sending Boozer back here?"

"He's busy."

"Well, unbusy him, I got a few questions for him."

Flores went out to spell his employee at the bar, and Boozer entered the back room. A few minutes later he went back to his job, and Flores returned to the messengers.

"What was that all about?" Flores said.

Mo rubbed his chin. "Wanted him to know that Vinnie appreciates his work."

Frankie opened the door while Mo put his arm around Flores and pointed to the girl at the stripper pole. "Nice piece, how much for her?"

"She gets off at three. You want an appointment?"

Sucking on the toothpick, Frankie nodded. "Damn right."

Mo tugged on his horny partner's arm. "Gotta go, keep it in your pants. Which way is Lucky's?"

Cecil pointed to the front door. "Take a right, about five blocks down."

He watched Mo and Frankie exit the club, and picked up his cell phone. Cecil called his best pal . . . Angel Salinas.

▲

As usual, Brick, Sharky, and Lucky were in the pawn shop, but so was Biggie, who had recovered from his gunshot wounds. He now hung out at the shop, an unlikely place for him to be since Lucky was never fond of him or Vegas. However, Biggie had convinced Lucky that an extra guard would be a wise investment.

When Lucky's door opened, Sharky growled, and Brick stopped the strangers. "You cops too?"

Biggie froze, recognizing the suited businessmen. "Fuck no," he yelled to Brick. "Hold Sharky back."

"Vinnie says 'hi,' fat man. You don't look so good."

Lucky and Brick looked at each other.

"Which one of you two is Lucky?" Mo said.

"I am," Lucky answered from behind the counter. "Who the hell are you?"

Mo tipped his fedora. "Tell him, fat man."

Biggie turned to Lucky. "These are Vinnie's boys."

"Boys?" Mo said. "Do we look like boys?"

"Sorry."

"This place smells like a pot farm. You got a nursery back there or something?"

Biggie reached over to the counter nearest him and handed Mo a joint. "This is on me. There's more under the counter."

Mo slapped the weed stick away. "You stupid? We're businessmen. We don't want that stink all over our suits." Mo stared into Biggie's eyes. "I want to know a few things. By the way, nice shootin'. Heard you took out Vegas with a shotgun."

"Motherfucker thought I was in on the money, and had somethin' to do with Jenkins escaping."

"Yeah, well, bottom line is Vinnie wants his money, and he's tired of nobody knowing nothing. You gotta find Jenkins."

"Nobody knows nothing, except the ambulance was in the warehouse and he's gone."

"Well Vinnie has a message: 'Find the bastard and the money.'"

Biggie paced the floor. "And how we supposed to do that?"

"Just like you're doin' fat man. Keep walking until you get to the money, might even shed a few pounds."

Lucky tossed Biggie a shotgun, and Mo turned to Lucky. "Really? You some kind of moron? Vinnie wouldn't like what you just did. You got smoke detectors in here? This place could go up real fast. Know what I mean?"

"This thing ain't even loaded," Biggie said.

"Tell the idiot behind the counter that. Gimme that shotgun," Mo said.

He looked at Lucky. "Hand me some shells, smart ass."

"Hell no," Lucky said.

Frankie pulled out his Glock. "This one's loaded. Wanna see?"

Brick held onto Sharky's leash, and a few seconds later Frankie spit his toothpick on the floor, aimed his weapon at the big Rottweiler and he pulled the trigger. The dog was still shaking and leaking blood as it fell lifeless next to Brick.

"What the fuck!" the stunned Brick said. "You shot my dog! You shot my fucking dog!"

Mo tossed the shotgun back to Biggie. "You could be next, shithead. On second thought, give me back that shotgun."

He looked at Frankie still holding his warm gun, and went behind Lucky to grab some shotgun shells. "Come on, Frankie. I think they get the picture."

Lucky, Brick, and Biggie watched Mo and Frankie casually walk out the door. The messengers got into the Caddy. Mo handed his partner the shotgun and he called Vinnie. When their short conversation ended, he turned to Frankie. "Load that thing. We have work to do. I'm not happy with what Boozer had to say. Fucking Flores is stealing liquor and cash."

CHAPTER 35

Dan and Scotty arrived at Landon Place as Sally was pulling into her space. She exited her car and opened the office door. Her black pant suit clung to her perfect shape. Inside the office she turned on the lights and started the coffee maker. "You guys want a cup?" she said.

"Thanks, Dan replied. "We can wait until after we see Flores. I'd like to do that now."

"Maybe I should give him a wake- up call before we head over."

"Good idea," Dan said.

She picked up the office phone and called Flores. "Hello," a nasally voice said."

"This is Sally, Okay if I come and deliver that package?"

"Sure."

She hung up. "He's waiting for his package. He sounds like he's got a cold."

Dan saw an empty cardboard box in the corner. "How about taking that?"

⋏

The detectives stayed a few steps behind her. When they approached Flores's unit, Dan noticed a black Ford F-150 pickup parked in front of the garage.

Sally rang the bell and the door opened. Angel Salinas had a worried look on his face, and Dan was surprised to see the ex-gang member standing in front of him. "Long time no see, Angel," he said.

"No shit. I'm clean. Where's Cecil?"

"You mean he's not here?"

"No. I been trying to call him all night. What's that package? I heard the message."

"Nothing, don't mind it. Let's have a chat."

They entered the unit, and Flores's cocker spaniel greeted them as they stepped into the living room. The smell of marijuana was evident and Dan saw a couple of joints in an ashtray on a table underneath a sixty- inch TV that was hanging on the wall. He also saw stacks of porn on the fireplace mantle.

Their shoes sank into the plush green carpet as they walked with Salinas to the sectional in the middle of the room. Dan saw Angel staring at Sally. "What are you doing here?" The detective said.

"What's it to you? I'm here a lot. Have my own key. Not like him to not call me back, and I don't think he's been here. Corky needed to go real bad when I got here, and for sure he wasn't fed."

"So Cecil hasn't been here all night?"

Sally took a quick look around, and after seeing the pile of X-rated videos, and pictures of naked women strewn around the place, she excused herself and went back to her office.

Salinas sneezed. "Think I got something." He grabbed his hanky. "No, talked to him yesterday afternoon. I was supposed to meet him here around nine. Nice of you to stop by, I gotta go to work."

"Still selling pot? Where you working these days?"

Salinas stared at the joint in the ashtray. "Lenko Roofing."

"They pay you well?"

"Enough. I gotta go."

Dan leaned forward. "Hold it. I'd like to ask you a few questions."

"Like what?"

"The suicides, you know what happened next door, and you know Cecil found the bodies."

"So?"

"Come on, Angel. What really happened that night? You knew Yolanda Gomes and Cosby Davis, right? You said you're here often. You must have known them."

Angel sat back. "I met em."

"You think they committed suicide?"

"What you getting at? You think Cecil had somethin to do with it?"

"Maybe, so what's the real story?"

Angel tensed, and gave Dan a scornful stare. "What the fuck? You really think Cecil killed them?"

Dan stared back, and raised his voice. "Did he? You're here all the time, maybe he had help."

Angel shrugged, and angrily replied. "Now you're crossing the line asshole. I'm outta here."

"Wait. I'm not done yet," Dan said.

"Eat my dust, unless you arrest me for something. I'm gone. See you around."

"Next time I see your sorry ass, I might have an arrest warrant."

"You better come up with something good, 'cause I'm clean. Ain't got no plans on going back."

Dan and Scotty watched him speed away in the truck.

"Let's take a peek around. Guess Sally isn't into porn. She sure flew out of here fast when she saw this stack of crap," Scotty said.

Flores's kitchen cabinets were filled with bottles of liquor. Scotty found a pot stash on top of the bedroom bureau. The bed was unmade, but there were two sets of panties and bras hanging on the shower door.

"Definitely different sizes," Scotty said.

Come on, pal," Dan said. "He's not getting any award from *Good Housekeeping*."

λ

As they left the apartment, they saw a middle-aged man sitting on his front porch across the street, shaking his head and looking in the direction in which the truck had disappeared. The detectives crossed the street and approached him.

"That guy speeds all the time."

Dan and Scotty introduced themselves, and the man replied: "Ainsley Waterman."

"Mind if we ask you a few questions?" Dan said.

Ainsley pointed to the bench next to him. "Have a seat."

"So you've seen that truck before."

"Many times."

"Do you remember Yolanda Gomes?"

"Pretty girl. I still can't believe she and her boyfriend locked themselves in that car and killed themselves."

"Were you home that night?"

"I was."

"Do you remember seeing or hearing anything unusual?"

"No, but I know that guy that was at Flores's place was here."

"How can you be so sure?"

"He sometimes walks Cecil's dog. I remember yelling at the guy that night when the news was over. That dog is a yipper, and I looked out my window and saw it poop in my front yard. I opened the slider and told the guy to pick up the crap."

"Did you see Cecil, or the victims, that night?"

"No. I just saw that guy."

"What about the next morning? Flores found the bodies around seven thirty, with the car running. Did you hear it?"

"No. I'm a retired teacher. Now I volunteer at the senior center. I left at about twenty after seven. I didn't notice any car running."

"Are you sure of the time?"

"Positive."

"What about Cecil Flores or Yolanda Gomes?"

"I've been here for five years and didn't run into them much. I did complain about a party once, and I know he drinks. The girl, she kind of comes and goes. She was a TSA employee. Her uniform gave it away."

Dan and Scotty got up to leave. "One more question: Anyone from the police department ever talk to you about this?"

"No. I was already at work."

"Thanks. Have a nice day."

The detectives left Waterman's. "Gotta tell Sally we're done." Scotty said.

"Go, but don't take too long. I'm sure she's got work to do."

"Don't worry. I'll meet you in the car."

A

As the detectives headed back to headquarters, Dan's cell rang. He tapped the screen on his dash, saw the call was from Syms. "Where are you now?" the captain said.

"On our way back."

"You guys need to make a detour. Get over to the Hi-Hat. Cecil Flores has been killed."

"What?" Dan said, how?"

"His body is in the front seat of his car in back of the club. Plenty of uniforms are at the scene."

"Holy shit!" Scotty said as Dan disconnected the call. "Think Salinas knew, and was covering for himself?"

"I don't know, but I sure got the feeling Salinas was hiding something from us."

A

By the time the detectives arrived, the street was full of emergency vehicles as well as unwanted onlookers. The uniforms kept the crowd away as Dan and Scotty walked through the alley to Flores's vehicle. One officer saw the detectives approaching. "Better take a deep breath before you look."

"What do we have?" Dan said.

"One fucking mess, looks like his head was blasted by a shotgun. The coroner is here, and they'll be taking him soon."

"Any witnesses?"

"None. The lab guys are checking the vehicle. Strange thing, though. The weapon was left behind."

"Really?" Dan said.

"Yeah. Nice shotgun."

Scotty nudged Dan. "Lucky's?"

Dan took a look at the shotgun and turned to Scotty. "We've seen one like this before. Looks like the one Biggie used to kill Vegas. It still has the pawn tag on it."

"We have that one in custody," Scotty said. "We know that one came from Lucky's"

"Let's go pal," Dan said. "I'm sure Lucky will be happy to see me again."

A

The brash detectives walked into Lucky's and Brick stared at them. "Nice to see you too. Where's Sharky?" Dan said.

"At the vet. Didn't think we'd see you again. Who's your friend?"

"Scotty's my Kung Fu black belt partner."

Dan's eyes turned to Biggie. "You look like you've lost some weight. So, which one of you shot Flores?"

Biggie got close to Dan and screamed in his face. "Get the fuck out of here, unless you got an arrest warrant."

Dan turned to Lucky. "You sold any shotguns lately?"

"Can't remember."

Dan eyed Biggie, who still stood face to face with the detective. "Back off fat man, you need to brush your teeth."

Brick started to walk away, and Scotty grabbed the guard's arm. "Not so fast. My partner's still talking, so don't be rude."

Dan drew some distance between himself and Biggie. "In case you didn't know, Flores was killed with a shotgun, just like the one you took out Vegas with. It still had a little white tag on the trigger." Dan pointed to the gun rack. "I happen to think it was right back there in one of those empty rack spots."

He stared at Lucky. "Am I right?"

"You know, you ask as many questions as Alex Trebek," Lucky replied. "You guys need to be leaving now."

"Or what?" Dan said. "Anyone want to spend the night in jail?"

He looked at Biggie. "You'd like the new cells. Pretty comfortable."

"Get the fuck out now," Biggie screamed. "You ain't got shit on any of us."

The detectives turned to walk out. "You haven't seen the last of us," Dan shouted.

CHAPTER 36

Clouds blanketed Hartford as a light mist fell, adding to the ominous task that Syms was about to undertake. He was inside his office praying for thunder and lightning. Standing at his window, he looked down to the parking lot and spotted every news van in the city. He also saw the podium where he would be standing in a few minutes.

With all the media vehicles in the lot, Dan had to find a spot across the street in front of the cab company before plowing his way through the sea of reporters just to get into the building. Earlier that morning, Chief Hardison had informed Syms, who in turn told his men, that it was the coroner's office who had leaked Cosby Davis's identity.

At exactly nine a.m. Dan watched the captain walk outside under murky, overcast skies, and stand at the podium. Syms peered over the crowd, and adjusted the mic.

"Good morning. You're all aware that the body found in Tolland has been identified as Cosby Davis. I urge you to please respect the family's privacy and stay away from them. You also know that Mr. Davis had been interred at City Cemetery, yet his body was found on property belonging to Amanda and William Merline. Please respect their privacy and do not contact them."

The TV cameras were rolling. Syms ignored the few hands in the air and continued. "I shouldn't need to remind you this is an active investigation, and I will be the sole source of information."

Syms paused and looked around at his large audience. "You'll know what you need to know when I tell you, so please do not pressure me or any of my officers. I will cooperate as best I can on my terms, but at this time I'm not at leisure to divulge any other details of this case, and it's not appropriate for me to answer any questions."

A burst of thunder came from above, and a few umbrellas popped open as light rain began to fall. From the gallery came a shout: "But captain, just one question!"

Syms yelled back. "Let's start this off right. I said no questions, and that means no questions. We all have work to do, so let's hit the road." He ended with, "Thank you for your understanding, and good day, ladies and gentlemen."

It was over. The captain turned to Hardison. "Thank God for little things like thunder. Damn reporters, I'd like to lock the whole bunch up and throw away the keys."

⅄

Dan and Scotty followed Syms into his office as Hardison went back upstairs to his quarters. The captain picked up the generic pill bottle. "Can't remember how many I took before the sermon, but this is nearly empty."

"I may need some too," Dan said.

"Good; you can stop at that drugstore and buy me a new bottle…The real medicine not that store crap."

"Listen," Dan said. "There's a lot of crazy stuff going on with Flores being killed and us digging around at Landon Place. Is it a coincidence that Angel Salinas happened to be at Flores's apartment?"

"What's he up to? I thought Salinas went his own way."

"He's working for a roofer, but he was obviously still buds with Flores."

"Any witnesses at the Hi-Hat?"

"No. But there *was* something unusual. The murder weapon was left at the scene, and we know it came from Lucky's because it still had the tag on the trigger. It'll be interesting to see if we get a match on prints."

Dan shrugged. "Lucky, his goon Brick, and Biggie all clammed up."

Syms downed the last two pills and tossed the empty bottle to Dan. "Next time you come in here, you better have a full bottle of Advil." He looked at Scotty. "And where the hell have your muffins been?"

Dan and Scotty had their orders, marching out of Syms's office.

"Think Connie's still around?" Dan said.

"I'm game, let's get out of here."

⅄

Connie's Place was still standing, although the wrecking equipment was parked across the street. Dan and Scotty saw a sign on the door: LAST DAY—THANKS FOR YOUR BUSINESS.

When Dan and Scotty entered the nearly deserted restaurant, Connie smiled. "Well, one more for old times' sake."

"Yeah, babe," Dan said. "Good to see that smile." She followed them to a booth, coffee pot in hand. "You know, I'm going to close the door after you leave, box up the leftover food, and take it to the shelter. I'll lock up and throw away the key." She looked at Scotty. "Seen Bev?"

"Yes, she was in with the babies a few days ago. She quit, and I kinda miss her."

"Drink all you want. I'll leave the pot, gotta pack up."

The detectives looked around the place once more. "Can't wait to retire," Dan said.

"We keep going to Lucky's and it may not be long pal."

Dan pushed the pot aside, not bothering to fill his or Scotty's cup. "We still have a lot of crap to do. Did you tell Sally about Flores?"

"She knows. I talked to her last night."

Connie returned, presenting Dan with the last green-papered check. It said *Thanks, boys. Stay safe. I'll miss you.* Her home address and phone number were written on the back.

The detectives got up. "I wouldn't feel right without paying," Dan said.

"Shush. Get out so I can go home. One last hug, boys."

Dan placed the stub in his shirt pocket, and the detectives exited the diner for the final time.

⤙

A copy of the incident report from the Hi-Hat sat on Dan's desk as he and Scotty re-entered the squad room. "Hey come on over. Look at this."

Scotty looked over his partner's shoulder. "No one saw anything," he said.

"No one ever sees anything in that neighborhood," Dan replied. "But why in hell would the killer leave the shotgun? That doesn't make sense, unless they were trying to frame Lucky, or Biggie."

"What makes you think Biggie didn't do it? He fired a shotgun once before."

"That's the point. He may be fat and worthless, but he isn't stupid. We could wait for DNA, but whoever used that gun wasn't stupid, either. I think we should put pressure on Biggie. He may be innocent, but he might sing like a bird this time, because we're going to get a warrant and charge him with murder."

Scotty sat back. "We don't have any proof yet. We can't get a warrant."

"Biggie doesn't know that. I want his ass for good this time."

Scotty looked at Dan. "Know what? It's getting a little too personal with you and Biggie. Cool it. Let's follow the trail."

Dan stood, leaning on the cubicle, he took a deep breath. "You're right." He paused. "Know what else, pal? We don't know jack-shit about Yolanda Gomes. All we know is that they were in Cosby Davis's car. Where's hers?"

Scotty plucked Gomes's file from his basket and opened it.

"According to her file, she had a two-year-old Honda coupe with Louisiana plates."

"We still have the airport to check out."

"What about Colton and the Merlines?"

Dan shook his head. "I get the feeling somehow all this stuff is tied together."

"You mean Vegas and Biggie, too?"

"Can't say, but if it is, then Willingham is back in the picture, and Syms will have to deal with him."

CHAPTER 37

Scotty had tossed and turned all night, rising at five a.m. This day had finally come, and the weather was cooperating with him. Meeting Sally in the park for a picnic was all he had thought about. As the clock ticked toward noon, he drove to their meeting destination in his red and white 1957 Chevy.

Sally was on time, wearing black designer jeans and colorful butterfly-patterned top. Her hair was mostly covered beneath a white-striped sun hat. Purple sun glasses shaded her eyes. "Great day, isn't it?" she said eying his car. "Let me look at this thing."

"Thing?" Scotty grinned, as he pulled his Aviator's from the pocket of his short-sleeved blue shirt. "This is a piece of American beauty."

"It is. I love it. You'll have to take me for a spin sometime."

"Play your cards right, and I'll take you around the park later."

She smiled at the picnic basket on the back seat, and Scotty pulled the front seat down to retrieve it, then he opened the trunk, grabbed a checkered blanket and handed it to Sally. "Do you mind carrying this? Don't worry, I washed it."

The park was getting crowded, but they were able to find a fairly quiet spot beneath a large oak tree to lay the blanket down. Sally sat cross-legged across from her date as Scotty unpacked the food and a bottle of red wine.

"What's in the Tupperware?" she asked.

"Chicken salad."

"Homemade?"

"Sort of. I know someone at the store made it."

Sally smiled. "What about those chips?"

"Can't take credit for those either. Someone named Frito-Lay did those, and the Italian bread came from Mazo's."

Scotty opened the wine. "This I did make in my bathtub, vintage yesterday."

They both laughed. "The muffins are mine."

They enjoyed the food. "So where did you grow up?" he said.

She sipped the wine. "Boston. My sister's there. My father was killed in a terrible car accident seven years ago."

"I'm sorry to hear that."

"Thanks. My mom's from Hartford, so she moved back here a while ago. You grow up here?" she asked.

"Yeah, home town boy, played football in high school. My folks are in Florida. Don't see them much."

He hesitated as he stuffed a few chips into his mouth. "I'm divorced. Have a little boy named Eli who lives with his mom, not too far away. You ever been hitched?"

Sally finished her wine. "I was engaged once to a navy lifer, but I think he loved his ship more than he loved me, so I let him drift off to sea. I was only twenty-two then."

"How about a walk around the park?" Scotty said.

"Great idea."

"I have a bag of popcorn for the ducks."

They strolled by the pond, sat on a bench and tossed popcorn into the water. "You have hobbies?" Scotty asked.

"I dabble in painting. I'm not very good, but I try. I like horses. My aunt had a farm and we used to ride them. Haven't ridden a horse in years. What about you?"

Scotty threw the last of the popcorn to the ducks. "Never been on a horse, but I'd be willing to try. I guess the Chevy is a hobby. I'm a sports guy, die-hard sox fan. Bet you are too."

"Got that right."

The afternoon was passing quickly, and Sally looked at her Tiffany watch. "It's almost four, and I promised my mother I'd take her to dinner tonight."

They rose from the bench and walked back to the blanket to pick up the picnic items, before heading back to the parking lot.

"I had a great time," Scotty said.

"Me too, and you owe me a ride in the Chevy. Call me."

"Definitely."

All Scotty could do was stand and watch her drive away, hoping he wasn't going to blow this one.

Chapter 38

Scotty whistled all the way down the squad room corridor, toting a round plastic container to Dan's desk. "Muffin?" he said.

"About time," Dan replied. "So what's with that shit-eating smile, I take it things went well with Sally?"

"Couldn't have been better."

Dan furrowed his brow and grinned. "You get laid?"

"Jesus H. No, never touched anything but her hand, but I know she's up for another date."

"Tell me the story, lover boy."

Scotty sat beside Dan. "You should have seen her tight jeans. I don't know what perfume she was wearing, but whatever it was, it smelled great."

"You know as well as I do, she would have smelled great if she was wearing motor oil."

Dan took a muffin and bit into it. "You bake these this morning?"

"I was up early. Couldn't sleep, kept thinking about her."

"So when's the wedding?"

Scotty smiled. "Don't worry, you'll be invited."

Dan held up the Courant's sport's page. "By the way, noticed the standings? I think it says the Yankees are in first place. Sox are four back."

"Give me that muffin. You sure know how to ruin a good day."

Dan turned to his computer. "Let me show you this." He brought up the PINE State Vacation CABINS website. "Nice place. I called the manager. The Merlines registered and stayed in cabin fourteen."

"You thought it would check out, so that confirms their alibi."

Dan finished his muffin. "Does it? I asked the manager if he knew the Merlines. He said he didn't. I asked if he knew how many people stayed in the cabin, and he couldn't tell me." Dan shook his head and looked at Scotty. "My point is, we don't know if Will was there, or if only Amanda and the kids stayed there."

Dan stood, picking up a giant bottle of Advil from his desk "I have to deliver this."

As he approached the captain's office, Syms came flying out, uttering profanity all the way out the front door.

"What the hell is going on now? He's probably going to kill some reporter," Dan said.

⋏

Syms wasn't going to kill a reporter, but he was damn near going to kill someone else. The phone call he'd received from Sergeant Streeter had set off a firestorm.

The captain was headed to Eastside Hospital, where Kim Patton had been taken by ambulance at one a.m... Marty was at the Manchester police station, being booked again for domestic violence.

Syms sped to the hospital and barreled his way to Kim's room, where a uniformed officer stood outside the door. "How bad is she?" Syms said.

"He beat the shit out of her."

Syms bowed his head. "God damn it. I'm going to kill him."

The captain opened the door and a doctor looked up. "Sir, would you mind stepping out until I finish my exam?"

"Go ahead. I'm Captain Syms."

"It should only be a few minutes."

Five minutes later the doctor allowed Syms into the room. Kim lay in bed, alert, with a swollen face, a black eye, and an IV hookup.

She saw Syms and began crying. "Here, take this Kleenex," he said. "Tell me what happened."

Her voice trembled. "You see what happened. He was out drinking. Marty's been a wreck since being released from jail. I was in bed; he woke me up about twelve-thirty, held my arms down and raped me again. This time after he climaxed he threw me off the bed and began hitting me. I think it was only when he saw the blood on my face that he stopped. He left and I managed to crawl to my cell phone and call 911."

Syms looked into her wet eyes. "I thought he was staying with his parents?"

Kim winced, as the pain killer for her bruised ribs couldn't rid her of all the discomfort. "He was, but I took him back because he promised he was going to change and I believed him. The funny thing was that for a while he *did* change, but then he went crazy. It all came crashing down on him. He started showing up at the gym again, and he kept ranting at me, wondering how many of the young studs I'd slept with when he was in jail. He always called Silver's a glorified whorehouse, and wanted me quit, but I told him that one of us had to have a job"

She sobbed harder. "Damn that bastard'" she yelled, feeling the sting in her side. "I was hoping he'd be happy when he found out."

Tears flowed down her puffy face, and she reached for more tissues.

Syms squinted. "Found out?"

"I hadn't told Marty yet." She uttered. "I was two months pregnant. The doctor told me I lost the baby."

"So he doesn't know?"

She nodded. "I was waiting for the right time."

Syms held her hand until her sobs quieted down. "Please get some rest, and I'll see you again."

Syms left the room. Her doctor was still outside. ""Lucky she's in great shape, because there are some pretty bad bruises, and a couple of broken ribs. It could've been a lot worse," the doctor said.

"Not really, Doc; she lost her baby."

"You're right. I didn't mean that."

"How long will she be here?"

"I don't think any more than two or three days." Syms was about to walk away when the doctor stopped him. "Captain. There's one more thing I have to tell you. She has a lot of bruises, but not all of them happened last night."

"Son of a bitch!" Syms was even more enraged as he stormed out of the hospital and drove as fast as he could to the Manchester police station.

⋏

He knew where to find Streeter, and stomped his way to the sergeant's desk. "Where is he? I should have strung that bastard up last time! What have you got him on?"

"Domestic assault, public intoxication, disorderly conduct, and resisting arrest."

"Where'd you find him, anyway?"

"That was easy. He was passed out in his car outside the apartment."

"I want to see his ass, and you can add involuntary manslaughter to the list of charges."

"Murder? I thought her injuries weren't life threatening."

"Not Kim. She was pregnant and lost the baby. He's a murderer."

The sergeant picked up his phone and told an officer to bring Marty up to interrogation.

⋏

Syms left his gun at Streeter's desk, and the police officers entered the room waiting for Marty. A couple of minutes later, a uniform appeared with the cuffed prisoner. Marty wasn't totally sober. His face was as red as his bloodshot eyes. He saw Syms standing next to Streeter and squirmed down in his chair.

Syms didn't hold back his tirade, but he waited to drop the bombshell on Marty. "What the fuck have you got to say for yourself?"

"How's Kim?"

That response drew a hailstorm from Syms. "You fucking bastard! If you cared how she was, we wouldn't be here in the first place. What's going on with you, Marty? Drinking, and what else? Wife punching? Is that your sport of choice?"

Marty bowed his head. "I'm sick. I need help."

Standing a few feet from Marty's face, Syms raged on. "You needed help a long time ago. You quit AA and never showed up at anger management classes. What happened? Tell me you were hearing voices Marty, voices like Jack Daniel's, and Johnnie Walker. You love them more than Kim and your baby."

"We don't have a baby."

That was the moment he'd been waiting for. Syms got right in Marty's face and raised his voice to a fever pitch. "Not now, you don't! You fucking asshole. Kim was pregnant, Marty! She was pregnant! She lost the baby—you killed your baby! That's manslaughter. Sergeant Streeter, please advise him that he is also going to be charged with involuntary manslaughter."

Streeter looked at the stunned Marty. "You heard the captain."

Syms took one last look at Marty before leaving. "I'm done sarge. Get him back to lock-up before I *really* get angry." The captain said as he tugged on his empty holster.

Marty was escorted back to his cell, and Streeter looked at the spent captain. "I think if you had your gun, you really would have shot him."

Streeter handed Syms his pistol. "I haven't fired this thing in years, but it would have been tempting."

⅄

The steamed captain drove back to headquarters and returned to his office as his entire crew stared at him.

Dan went to Scotty's cubicle. "Come on, let's see what bug is up his ass."

"You sure you want to barge in on him?"

"I have to, you coming?"

Syms looked up at the fearless detectives who were entering his office. "Get out, the captain said."

Dan held up the new bottle of Advil. "Okay, but if you want these babies, you have to let us stay."

"Give me those things. One of you get me some water and close the fucking door when you return."

Dan sat and watched the captain unseal the bottle and line up three pills on his desk. "Anyone care to join me?"

"Maybe after you tell us what's going on," Dan said.

Syms stared upward. "See up there, boys?"

"The ceiling?" Dan said.

"Nope. Higher. Think God's watching us?"

Dan glanced at Scotty and he looked back at Syms. "What are you getting at?"

Syms leaned forward, staring at both detectives. "God. Why does he let crap happen? Why does he let people like Marty live and breathe?

"Oh shit," Dan said. "What's he done now?"

"Bastard's in jail again, and he's going away for a long time."

The detective's faces went blank.

"The son of a bitch beat Kim like she was a punching bag. She looks like Muhammad Ali used her for a sparring partner. The good news is, she has a few fractured ribs and bruises that will heal. She's in Eastside, will be there a few days, but here's the kicker: she was pregnant, and Marty didn't know it. She lost the baby, and Marty has a few charges, including involuntary manslaughter."

Dan was sickened by the news. It brought tears to his eyes. "I could've helped. Shit, I could've helped him if I'd been on him."

Syms slammed his fist on his desk and leaned forward. "Dan, you couldn't have done a damned thing," he said. "Marty had his chances, quit AA, ditched anger management, served a few months in jail, and wouldn't help himself. It's Kim I can't help thinking about. I'm thankful she'll be fine, physically anyway."

CHAPTER 39

D an didn't have fond memories of the airport, nor his last flight four years ago. That was the summer he'd taken the family to Orlando.

Aside from the fact that Disney had been a lot more expensive than he'd anticipated, the flight down had hit heavy turbulence, and with the cabin bouncing around like a pinball machine, Kate had thrown up. Luckily, Phyllis pulled the barf bag from the back of the seat in front of her, and they'd avoided a mess. The clincher came on the return trip when their luggage had been placed on the wrong baggage carousel, and it took Dan two hours to retrieve their bags.

As the detectives got closer to the airport, they began seeing planes flying low overhead.

The Accord followed a couple of buses around to the drop-off area, and bypassed the garage. Dan stopped next to a security car, and Scotty lowered his window and flashed his badge, asking the driver where they should park. They were directed to the restricted parking area where Dan pulled into a spot next to a state police vehicle.

The detectives headed to the terminal, passing the curbside check-in, entering through the sliding glass doors along with several frantic travelers. Lines were long at the security checkpoint. "If I remember right," Dan said, "baggage is downstairs and there's an elevator to our left."

His memory hadn't failed him. As soon as they got downstairs they saw the rows of conveyors and pacing passengers watching luggage go around and around. Scotty pointed to a blue and white sign that read BAGGAGE OFFICE.

"Good eyes," Dan said.

⋏

Scotty opened the door and they walked into a room where suitcases had been placed in one corner. Standing behind a counter, checking a bag, was a middle-aged woman wearing a photo ID lanyard. Brenda Simmons had short dark hair, and was dressed in airport- issued employee garb: khaki pants and a blue top with a silver airplane insignia. She looked up and saw the detectives.

"Can I help you?" she said.

"We're detectives Shields and Scott from Hartford," Dan said. "We'd like to talk to you about a former employee named Cosby Davis."

She peered over her wire-rimmed glasses, stopped what she was doing, and sighed. "A tragedy, Cosby was a good man. I don't understand it. Never would have suspected anything like that to happen, and what's this I read about his body in some grave?"

"That's why we're here," Dan said. "We've reopened the case, and you may be able to help us."

"I don't know what I can tell you."

Dan saw luggage sitting on the floor. He also noticed a room behind the counter, racks loaded with bags and asked.. "Are those unclaimed suitcases in back?"

"You'd think there was an epidemic of runaway suitcases with all the ones we have here." Brenda replied.

As they stood talking, an airline attendant wheeled a suitcase into the room. "Got another one," the man said. At least it has a tag."

"Thanks. I'll try to contact the owner."

That action gave Dan a way to ease into the conversation.

"I can see what part of your job is. What exactly do you do here, and what specifically were Cosby Davis's duties?"

"Same as mine."

She pointed to the bag she had just tagged. "This one's easy because there's an ID card on the outside, unless, of course, the owner doesn't respond to my call."

"So what's the procedure?" Dan asked.

"First, I'm going to log the bag in."

She took a numbered yellow tag from below the counter and attached it to the suitcase, then entered the date, time, description of the suitcase and any other pertinent information into the computer that sat on the counter. "Now the suitcase goes on a shelf in the back room. Not that complicated."

Scotty stared into the back room. "How many never get claimed?"

"Hard to say, more than you would think though, but after six months they get auctioned off."

"How long did Cosby work with you?" Dan asked

"About three years. He was very consciences, never missed a day, and always polite."

"Did you know Yolanda Gomes?"

"I know she was a TSA agent, and I'd seen her with Cosby, but I never spoke with her."

"Did he ever talk about her?"

"Not really?"

"So he said something?"

"Only that she came from New Orleans, and he liked her Southern accent."

"We're going over to TSA to see what they can tell us about her. Can you point us in the right direction?"

"The office is upstairs to the left of the first security line."

Dan and Scotty thanked Brenda, then the detectives took the escalator up one flight to the main terminal. They spotted the TSA office right where Brenda said it was.

⋏

The detectives entered the TSA office. They approached an agent who was sitting at a desk and Dan displayed his badge. "We'd like to speak with the person in charge," he said.

"That's Mr. Quince. I'll tell him you want to talk with him."

Peter Quince, a man who facially resembled Tom Hanks appeared in a TSA uniform. "Detectives, what can I help you with?"

"Can we go into your office?"

"Sure."

Once inside Quince's office, he shut the door and they all sat.

"We're here to ask you about Yolanda Gomes," Dan said.

Quince shook his head somberly. "That was a shocker. She was a good employee, a little flamboyant at times, but a reliable worker."

"Did she have any friends here?"

"Everyone liked her, especially Cosby Davis."

"Did you know him too?"

"I met him a few times, seemed nice enough. What's going on? I saw the news."

"That's why we're here. We're reinvestigating the case. Tell us more about Yolanda. Do you have her personnel file?"

Quince turned to a cabinet behind him and removed her file. He held onto the folder and read from it. "She transferred here from New Orleans, had a sweet twang in her voice."

"She ever talk about her personal life?"

"Not to me. She was kind of private, although all the men passing through her station noticed her, if you know what I mean."

Dan smiled. "I do. She was a pretty gal. Can I get a quick look at that file?"

Quince handed it to the detective. Dan looked at her photo, a better shot than the one in Colton's file. "Really nice looking girl," he uttered. He also noticed her salary was nowhere enough to afford the rent at Landon Place. "Think we can get a copy of this file?"

"You mean without a warrant?" Quince took the file back and smiled. "Just kidding. I'll be right back."

"Sharp guy; I like him," Scotty said.

Quince returned, handing Dan the copy. "Anything else I can do for you?"

Dan stood. "There is one more thing. She drove a fairly new Honda coupe that has never been found. Do you know if she drove to work?'

"I know she did. Sometimes she and Cosby drove together. But her car was found here in the employee lot and impounded."

Dan looked at Scotty. "Sloppy Joe did it again." He smiled at Quince. "Thanks for your time."

Chapter 40

Captain Syms had a smile on his face for a change. He waved a finger at Scotty when he walked by the detective's cubicle. "Grab your partner and come on down."

Dan heard that. "No need for grabbing, I'm coming."

Syms leaned back in his new chair. "I talked to Kim before I came in. She's home, feels good. She could be back to work in a few weeks. Marty is locked up. He was arraigned without bail.

The captain looked at Scotty. "So you want to tell me about your hot sweetie?"

Scotty looked at Dan. "You told him?"

"Must have slipped out."

"Heard she's a beauty."

"Don't worry; you'll be invited to the wedding."

Syms sat back. "So hit me with the latest."

"We've got to find out more about Cosby Davis and Yolanda Gomes." Dan said. "We were at the airport and learned a few things, like Sloppy Joe never reported they found her car and impounded it. I checked with Dixon, and he traced the car. According to his records, the vehicle was sold at auction two months ago. I also don't know how she could afford Landon Place. She only made twenty-eight grand at the airport. Unless she had another job, I can't see her living there."

Syms twirled his bottle of Advil around. "What are you thinking?"

"She was good looking girl. Maybe she was making money off the clock."

"Hooking? You think she might have been a prostitute? "

"It's a thought." Dan paused. "She certainly knew Flores, and you know what he was. I want to find out more about Yolanda Gomes. She came from New Orleans and I want to know what brought her here." Dan grinned. "Think we can take a trip south?"

"By south, you mean six feet under?"

"You know anyone in New Orleans?"

"I bet Hardison does. I'll see if he can get help us."

"Thanks, but I really think sending us to New Orleans would be better."

Syms pointed to the door. "You have a better chance of being sent to Sing Sing. Close it behind you."

Dan tugged Scotty's arm. "Let's do some police work. Hopefully Hardison will get us a contact. I've got Cosby's address and the landlord's name."

Jasper Olden's house was a two-story duplex situated on the corner of Framingham and Sexton. The residence had white siding and sage green shutters by the windows. Dan parked on Sexton, and the detectives walked up the front steps, where two doors that appeared to have been recently painted a lighter shade of green, separated the two living spaces.

Dan rang the bell and a gray haired man came to the front door, and introduced himself as Jasper Olden. He stood, slightly hunched over with a cane in his left hand, as Dan and Scotty showed the man their badges. The landlord invited the detectives into his living room where they sat on the sofa, while he eased into his recliner.

"It's nice to meet you Mr. Olden," Dan said. "I like this neighborhood."

"Should have seen it a few years ago. You wouldn't have said that then."

"This is a very nice home, you have good taste."

"Thank you. I'm all alone now, but my late wife would be proud of me."

Dan watched him rest his cane on the edge of his chair.

"I'm sure she would. We came to talk about Cosby Davis. We understand he lived here for a few years."

"Upstairs. It's still empty. I haven't rented it out again because my nutty sister-in-law wanted me to hold it for my nephew. She never mentioned that he recently got out of jail in the Bronx and is in rehab."

"Tell us about Cosby Davis."

"He was a good tenant, and it was a shock when he and that pretty little friend of his killed themselves."

"Did you ever see any of his friends?"

"Cosby was pretty much a loner, except for that girl."

"Was she here often?"

"She came here enough."

"You said you haven't re-rented his apartment. Is it empty?"

"Yeah, his brother came and took everything. I let him in and helped a bit. It looked like Cosby and the girl may have been planning a trip, because there were two large suitcases behind the couch."

Dan immediately thought about the airport. *Nobody had mentioned a vacation: not his mother, brother or Brenda Simmons.*

"Do you know what happened to the bags?" Dan asked.

"His brother and friend took them."

"Was anyone else here?"

"No, that's all I remember."

"Mind if we take a quick look upstairs?"

Olden grabbed his cane. "Sure thing. Mind if I give you the key?"

Dan took the key, and the detectives walked out to the porch. Dan opened the other front door. They walked upstairs, Scotty placed the key in the lock and he opened the apartment door. The furnished space smelled a tad musty. "One thing's evident," Dan said. "No one's lived here for a while."

They checked each room and found nothing out of the ordinary.

Dan locked up and returned the key to Olden. He asked the man, "What made you remember the suitcases?"

"I don't know. It's just that if he was planning a trip, he should have told me so I could watch the place."

"Had he traveled before?"

"Not that I remember."

"Thanks, Mr. Olden," Dan said, eying the old man's cane.

The detectives got into Dan's car, and Scotty remarked, "What do you make of the bags?"

Dan shook his head. "I don't know, but it does have my mind going. We have to see the Davises again."

Chapter 41

Dan saw the note on his desk. It was the phone number of Eugene Mumford, a New Orleans Lieutenant.

Scotty approached with a copy of the newspaper in his hand. "Read the sports?" he said to Dan.

"I listened to the radio on the way in. I know the Yankees have lost four in a row."

Dan held up the note. "Hardison came through. I'm gonna call a Lieutenant Mumford. Get yourself a coffee and pull up a chair. I hope this guy can help us."

Scotty returned and placed his hot cup on Dan's desk as his partner called the Lieutenant. "Mumford," The New Orleans's officer said.

"Good morning sir. This is Detective Dan Shields from Hartford. My captain left me your number and said you might be able to help us.'"

"I got a heads-up. What can I do for y'all?'

"We had a double suicide up here a few months ago, and a young girl named Yolanda Gomes was a victim. We don't think it was suicide."

"Y'all think there's a connection down here?"

"I can't say that, but she was from New Orleans. We want to know more about the girl. I'll run down what we have, and you can take it from there."

Mumford paused. "Can y'all fax it down?"

"I can. But first let me brief you. Gomes was a TSA worker at the airport here. She and her boyfriend, also an airport worker were suicide victims, but we

179

don't think that's the case. We need to know more about her. That's where you may be able to help us. I'll fax the details right down to you."

"Y'all think she has priors down here?"

"It's possible. We're hoping you can tell us."

"Send the fax. I'll be waitin, and get back to ya."

Mumford recited his fax number and Dan wrote it on his pad and handed it to Scotty. "How about faxing Yolanda's file to him?"

Dan spoke into his phone. "The file is being faxed now. Thanks for your help."

While Scotty was doing his task, Dan called the Davis home and Barrett answered. "Barrett, this is Detective Shields. Mind if Scotty and I stop by again? We have a couple of things to discuss with you."

"Yeah it's all right. Mama's in the kitchen like usual."

"By the way," Dan said. "Is the press hounding you at all?'

"Some. I tell them to go away, and once I threaten to take the dogs off their leashes, those reporters run like Secretariat."

⋏

The aroma of fresh baked something hit Dan's and Scotty's noses the second they entered the Davis house. Martha came out wearing her apron and she greeted the detectives. Dan had to stop and think for a second. He was safe: he felt his EpiPen in his coat pocket before asking, "What's that wonderful smell?"

Barrett's dogs were at his side as Martha smiled. "Goodies; I call them specials. My hot cross buns would make Betty Crocker jealous. I'll fetch a few before you leave."

"Any nuts or nut oil?" Dan asked.

"Not a drop. Can't have you scaring us like that again."

The detectives took seats where they had before, and Barrett stood beside his mother.

"Barrett," Dan said. "We went to visit Cosby's old apartment and spoke with the landlord. He told us you were there to clean out your brother's belongings."

"Yeah. Still have a lot of it in the basement."

"Would you still happen to have a couple of suitcases?"

"Sure do."

"Did he mention any travel plans?"

"No. Funny thing. All that was in those bags were rags. They were both filled with rags. Looked like the cases came from the airport."

"What makes you say that?"

"The yellow tags."

"Do you mind getting the luggage? We'd like to take a look at the bags."

Barrett turned and walked toward the basement door.

"You need any help?" Scotty asked.

Barrett smiled. "I can manage." He made a muscle. "These still work pretty good."

While he made his way to the basement, Martha walked back into the kitchen. Before Barrett could return with the suitcases, she brought out a plate with six warm, frosted hot cross buns. "You want coffee or something?" she asked.

"Would you mind?" Dan said. "These look great."

She went back to make a pot of coffee, as Barrett entered the room with both suitcases, one green, the other blue. He placed them in front of the detectives. "Mind if we open the bags?" Dan asked.

"No problem," Barret replied. "Nothing in them, I ditched those rags a while ago."

Dan unzipped the empty suitcases, and ran his hand along the linings and inside pockets. He saw the yellow tags still attached to the handles. They each had a number and date written on them. Surely the luggage had been logged in, but why would Cosby have had them, and why rags? He looked at Barrett. "When you say rags, were they cloth, paper, old clothes, or anything unusual like a shirt with a name on it?"

"Looked like a bunch of torn up tees and shirts."

Dan zipped up the bags, and placed them next to the sofa.

Martha poured four cups of coffee, and the aroma of buns whet Dan's pallet. She handed the detectives napkins. "These buns can be a little sticky."

Dan and Scotty weren't the only ones eager to dive into the treats. Hide and Seek poked their noses at the table before Barrett pulled the dogs back.

Scotty bit into his first. "My God, these are out of this world. You have to give me the recipe."

Martha smiled. "You'd have to watch. There's nothing written down", she replied

"Mind if we take the suitcases? I promise, we'll give them back," Dan said.

"Take them," Martha replied. "They'll only gather more dust in the basement."

The detectives rose, wiping crumbs from their faces, and thanked the sweet baker. They each grabbed a suitcase by their handles and carted them out. "Thanks again," Dan said.

He opened the Accord's trunk and put the bags in. Driving away from the house Dan said. "Looks like we're going back to the airport."

CHAPTER 42

Phyllis's car wasn't in the driveway because she'd gone to pick up Kate at gymnastics. When Dan entered the house, Josh was at the dining table doing his math homework, and Nana was seated on a kitchen chair while her lasagna was in the oven. Dan saw his tired looking mother. "You okay?"

"I'm fine, and you still have your shoes on. Go put them where they belong. Even the kids know better".

Dan kissed his mother on the cheek. "Sorry. Don't tell my other boss."

He placed his loafers on the front hall mat, returned, and looked Nana in the eye. "Phyllis said you seem to get out of breath lately. What's that all about?"

"Just a little run down, not to worry."

"When's the last time you saw your doctor?"

She frowned. "Don't worry about me. I'm not going to keel over like your father. I'm strong as an ox."

Dan sighed and he raised his voice. "Stubborn as one too, that's the point. We don't want you to keel over; we want you to see your doctor soon. Like this week."

"I don't need to. All I need is a little rest."

Dan couldn't remember ever confronting his mother as he was about to. "You can get as mad at me as you want, but you're going to the doctor. You can kick and scream all the way, but you're going, because we love you more than anything."

Nana huffed. So you talk about me behind my back?"

The front door opened. Phyllis and Kate entered the kitchen, and Dan pointed to his little girl. "See her. I want to see you at her wedding."

"Go wash up and tell your brother to do the same," Phyllis said to Kate.

"Mom and I were having a chat," Dan said.

Phyllis looked at Nana and Dan. "I can see that, and by the looks on your faces, it must have been quite a chat."

Dan kissed his mom on the cheek. "We're good," he said.

The kids washed up for dinner and were ready for Nana's tasty lasagna.

Dan headed upstairs. "I'll be back. I want to change."

Nana opened the oven door. "You got five minutes, and don't forget to scrub those hands good."

Phyllis helped placed the meal on the table. "I know he talked to you about seeing your doctor, you really should."

"You know he doesn't take his shoes off without being reminded. Always did that even as a kid, hard to train him."

Dan returned and sat at the table with the rest of the family. He looked at Kate. "How was gymnastics? You balancing on the high bars?"

"She shook her head. "No, but I can do a handstand."

"You'll have to show me. I've seen a ton of cartwheels around here."

Dan turned to Josh as he scooped mashed potatoes onto his plate. "You staying out of trouble at school?"

"Yeah, I got a ninety-eight on my math test."

"Nice. You're smarter than me."

Phyllis noticed Nana's plate. "You not hungry?"

"I cheated and had some bread before. You finish up. I think I'll head home."

Dan looked at her and pointed. "Don't forget what we talked about. You call your doctor tomorrow."

Nana got up, grabbed her purse and headed out the front door.

Phyllis eyed Dan. "I'm worried."

"Me too, I'll make sure she sees her doctor."

Chapter 43

Dan wondered why Cosby Davis would steal suitcases.. Then again, he thought, maybe he didn't steal them. Maybe they were unclaimed and he bought them at auction. That would make sense.

He tapped on Scotty's cube. The empty suitcases were inside his cubicle. "How about bringing these to the airport? We owe Brenda Simmons another visit."

"You called her?"

"No. Let's drop in."

λ

Dan knew where to park this time so he drove around to the restricted lot and found a space for his sedan. Scotty lifted the suitcases out of the trunk and the detectives rolled them along the hard surface.

They entered the terminal through the sliding door again. There was less traffic inside than the last time, and Dan could hear and feel the squeaky, wobbly wheel on his suitcase as they made their way to the baggage office. Dan opened the door. Brenda Simmons wasn't in sight, but there was music coming from the storage room. Dan rang the bell on the counter, and Brenda came out seeing the detectives, and two large suitcases. She looked at the yellow tags on the handles. "Where did you find these?"

"Funny you should ask," Dan said. "In Cosby Davis's apartment, and we were wondering how he might have gotten them."

She came around the counter, and her hand shook as she inspected the tags. Brenda logged into the computer and found items 22126, and 22127.

"They were logged in ten months ago and they still show as unclaimed."

Something registered with Dan. "Didn't you tell us these bags are auctioned off after six months?"

She drew a blank look "They are, but it's usually noted in the register. These were never noted. You think Cosby took them?"

"That's what we want to know. Can we get a printout of that log?"

Brenda printed out the information, her hand unsteady as she handed the pages to Dan. "Hope this helps."

Dan stared at Brenda. There was an uneasiness about her that made him think she knew something about the suitcases. "If you wanted to steal a suitcase right now, how easy would it be?"

Brenda gave Dan a blank stare, before uttering. "I suppose it could happen, but Cosby never would have done that, he was as honest as they come."

Dan had heard statements like that before, and he knew he couldn't take that comment to the bank. "I'm sure he was honest. Anyone else work here?"

"I've got three part-timers now, but none of them were here when Cosby was."

"Who was here with Cosby?"

"Me, Sarah Riley, and Rex Parandis."

"What can you tell us about Sarah and Rex?"

Brenda smiled. "Rex was here before I was. He was a nice old man. He retired. Sarah was here for two years and went back to school. UMass."

Dan paused. "So how do you suppose these two suitcases got out of here without anyone noticing?"

She eyed the bags and hesitated before saying. "I don't know. I guess it's something I never thought about."

Dan pulled out his card and handed it to her. "If you think of anything unusual about Cosby or these suitcases, please let us know."

Brenda took a deep breath and Dan saw it as he turned to leave.

"One last question. If Cosby stole the suitcases, why do you think he'd leave the yellow tags on them?"

"I have no idea."

The detectives rolled the suitcases all the way back out to the car and placed them back into the trunk. Dan handed Scotty the printout. "Why would he take suitcases full of rags?" Scotty said.

"I don't know, and I don't know if he emptied them and stuffed rags inside them himself. And I don't know why he would do that? But I'll tell you what I think. Brenda knows something. Did you see her hand shaking, and how uneasy she was?"

"So what's this all about?"

"We'll see. We're not done digging."

"True, but I'll be digging Sally tonight."

"Tonight?" I thought you were seeing her tomorrow night."

"That's what I thought, but she's going to Boston to stay with her sister this weekend, so we switched to tonight."

Dan eyed Scotty. "You sure she isn't shacking up with some other stud?"

Scotty moved his hand underneath his jacket toward his holster. "You want me to shoot you now, or later?"

"Save the bullet. I'm coming to the wedding. Got a best man yet? You gonna try to score?"

"I'm making a nice dinner. Already have the wine. I'm stopping at Mazo's to pick up some Neapolitans for dessert."

"Sounds good. Main course?"

"Salmon, green beans, and rice pilaf."

Dan grinned. "Sounds like you're trying to score to me."

Scotty laughed. "I'll take first base, if I can get it."

"Hope it goes well, pal."

Chapter 44

Dan's weekend was uneventful. The same couldn't be said for the city. There had been a drive-by in the south side, a stabbing at a downtown convenience store, and another shooting that killed a teenager in the north end.

It was seven fifteen, and Dan was itching to take a look at the weekend's roundup of thugs. He walked to the secure entrance where he was buzzed in by the guard at the desk. As Dan passed through the corridor, he looked to his left and right. Some things didn't change: the smells of alcohol and urine were unmistakable.

The cells were half full, some detainees sleeping, others paced their enclosures. As he got near the end, Dan heard a familiar voice.

"Comin' to get me out, Shields? They can't keep me here, and you know it."

Dan didn't have to look at the shit-faced felon occupying cell six, but he did. "Nice to see you, Slash. You the robber I heard about on the radio this morning?"

"Me? You know me better than that."

"You know something Slash. I kinda like having you around here. How many times have you been here?"

"Here? The new place? This is my second, pretty nice. Sasser will be here to get me out later."

Dan shook his head. "Don't count on it this time Slash. The store clerk died."

"No way."

"Way" Dan said, walking away.

He exited the holding tank and took the stairs up to the squad room.

⋏

Dan approached his desk. "Cheer up," Scotty said. "You look like shit."

"I'm okay, just visited the tank. Guess who's there? Slash, and this time he's not walking. He killed a convenience store owner last night."

"That was him? I heard about it."

Dan broke into a huge grin. "I see you're on cloud nine. Tell me about your date."

"It's all good."

Dan and Scotty went into Dan's cube, Scotty smiling from ear to ear. "She loved my dinner."

"She love it enough to put out?"

"Jesus. Never got close, although her red dress had me drooling all night."

"You at least reach first base?"

"Knock it off. We had a very nice evening."

"You're slipping. You never made a move?"

Scotty paused and grinned. "Well, nothing beyond a few kisses. I did sorta made my way toward second, base, but her hand stopped me right in the base path."

"You got another date set?'

"She's taking me to the museum next week, and I'm giving her a ride in the Chevy."

Syms appeared at Dan's cube. "Boys, we have to talk. Come on down to my place."

⋏

Both detectives followed Syms into his office. "You two look like happy campers," the captain said.

Dan looked at Scotty as Syms grew serious. "Uh oh. What did we do now?" Dan said.

Syms picked up his Advil and leaned forward. "You didn't do anything, but somebody else did, and you won't like it any better than me."

He spun around in his chair and leaned forward again. "I don't know what's going on, but remember the exhumation order we asked for? It's on hold. Somebody doesn't want Cosby Davis's grave dug up."

"What?" Dan said. "Who the hell put a freeze on it?" He thought for a second and opened his mouth to speak.

Syms cut him short. "Don't say it."

"It? You mean *it*, as in 'Willingham' it?"

"Don't know for sure, but I want to talk with him again."

Dan rolled his eyes, and he stared at Syms. "I have a hunch that somehow Cosby Davis, Gomes, Flores and a few others are tied to the money. Those suitcases may have contained something other than rags, and Willingham may still be dirty."

⋏

Two hours later Ted Willingham placed his hat on a table in Syms's office. The commander shut the door and took a seat. The captain silently stared at him before looking up to the ceiling. He turned to Willingham and picked up the headache pills. "You believe in God, Ted?"

"Of course I do, although my divorce is putting my faith in him to the test."

"Anything else bothering you? You wouldn't lie to me, would you?"

"What are you getting at?"

"I'm getting at, what the hell is going on? We haven't spoken since the drug bust and the vanishing money, so what the hell has Cosby Davis got to do with that?"

"What are you talking about?"

"Damn it Ted, don't play games with me. I know you got us pulled off the money chase, and you had Judge Zimmerman put a hold on exhuming Davis's grave. What's the deal? Level with me."

"The dig is premature. We'll get it dug up."

"Why not now? What's going on?"

Willingham leaned in close to the captain. "Look, this is far more complicated than you would understand. I have my orders, too."

"What are you saying? My guys are spinning their wheels while you sit back and watch."

"No. It's a lot bigger than you could imagine. Believe me. I would tell you if I could. I can't; at least not yet."

"So you plan to let us in on your little secret at some point?"

"Be patient."

Syms growled at Willingham. "Like, how patient? Until it costs one or both of my guys their lives?"

"No. We won't let that happen."

Syms caught the significance of the *we* comment. "We?

You mean you and someone else. Could it be someone else like the FBI, or DEA?"

He could tell by Willingham's expression he'd struck a nerve. "So be it Ted. I'll be in touch like a bug up your ass. You can leave, unless you have something more to say."

Willingham stood. "God damn it. You don't understand. I can't tell you right now. Okay?"

Syms got up and pointed to the door. "No, it's not okay, and you better leave God's name out of this."

Willingham picked up his hat and marched out of headquarters.

Without a clue as to what had happened, Dan and Scotty saw Willingham tread heavily through the back door of the police station, into the parking lot, and getting into his truck.

"He and Syms must have had some conversation," Dan said.

"Let's go find out."

Syms rushed into the men's room before his detectives got to his office. Dan detoured into the bathroom as well, pulling up to the next urinal. "Do you have to?" Syms said.

"I do. Can't you hear the tinkling?"

"Funny, Dan. Get your ass in my office."

"Can it wait until I'm done?"

Syms zipped up, washed his hands and went back to his office where Scotty was already seated. "Your partner is a very funny fellow, you know that?"

Dan walked in. "I heard that. Thanks for the compliment."

"Close that door and sit down."

"We saw Willingham leave like his ass was on fire," Dan said.

"Damn right it was. Son of a bitch is hiding something big. He had the dig stopped, said it would get done, but not now."

"What do you think he's up to?"

Syms sat back. "Them, it's them. It's what they're up to."

Dan wrinkled his brow. "Them?"

Syms leaned forward. "Can't say for sure, but it smells Feds."

"So what's Davis and Gomes got to do with it?"

"That's what we have to find out. Go try to connect the dots."

"You think Willingham might be one of those dots?"

"I don't know. All I know is that it's a big puzzle and Willingham seems to have pieces we're missing."

PART THREE

Chapter 45

Jacksonville was home to Vinnie Martinez, and he seldom left his estate, partly because he liked his seclusion and partly because he was a wanted man. His sixteen-room refuge on top of a hill overlooking the St. Johns River was far away from neighbors.

The skinny drug lord always looking for new employees for his clubs, suffered no shortage of talented ladies. Hairless on top and sporting a goatee, the heavily tattooed businessman made sure every working girl passed his rigid interview. The olive-skinned, dark-haired new hire standing before him had earned her diploma. Honey was still wet from a dip in the round pool, and placed a robe around her naked body as Vinnie got off his lounger, grabbed a towel and wrapped it around his waist.

He opened the sliders and they entered his living room. Pouring himself a bourbon as he watched his employee head for a shower, he slipped on a yellow sleeveless shirt, and a black silk robe.

Vinnie poked through a pile of videos that he planned to watch with Honey, before sending her off to work. He plopped himself on the couch and leaned his head back as he waited for her to join him. Hearing a vehicle coming up his driveway, Vinnie jumped up and he looked out the bay window seeing a black Cadillac parking in the semicircle. Watching Mo and Frankie get out, Vinnie opened the front door of his estate, and looked up at Mo. "You need to call more often. I just finished an interview."

"I can tell," Mo said.

Honey entered the room wearing tight shorts and she picked up her bra from the couch as Mo watched her put it on.

"Nice tits, she hired?" Mo said.

"Get in here and sit down. God damned right. Honey's as sweet as her name."

"We get a taste?"

Vinnie opened his robe. "Suck this, you asshole."

He motioned to Honey and she left the room.

"Where's my cash?"

"Don't know," Mo said.

Vinnie chugged his shot. "What's Flores got to say?"

"Not much, at least not anymore."

The boss didn't say anything, and he glared at Mo because he knew bad news was coming.

"It's like this," Mo said. "He was robbing you Vin, and you know what he did to Yolanda."

"So you took him out. Is that what you're telling me?"

Frankie chimed in. "It's more like his head and body are in two different places."

"Wanna pour me one of those?" Mo said.

"Not now. So you two executed him. Jesus, I wanted you to squeeze the truth out. I didn't mean dump his ass."

"I don't think he was gonna talk," Mo said. "I drilled a hole in his head with a shotgun in the back alley of the Hi-Hat. Made it look like Biggie did it. Same kind of rifle he killed Vegas with, took it from Lucky's."

"Who the fuck did you leave in charge of the club?"

"Boozer. He ratted Flores out, so as a thank you, we promoted him."

Vinnie picked up his remote. The lights went down and his TV dropped from the ceiling. "You guys get the fuck out—me and the lady are gonna watch a movie."

He stared at the TV as Mo and Frankie were about to leave. What he saw and heard stunned him. "Hold it, buttheads. Look at this."

Vinnie motioned to his henchmen. "What the hell happened while you were up there? How the fuck did Cosby Davis's body wind up in Tolland?" He scowled at the news report. "What the fuck is going on? I thought Flores took care of Yolanda and him?"

Mo and Frankie sank down on the couch. "Shit, we just came back from there, and no one said nothing," Mo uttered.

"That's 'cause the police just let the story out. You guys have to get back and find Salinas. Last I knew he was working for some roofer named Lenko."

"I thought he went clean, got out of Vegas's gang."

Vinnie stared at Mo. "No one ever quits. He may look clean, but you know the drill: once you're in, you're in for life. He couldn't have simply left and still been pals with Flores. I remember when I got in. Julio's brother Santiago was running things. I was with Santiago when he got shot. It was a drive-by. We was sitting on his porch smoking and a dark van pulled up, stopped for a second and fired several shots. I ducked and never got hit, but he was bent over in his rocker bleeding bad. Ambulance showed up and he was still alive, but he didn't make it to the hospital."

Vinnie pointed to the door. "We're far from done, and if I have to get up there, you, me, and the rest of our posse will make it to Hartford and go door-to-door until I get my money, but you're going back. I have to make a phone call."

Mo and Frankie got up to leave. "Not so fast. You think Honey would be a good replacement for Yolanda?"

"Damn right. I'd pay a hundred right now."

"Get out of here."

As Mo and Frankie walked away Vinnie said. "Hold on. Frankie go out to the car, I gotta tell Mo something"

Frankie left the room and Vinnie looked up into Mo's eyes. "Do me a favor and take Louie with you, and make sure that useless shithead doesn't come back. The Colombian's want him out."

Jessie Colton's workday had been like any other until his phone rang. He knew by the caller ID who was on the other end. Taking a deep breath, he finally picked up on the fourth ring.

"Hi Vin. How's the weather down there?"

"Nice Jessie. How's the weather up there? What's going on?"

"What do you mean?"

"I mean Cosby Davis. What's that all about? I know Flores is out of the picture, so what's going on? How'd Davis's body end up in Tolland?"

Jessie turned to his liquor cabinet, opened a bottle of Dewar's and poured some into a shot glass. "I don't really know, but there were a couple of detectives here asking about the house, Flores, and Yolanda. They reopened the suicide case."

"What did you tell them?"

"Nothing, I told them we lost Flores's and Yolanda's files."

"What about the property? You know if they connect me to that property and Davis, there's gonna be trouble."

"Vinnie, come on. There's no way they can trace that property back to you. The deed is in Manuel Vinton's name and all they know is that he lives in Florida."

"No shit. I'm in Florida, did you forget that?"

"Look. I filed the paperwork, deed and all. Don't worry about it." Colton sat back and thought for a second. "You use that Vinton alias much?"

"Only one bank account, gotta launder the money."

Colton wondered if that could spell trouble, and chugged the scotch.

"Why you asking?" Vinnie said.

"I was just asking. No reason."

"Jessie, if those cops come around snooping again, you let me know."

Colton hung up and stared out his window at the walking trail. He poured another shot, slugged it down, and then left his office, passing his secretary on the way out. "I'm going for a little walk; I'll be back."

As he strode slowly, he wondered what he'd gotten himself into by managing the property of a known criminal, and hiding information from the police. In his mind, he'd had no choice.

Chapter 46

If Lucky had ever been lucky, that luck was about to run out.

Sharky had been tossed into the dumpster out back, and Brick rescued a pit bull from the pound two days ago. The puppy was getting used to its new surroundings, and needed to be fed.

Biggie was hungry too. "I'm getting some burgers. Be back."

Lucky tossed him a twenty. "Bring me a double cheese."

Brick nodded. "Get me a Big Mac, and the pooch wants a Happy Meal."

"You better take that dog out for a walk," Lucky said. "He craps in here again, and you're eatin' it."

"He's a pup, man. He'll get the hang of it."

Brick and the pooch went outside into the dark street. They headed toward the side alley when the dog squatted and crapped on the sidewalk. Brick tugged on the small dog's leash and with a brown deposit sitting on the walk, he guided the mutt back inside the store.

Biggie arrived with the food. "Let's eat," he said as he placed three bags, and a red box on the counter.

"Where's the Happy Meal?" Brick said.

"In the box."

Brick took out the dog's food as well as his own sandwich.

"When you gonna name that pooch anyway?" Biggie asked.

"Just did. Big Mac."

Biggie stuffed a few fries into his mouth and flipped one to the dog. "Hope he likes chicken nuggets."

Lucky took a bite of his burger, studying the gun rack and the two empty spaces where the shotguns had been. "Never did tell us the whole story, and you know who we haven't seen in a long time? Your boy Salinas," Lucky said.

Biggie swallowed half of his burger. "Nothing much to tell. Everything happened so fast, before we knew it, we was jailed and Jenkins was gone. Don't know where Salinas was. Vegas had let him split a while ago, but he was still hanging with Flores."

"You see any connection?" Brick said.

"What do you mean?"

"I'm sayin' Jenkins was hauled out by two ambulance dudes, and Vegas knew where to find the damn thing. Salinas and Flores was pals. Think they was in cahoots? You know, playing paramedics, and takin Jenkins out to bury the money?"

Biggie took out his second burger. "Jesus, you think Salinas and Jenkins is sittin' on the cash?"

"I'm just sayin', what could be could be. Nobody ain't seen Jenkins. He could be dead too, and maybe Salinas is sittin' on the bread."

"Jesus, I gotta see that slick dude."

Lucky looked at his Rolex. "Time to pack it in. Clean up your shit and let's get out of here."

It was around nine-thirty p.m. and a car pulled up outside the pawn shop. When the store's door opened, Lucky, Brick, and Biggie all froze.

Mo, Frankie, and another associate named Louie, entered the store, all pointing loaded weapons at each of the stunned thugs. "Nice to see you guys again," Mo said. "Vinnie says hi. We got a little more business to discuss."

Frankie shut the door, drew the shades, and he turned the window sign to CLOSED.

Brick made a move toward Mo, and was dropped like a fly as Frankie, chomping on a toothpick, put a round between the goon's eyes, and when Big Mac bared his teeth, Frankie fired another shot turning the puppy into a floor ornament.

With his Glock pointed at Biggie. Mo said. "Sit down." He eyed Lucky. "And you turn your ass around."

Mo saw Lucky peeking at a handgun. "Don't even think about it asshole." Louie slipped a pair of handcuffs on Lucky before tying him to a chair.

Biggie sat and Frankie cuffed him. "Sing," Mo said. "Vinnie wants his money and he doesn't give a shit what we have to do to get it."

Biggie was sweating bullets. "Fuck, you think if I knew, I'd still be 'round here?"

"You still don't have any idea who sprung Jenkins, or where they went?"

"Fuck no. All I know is we found the ambulance, and you know what happened after that."

"That's it? That's all you got? You stickin' to that bullshit?"

Biggie's eyes widened in fear. "I don't know, Mo. You gotta believe me. Maybe Salinas drove the ambulance."

"Really; that's interesting. Salinas may be next, unless we find Jenkins. Is that it? Any other last words?"

"What the fuck? Don't shoot us!"

"Who said anything about shooting you?" Mo turned to Frankie. "I believe we left some things in the car. Go get them."

Louie pulled Lucky's chair around to Biggie's, put the two helpless men back to back, and taped their mouths. Frankie brought the rope in and helped Louie tie the two captives together so they couldn't move. Then he spread rags on the floor. The fear in Biggie's eyes said it all.

Mo turned his gun on Louie and shot the unsuspecting accomplice in the back. "Blindfold them, Frankie. I don't think they want to see the fireball."

Frankie poured gas onto the rags, and as he neared the front door Mo tossed a match into the shop and they waited in the car until orange flames appeared, before speeding away.

"Why'd you shoot Louie?" Frankie said.

"Vinnie told me to. He was excess baggage, and the Colombians wanted him out."

Chapter 47

Dan's house phone rang at four-fifteen a.m. and he knew it wasn't good news. He flipped on a light and answered the call as Phyllis rolled over. "What?" Dan said, then paused. "I'll be down in an hour."

He knew Phyllis heard him. "I gotta get going. Have to meet Syms at the station."

"What happened?" Phyllis said.

"A fire. I have to call Scotty."

⋏

Syms was in his office and he yawned as Dan walked in. "Coffee's not even made yet. You call Scotty?"

"Yeah, he should be here soon. What's the story?"

The captain leaned forward. "I was notified about Lucky's a little while ago. Landry was on call and he's on his way down here with the incident report." Syms saw Scotty approaching "Looks like your partner's here."

So Lucky's burned," Scotty said as he entered the room. "Who do you suppose set the place on fire?"

"That's what we want to know," Syms said. "Landry should be here soon with the details"

No sooner had Syms uttered those words than the husky detective wearily appeared. In need of a shave, his chinos and zippered jacket still smelled of smoke. Landry placed the incident report on Sym's desk. "Have a seat," the captain said.

Syms read the document. "Two alarms, four bodies that may not be identifiable."

Dan said. "I'm guessing Lucky, Brick, and Biggie, but I'm stumped for a fourth."

Suddenly, struck by the fact that Biggie may have been turned to ashes, Dan's eyes became glazed. He heard the gunshot that had penetrated his body, and he felt the warm blood gushing from his abdomen as he looked up and saw Biggie's fuzzy image running from that alley. Six years, he'd lived with that thug still on the loose. Dan didn't know whether to feel relieved or gypped out of the chance to kill that bastard himself. Then again the fat asshole who'd nearly killed him, deserved to die slowly…burning in hell.

Syms stared at Dan. "Hey what are you thinking?"

Dan snapped back to the present. "Holy crap. The fourth. It could've been Jenkins."

"Jenkins?" Syms said. "You mean the two fake paramedics could have done this?"

Dan sat back. "It's possible."

Syms glanced at the veteran Landry. "I see this guy Hector Ortiz was a witness."

Landry nodded. "There may be more, but he's the only one that would talk. He was in the convenience store across the street. Heard a couple of shots around quarter to ten, and he was sure the noise came from Lucky's. Later he saw a black Caddy pull away, and then the fireball."

"Any descriptions?"

"Not really; he thought he saw two or three guys inside the car as it drove off."

Syms excused Landry. "I know you have more paperwork to do."

"How about a shower and some sleep. I'm headed home."

The captain took a deep breath. "We could all use a little shut eye."

"I think the caf is open. I could use some breakfast," Dan said. "You guys coming?"

"You two go," Syms said. "I'll stay here."

⋏

Dan and Scotty entered the cafeteria and got into a crowded line behind Dixon as first shift uniforms were piling in. "What are you guys doing here?" Dixon said.

"Slumming," Dan replied. "Can't go to Connie's. We got called in because of the fire at Lucky's. Syms got us up around four. Landry just went home. He's been up all night."

"Good luck. Stick with the scrambled and hash browns."

The sleepy detectives stepped to the counter and got their breakfasts. They found a table in the rear right corner, next to the bathrooms. "Let's take this stuff upstairs. We can get free coffee up there," Dan said.

⋏

They sat at Dan's desk with their eggs, hash browns, toast and coffee. "I want to look at those suitcases again." Dan said.

"I'm done. I wanna go wash up," Scotty said as he dumped his plastic dish in the basket.

"Me too," Dan said as he tossed his empty plate in the trash.

When they returned from the bathroom Scotty placed the two empty pieces of luggage beside Dan's desk. Turning to the printout, Dan noticed something they'd overlooked. "Take a look at this. These suitcases were logged in October 19th. That's the day after the drug bust." Dan took a close look at the luggage. "This is weird. Brenda said they keep accurate records. You see the brand name on those suitcases?"

"American Flyer."

"Right on, my man. Only problem is, the log says these are American Tourister. Something's off. I hope Brenda can explain this discrepancy." Dan punched his desk softly with his fist. "It's the money. The damned money. Ten million dollars. I think Cosby knew there was money in the bags and he stole them."

Scotty looked at the luggage. "Okay, but where'd he stash the money, and why the rags?"

Dan stood and stared at the wall clock. "I'll tell you why. Cosby was planning to return the luggage to storage knowing no one would ever claim them, and they'd eventually be sold to an unsuspecting buyer at auction."

"But someone else had to know about the scheme."

"Brings us right back to Willingham, doesn't it? We gotta see Syms... that son of a bitch Willingham."

⋏

They raced down the hall, and entered Syms's office. "I knew it" Dan said. "It's all about the money. Vegas, the shootout, the drugs, Flores, Yolanda Gomes, Biggie, and Cosby are all somehow tied together. Willingham needs to level with us right now, and that weasel commander may very well be dirty."

Syms reached for the Advil. "Holy mother, so how's this all connected."

"We don't know yet, but our baggage lady has some explaining to do. Somehow, I think ten million dollars ended up at the hands of Cosby Davis."

Syms downed his tablets. "Oh, man. This will kill his mother if she finds out Cosby was on the take, or just plain took."

"We'll tread lightly until we know for sure, but we need to talk to Brenda Simmons one more time."

Dan and Scotty went back to the squad room. "You gonna call her?" Scotty said.

"I think not. I'd rather see the look on her face when we confront her. Let's take the bags again."

"You think she gets in this early?"

"I'm sure the airport's open, and we can wait around if we have to."

⋏

Once again Dan and Scotty wheeled the luggage down the main airport corridor as passengers passed them in both directions. As the detectives neared the baggage office, they were stopped by a state trooper whose black

Shepherd sniffed the bags. The dog sat beside the suitcases. "What's in those suitcases?" the officer asked.

Dan pulled out his badge. "Actually nothing, these are part of a case we're investigating and they came from this baggage office."

"Well they must have contained some kind of narcotics or pot at one time."

"Wouldn't surprise me," Dan said.

"Mind if I take a peek inside?"

Dan unzipped the cases. "Go ahead."

The trooper inspected them. "Okay. Good luck," he said.

"Thanks," Nice dog." Dan said.

⋏

Their first break of the day came when Brenda showed up early. The detectives opened the baggage office's door, and she looked at the suitcases. "You must like lugging those things around," she said.

"Not really," Dan replied. "Remember when I asked you if Cosby Davis could have stolen these suitcases and you said not likely?"

"Yes."

"Could he have stolen them and replaced them later without you noticing?"

Brenda's hands began to shake again. "I suppose so."

"Can you explain this discrepancy?" Dan showed her the brand names on both suitcases, and he pulled out the log pages she'd printed.

"Take a look at this. These bags are American Flyers, but they were logged in as American Tourister. We know Cosby entered the data and put the tags on the suitcases, because those are his initials on the printout."

"Looks that way," she replied.

"Didn't you tell us that accuracy is important?"

"Yes, but everyone makes mistakes once in a while. I could see where this could be an easy error."

Dan looked her squarely in the eyes. "I guess so, but I can't see how he could have tied the tags around the handles without noticing the discrepancy."

Her eyes widened. "I don't know. What difference does it make? He's dead."

"Precisely," Dan said. "And these suitcases may have cost him his life."

"I need some water," Brenda said. "Are we done?"

Dan kept his eyes on hers, and he raised his voice. "Are we? Are we done? You tell me."

Brenda took a cup of water from the cooler that was in the corner. Her face was flush. "I have a headache. Please leave me alone. I've told you what I know."

Dan pulled his card from his coat pocket and placed it into her trembling hand. "In case you lost my other card, here's another. I suggest you keep it close to the phone."

The detectives walked out, dragging the suitcases back to the car. "She knows something. I hope she's not in on it." Dan said. "I'm sure she's gonna crack soon."

CHAPTER 48

Dan was halfway home when his Bluetooth showed an incoming call from Phyllis. He pressed the accept button and heard her frantic voice. "Where are you?"

"I'm almost home. What's wrong?"

"Nana, the ambulance is here and they're taking her to the hospital."

"What? Holy shit, is she okay? What happened? Is it her heart?"

"Yes, I'm going with them. The kids are next door."

"I'll be home in ten."

"We're not waiting. Meet us at Woodland."

Dan choked up at the thought of losing his mother. He knew it was going to happen sometime, but like anyone else, he wasn't ready for it. He got off the highway at the next exit and turned back toward the hospital, speeding all the way.

Dan sprinted into the emergency entrance. Phyllis was in the waiting room, nervously pacing as he approached her.

"Where is she?"

"They're working on her."

"As in CPR?"

"As in defib. I don't know if she's gonna make it, she almost flat-lined in the ambulance."

Dan's eyes welled up as he held onto Phyllis who wiped her tears with Kleenex. "All we can do is pray and wait."

"What happened?" Dan asked.

"She was in the kitchen, and I heard was a thud. I thought she had died right then and there. I called 911 and they were at the house in five minutes." Phyllis breathed heavily. "I told the kids to go next door and called you when the paramedics were putting her on the stretcher."

An ER physician walked over to Dan and Phyllis. "I'm Doctor Kantor," she said. "Your mother is a strong woman who just had a major heart attack, but she's got a steady pulse and is breathing okay with the oxygen. She needs to be moved to the cardiac ICU on the second floor. You can go up there. Give us a few minutes."

Dan put an arm around Phyllis, and they made their way to the elevator up to the second floor. Nana was wheeled into room 244 and hooked up to a respirator. Her eyes were barely open and she didn't seem to know where she was. Phyllis took her free hand.

"Shh. Rest, Nana. You're at the hospital. You had a heart attack, but you're going to be fine."

Dan leaned over to plant a kiss on his mother's cheek. "You'll be cooking again soon. Do what the doctors say."

She nodded, and dozed off to sleep.

"You have to go now," the attending nurse said.

Dan and Phyllis walked out of the room hand in hand.

⅄

Needless to say, both Dan and Phyllis hardly slept with Nana on their minds. Dan still managed to drag himself out the door at his usual time.

Before heading to headquarters he stopped at the hospital to see his mother. She was sitting up, still hooked to monitors. "You look good," he said as he kissed her cheek, and held her hand. "You do what the doctors say and we'll see you home soon."

She smiled at her son, and squeezed his hand. "You're a good boy."

A tall, thin male doctor of Indian descent entered the room.

"I'm her son," Dan said.

"I'm doctor Bashir, I need to check her."

Dan released her hand. "I need to get to work, so take good care of her doc. See you later mama."

⚔

Dan entered the squad room, and he noticed the cell phone in Scotty's hand and the smile on his face. "You looking at porn again?"

"Shut up you jerk. These are pics Sally texted me from her Boston weekend with her sister. See?"

"Her sister is dark haired. Not bad looking, either." Dan said. "What's her name?"

"Kathy, she's two years younger."

"What's she do?"

"She's an ER nurse at Mass Gen."

Dan took a deep breath. "Let me tell you what happened after I left here yesterday. What a fucking day, my mom had a heart attack. I just came from Woodland. She's okay, scared the shit out of us."

"Glad to hear she's okay."

"Should be back to cooking soon. Seen Syms?"

"He's up with Hardison."

"That's never good."

Dan sat at his desk. "I got the drug bust file. Let's get into it."

Scotty pulled up a chair next to his partner, and they combed through every inch of paperwork. They checked both Vegas's and Martinez's gangs name by name, learning who went to lockup. The one guy still unaccounted for was Jenkins, but they didn't even know if he was dead or alive. The only one who could possibly tell them anything about Jenkins was Angel Salinas.

"We need to talk to Salinas again," Dan said. "He's the only one who might be able to give us some answers."

"He's not going to be easy to talk to. He's not going to pick up a call from us."

"No. He's not, but what if we bring him in?"

"You mean arrest him?"

"Yeah."

"On what charge? We can't tie him to anything."

"Let me work on that. I'll think of something to get him down here. He needs to be real scared in order to open up."

"I don't know if I like where you're going with this."

Dan's cell rang. It was Phyllis. "Get to the hospital. Nana's had another heart attack."

"What? I was just there."

"Go. I'll meet you there."

Dan's face was ashen. "Gotta go to the hospital, moms in trouble, tell Syms."

⅄

Dan rushed into room 244. There was no bed in the room, and no Nana. *Holy shit. I'm too late, she's dead.* He stopped doctor Bashir. "Where's my mother?"

The doctor's face told Dan everything. "How about having a seat in the second room on the right? I'll be right in," Bashir said.

Dan joined Phyllis in the room and held her hand. He didn't have to be told. Bashir entered and he looked into their eyes. "Believe me, we did all we could, but this was a massive coronary. Add that to the one she had yesterday, and she couldn't be saved. I'm sorry."

Dan bowed his head, and Phyllis cried, clutching the damp Kleenex in her hand.

"Thanks doctor," Dan said. Turning to Phyllis, he muttered. "What are we going to tell the kids?"

"We have to tell Kate and Josh that she's with God now. Mike's a different story. He has to know what happened. I'll call him later."

Phyllis held Dan's hand. "I think you have to sign some papers."

Dan raised his head; water in his eyes. "She wanted to be cremated you know."

Phyllis squeezed Dan's hand. "We'll put her on the mantle beside your father."

Dan and Phyllis left the hospital, Dan holding a bag containing Nana's wedding ring and butterfly brooch.

⚓

Dan remembered when his father died, and his mother had told him that life goes on. She instilled a *go on about your business* attitude in him, so he knew his departed mother would not want him to take time off.

The weary detective noted Scotty's and Syms's looks of surprise the next morning to see him at his desk.

"You okay? You should be home," Syms said.

"Tired, but mom would have wanted it this way, so I'm making her happy by being here."

"When's the funeral?" Scotty asked.

"That's another wish of hers. She didn't want one. She's being cremated, and her ashes will sit beside my father's on our mantle."

Syms strolled to his office.

Dan looked at Scotty. "We got work to do, too. You and Sally have a good time last night?"

Scotty sat next to Dan. "The best."

"Hold it, third base, home run?"

"I slept over."

Dan's jaw dropped. "You dog. So when's the wedding? She a true redhead?"

Scotty shrugged. "Thought you said we got work to do."

Dan smiled and said. "I've been thinking about Salinas. We have to get him."

Dan's phone rang. It was Lieutenant Mumford. "Shields," he said.

Mumford replied. "Y'all wanna hear what I got? Sorry I never faxed you what I found. Dang machine broke."

"Tell me. I'm putting you on speaker so my partner Scotty can listen."

"Ready? That little gal Yolanda Gomes was a native, went to school here, worked at Dabney's."

"A waitress?"

"Stripper."

"I thought she worked at the airport, TSA."

"She did. Dabney's was part time. I got us a rap shee too. Prostitution."

"How many arrests?"

"Two here."

"So how the hell did she get that job at TSA?"

"Good question." Mumford replied. "Talked with the head guy over there. He says she passed all the background checks." Mumford paused. "Here's a kicker: she was arrested in Jacksonville once, same deal. So what's the scoop? Who killed her?"

"Were not sure, but we've got suspects. Thanks for the news."

The detectives rushed off to Syms's office. "We just heard from Mumford. Turns out that Yolanda Gomes was no saint. She was a hooker with a rap sheet. That definitely ties her to Flores. There's still one guy who can sing to us. Angel Salinas."

Syms got up and stared out his window into the parking lot. "We have another problem boys. Willingham is missing."

"What?" Dan yelled.

"You heard me. He hasn't shown up for work in four days. His soon-to-be ex doesn't know where he is. Neither does his lawyer."

"He finally vanished with the money?"

"I don't know. You'd think that, wouldn't you?"

Dan eyed Syms. "Interesting timing, isn't it?"

CHAPTER 49

Mo and Frankie were back in town, and they were about to pay Angel Salinas a social visit. Mo took out his phone, googled Lenko Roofing and called the place. "Hi, is Angel Salinas there?"

"He's out on a job, should be back around five, anything I can do for you? Roger Lenko asked."

"No thanks." Mo said. He hung up and turned to Frankie. "Let's go. Salinas should be getting off work soon."

They headed to Syracuse Street and stopped in front of the roofing company. Mo noticed a bar next door, and chose to go in to wait for Salinas. He and Frankie sat on stools near the front window and ordered a couple of drafts. The place was beginning to fill with customers eager to take advantage of happy hour.

Frankie eyed two young ladies who had just entered the bar. "What do you think?" he said.

"I think you'd fuck any woman who could walk," Mo said as he put his hand on his sidekick's shoulder.

"Just sayin'."

"Go sit at that booth near the back door and keep your eyes off the jailbait. I'll stay here and look for Salinas. Try not to swallow that piece of wood in your mouth."

It was nearly five-fifteen when a truck pulled into Lenko's side lot. Mo was sure Salinas was driving. Mo gave Frankie a wave, and he exited the bar.

He stood at the edge of the lot and saw three men heading for their cars. Salinas approached his truck, but before he could shut the door, Mo tapped him on the shoulder. "Hold it, Angel."

Salinas turned to his left. "What the—?"

"You mean fuck," Mo said.

"Jesus. What the hell you doing here?"

"Three guesses. Now get out, and let's go to the bar next door. Frankie's waiting for us."

They entered the now crowded, noisy place and walked back to the booth.

"Greetings, Angel."

"Yeah. Same to you Frankie."

"Get in," Mo said as he slid his body next to Salinas. "Want a beer? It's on us. Matter of fact, go get us a pitcher, Frankie."

"Shit music," Frankie said as he got up. "A couple of guys are hittin on those two chicks I spotted."

"So what's up?" Angel said.

"You clean?"

"Damn straight, got a good job and a new lady."

Frankie returned, pouring beer into the three frosted mugs the waitress had placed on the table. "Drink up, Angel," Mo said. "You real clean or you still selling?"

Angel gulped his beer, "I'm clean except for the little side action pushing weed."

"I want to know everything."

Angel's eyes opened wide and he jerked back. "Wait a minute. You guys burn down Lucky's, and kill Flores, too?"

"What are you, the fucking FBI?" Mo said. "And keep it down."

"Sorry, but it's getting loud in here. Jesus, everybody's dyin."

"And if you wanna make sure you're not next, you'll spill your guts."

Mo picked up his mug and took a big chug. "Tell us about the drug deal, and Jenkins. You drive that ambulance?"

"You fucking insane? I was nowhere near that shootout or that jail."

"So where were you? Maybe waiting for Jenkins to arrive with the money?"

"You fucking ass. I wasn't even around that weekend. I was in Puerto Rico with my girl."

"Really? You can prove that?"

"Damn right."

Mo finished his beer. "Hate to see a good pitcher go to waste. Drink up, you two."

Angel took a drink. "Anything else I can do for you?"

"Don't get smart on us now, Angel. What happened with Flores, Gomes, and Cosby Davis?"

"Jesus. It all started when Gomes was workin at the club. She was some piece of ass, and Flores wanted to be her pimp, but you know he couldn't tell Vinnie that."

"So was Davis a steady customer?"

Angel almost choked as he chugged his beer. "Customer? Shit man, he was gay. They was friends, worked at the airport. I don't think he ever knew about her weekend job."

"So why did Flores kill them?"

"He was a jealous bastard. Yolanda was his high-priced meal ticket, and he thought Davis was banging her off the clock. Pretty funny, isn't it?"

"I don't understand. What's Davis got to do with anything?"

"Yolanda told Flores that Davis said he'd seen a couple of suitcases full of money. He stole them, but says when he got them home they was full of rags. Flores thought he was hiding the money, and Davis wouldn't tell him where it was. He thought Yolanda knew, and kept her lips tight, so he took them both out."

"How'd Flores make it look like suicide?"

"I was at Flores's place that night waitin for him to come home. I left around midnight after he didn't show. Cecil came an hour later; said he heard Davis's car pull into her garage. He went out and said he had to talk to them; couldn't wait. He poured them nightcaps."

Angel leaned in toward Mo. "Son of a bitch slipped drugs into their drinks, and they fell asleep, so he placed them both back into Davis's car, and started the engine. Later he took his dog for a walk, and called the police."

"That's the whole story?"

"That's it, except I have his dog now."

"So there's still a piece I don't understand. What happened with Cosby Davis? How'd he go from the cemetery to Vinnie's old place?"

Angel put his mug down and shrugged. "Nobody knows."

"Somebody gotta know dude. You saying you heard nothing?"

"I swear. No one knows."

Mo tapped his empty mug. "He have a funeral?"

"Yeah. Samuel did it; he's buried a lot of us."

"Frankie, I think we gotta go see Samuel."

Mo looked at Angel. "If you're holdin' out on us, you'll be seeing the man sooner than you think."

"I told you, I'm clean!"

"Here's my number, stay in touch."

The three men slid out of the booth and headed for the door. Frankie kept eyeing the jail bait. "Nice shit."

The henchmen headed for the Caddy and Angel walked to his truck.

⅄

A black hearse was parked by the side door of the Samuel Funeral Parlor. Cars were in the back lot as Mo's Cadillac pulled into the driveway. He drove to the last row and slid the vehicle into an empty space. He and Frankie approached the parlor, letting a few mourners pass them by. A dark suited employee was at the door and held it open.

"I'd like to speak with Mr. Samuel. Do you know if he's here?" Mo asked.

The doorman pointed to his right. "He's the man in the corner with Father Stevens."

"Do you think we could speak with Mr. Samuel?"

The employee walked over to Samuel, and politely interrupted the mortician's conversation with the priest. "Sir, the two gentlemen by the front door would like to speak with you."

Mo whispered to Frankie, "You shut up and let me do the talking, and no fucking toothpicks."

Samuel approached the two visitors. "I understand you want to talk to me?"

"Yes sir, may we go to your office? This is official police business."

"Again?"

"Yes sir, I'm Agent Maurice Harris, and this is Agent Franklin Cruz—we're with the FBI."

"My office is down the hall. Follow me."

Samuel sat behind his desk, and the phony agents took seats in chairs across from him. Mo placed his fedora in his lap.

"What's the nature of your business?' Samuel asked.

"It's Cosby Davis, sir."

"I already spoke with the detectives about him."

"We understand that sir, but we're following up on their work. Can you tell me about Mr. Davis's funeral?"

"I can only tell you what I told the detectives. Davis had a normal funeral, and we buried him in City Cemetery."

"You're sure it was Cosby Davis that you buried?"

"I can only assume it was. There was no open casket."

"So it could have been someone else?"

"Possibly, that's why we'll be exhuming the body soon."

"When will that be, sir?"

"I'm waiting for the detectives to tell me."

"And their names again?"

Samuel opened his desk drawer and took out Dan's card. "Dan Shields, and his partner's name was Scott."

Mo reached into his coat pocket, and came away empty handed."I don't have any of my cards, and Agent Cruz is new to the department. Can I write my number on the back of the detective's card?"

The funeral director handed Mo the card and the phony agent wrote his cell number on it. "I want you to call me the minute you hear about the exhumation plans."

"But can't you get that information from the detectives?"

Mo stared long and hard at the funeral director. "We can, sir, but for reasons I can't tell you, we need to hear it from you. This is the FBI, not local law enforcement jurisdiction. It's our case."

"Fine, I'll call you as soon as I get the information."

Mo grabbed his hat, stood and extended his hand to Samuel. Frankie got up and the two imposters turned, and walked down the corridor that had filled with mourners. Vinnie's boys exited the funeral home.

As soon as Mo got into the Caddy he called Vinnie.

⚔

Vinnie was by his pool with Honey, both drinking sombreros when his cell rang, and he pulled his sunglasses up to see who it was.

"Mo, what's shaking?"

"Trees, Vin, lots of trees. We spoke to Biggie and Salinas. I think we got a lead."

"Wait a sec." Vinnie motioned to Honey. "I'm going inside. You come in too and cover that sweet ass and get dressed. You have to get ready for work."

"Huh?" Mo said.

"Her, not you. Never mind." Vinnie stepped inside and sat on his leather couch. "Where's Louie?"

"Sleeping. So are Biggie, Lucky, and Brick."

"You shoot them?"

"Just one, two if you count Louie. Wait, three if you count the dog. They all burned. We also had a long chat with Salinas and some you ain't gonna like. I believe Salinas. He's clean, but Flores deserved what we gave him. Not only was he stealing from you, he was after your girl Yolanda. Tried to be her pimp right out from under you."

"What about the money?"

"I'm getting there. Salinas gave us a story about Davis stealing a couple of suitcases full of money, but he claimed they were stuffed with rags, and wouldn't tell Flores or Yolanda if he really had the cash." Mo coughed. "We're leaving the Funeral Home. Seems they're gonna dig up Davis's grave soon."

"You thinkin' what I'm thinkin'?"

"I think there's something in that grave, and it's not Davis. Anyhow, cops already talked to Samuel, and he's waitin' to hear from them when they're gonna do it."

Vinnie stood and watched Honey slip out the door in her shorts and a blouse that was tied below her breasts. "Make me a grand tonight," he said.

"You paying attention?" Mo asked.

"Yeah, so shoot."

"I told Samuel to call me the minute he gets the details."

"How'd you pull that off?"

"Vinnie, come on; give me a little credit. FBI Agents Harris and Cruz made sure he got the message."

Vinnie laughed. "FBI? Good one. Keep me posted."

CHAPTER 50

Dan had come up with a few not-so *by the book* schemes in the past, but what he was cooking up this time could cost him his badge. Salinas was his new hot button, but Dan knew merely confronting him would not make Salinas sing.

"What's going on in that head of yours?" Scotty asked.

"Salinas. We need a setup."

"A what?"

"A phony charge. We need to bring him in on a trumped-up charge."

Scotty squinted. "Are you crazy? We can get fired, or even go to jail."

"Don't worry about that. We know where he works, and we know what his truck looks like. All we have to do is plant a weapon under his seat, and let the uniforms do the rest."

"What?"

"Oh yeah, one more thing: you're going to have to go into the roofing place to distract the guy inside while I'm out back in the parking lot busting Salinas's taillight and planting the gun."

"Now I *know* you're nuts. So how do you intend to confront him?"

"I don't. Traffic cops will stop him for a broken taillight and search his vehicle."

"Why would they search his vehicle if he's clean and just has a taillight issue?"

"We'll need to have a warrant posted."

"What? How the hell are you going to pull that off?"

"Syms will have to help us."

"Help us? He'll send us packing like a couple of hobos."

"Bring the muffins and we'll have a nice chat with him."

Scotty picked up his Tupperware container. "Let's go."

Syms reached for his ibuprofen bottle as Dan and Scotty approached. "Keep the food container," he said to Scotty. "You two must be up to something good." The captain sat back, twirling a pen. "Let's hear it."

Dan leaned forward. "We need a favor."

"No shit, Shakespeare. I could read your face a mile away."

"Listen. We need to have Salinas arrested in order to get him to talk to us."

Syms sat forward, staring into Dan's eyes. "Oh, this is gonna be good."

"We need an arrest warrant put into the system."

Syms stood. "A false warrant? We'll all be fired. I can't do that."

"What if no one knows? It'll be quick and dirty, in and out."

"Oh my lord. You can't be serious."

"Dead serious. Audrey Pelman's the one who updates the system, right?"

"Yeah, but you can't simply walk up to her and say, you look lovely today, Audrey. Would you mind entering this false warrant into the system?'"

"Ever try it?"

"No, and I'm not going to do it now." Syms sat again." What's your plan?"

"I plant a weapon in his truck, I'm figuring he'll already have weed in it. We saw his F-150 at Flores and we know the vehicle has a broken taillight. He gets stopped for the broken light, the traffic cops find the warrant and search his vehicle. Now he's got a firearms charge as well as possession of pot."

Syms closed his eyes and spun his chair all the way around. He opened his eyes icily staring at Dan. "Have you lost your mind?" he shouted.

Dan tapped his hand on Sym's desk, and the captain gave his detective an incredulous look. "You so much as tell anyone about this conversation, and

I'll have your pink slip on my desk, and that goes for you too muffin man. This conversation never happened. Got it? Now get the hell out, and come back only when you have a real plan. Dumbest thing I've ever heard."

Syms picked up the Tupperware container and threw it at Dan. "Take this with you."

The detectives left Sym's office, and Dan picked up the bruised container. "I think the muffins are still okay."

They walked past the men's room. Meet me back at my desk," Dan said. "I'm stopping in here to empty my bladder."

When he got back to his desk, Dan saw Scotty using the computer. "What are you doing?'

"Hold on. Look at this?"

Dan walked over and read the screen. "You shitting me? Salinas has an outstanding warrant that's eight month's old. Failure to appear in court on a drug charge for possession and intent to sell marijuana." He tapped Scotty on the shoulder. "Our lucky day pal. That means he has a suspended license. All we have to do now is get a weapon to plant in his truck."

"Hold it. Why do we need that? If he's brought in on the warrant that should be good enough, and what the hell was that shit about the already broken taillight?"

"I couldn't exactly tell Syms I was going to smash it. All he had to know was that the vehicle was ripe for a moving violation. The weapon is another story. "I want to scare the shit out of Salinas. I want a weapons charge too. Let him stew until Sasser gets him out again. Come on pal. We're going to get a handgun."

"We can't just pop into the evidence room and ask for one?"

"Who said anything about the evidence room? I know the place. How much money you got on you?'

"Twenty. Why?"

"Great. I have forty, takes more than that to buy a pistol. We have to stop at the ATM downstairs."

Dan withdrew two hundred, and he knew just the place to go to complete his mission.

"Where are we going?" Scotty asked.

"Dewey's."

"Dewey? Pawn shop Dewey?"

"Dewey."

⚔

When the pawn shop door opened, Dan saw Dewey standing behind a counter of jewelry. Shaking his head, Dewey said. "Long time no see. What brings you here?"

"A little business," Dan said. "How have you been?" Remember Scotty?"

"Hey. You this guy's partner now?"

"I'm the lucky one." Scotty replied.

Dewey had done a few laps around the police station before. Selling stolen merchandise was nothing uncommon. The Harley tee-shirt was two sizes too large for his skinny body

"What happened to the long hair?" Dan said.

"Chemo, I been in remission. I feel okay now."

"Know what?" Dan said. "You look better in short hair, shows off your big ears."

"Funny. So tell me a story. I know you didn't come her to bullshit."

"I need a favor," Dan said. "Where are your handguns?"

"See those two customers at the counter to your left? Over there."

"I need a small pistol."

"What the hell's wrong with the one on your hip?"

"Anyone ever told you not to ask questions?"

"Just my mother, you didn't want to cross her."

Dewey pointed at Dan. "Anyone ever told you not to ask questions?"

The two customers moved away from the weapons counter and the detectives followed Dewey over there. "Pick one," he said."

Dan looked down through the glassed counter top. "This a Pico?"

"It is. Nice piece."

"What are you asking?"

"Two."

"How's one?"

Dewey laughed. "Come on make me a real offer."

"One twenty-five."

"One seventy-five it's yours."

"I think one-fifty sounds like a little more reasonable, don't you?"

Dewey shook his head, and he removed the gun from the shelf. "You win."

"Just one thing, I don't want you to write it up, I'll give you the cash."

"I'm legit Dan. You know that. What's the deal?"

"The deal is this. It somehow disappeared."

Dan looked around the large store, eying the electronics, and bicycles. "Don't give me that legit crap. You've got more stolen goods in here than we have in our evidence room. Want me to check out all the merchandise now?"

"Dewey smiled. "Got ya, get that gun out of here."

"Thanks Dewey. I knew you'd understand."

Dewey held out his hand. "You forget something? How about the cash?"

Dan handed him the money. "You know Dewey; it smells like a weed farm in here."

Dewey grinned. "Wanna laugh?" he said. "I used to smoke it all the time and even got busted a couple of times. Now they can't bust me. I have a card and medical marijuana."

"Thanks Dewey, it was nice doing business. I'd get some air freshener in here if I were you."

CHAPTER 51

Nana's ashes were inside the second urn on the fireplace mantle. Josh and Kate, saddened by the death of their Nana, had stayed home from school for a couple of days, while Phyllis began to deal with her mother-in-law's small estate.

A tear came to Dan's eye as he sat at the dining table and led the prayers. He looked at his young children. "It's okay. Nana still loves you."

Phyllis held her hand out to Dan. "We still love her, too."

In a sense the entire Shields family was still together, all residing inside their Suffield house, except for Mike, away at college, but his spirit was still home..

While they were at the dining table, ready to eat, the house phone rang, and Dan answered. It was Mike.

"How's it going? Josh and Kate okay?"

"They're fine. How about you? We're having supper."

"I'm okay, just wanted to check on those two little brats. Sorry. I forgot it's two hours earlier here."

Dan handed the phone to the young siblings and they both talked to their big brother. Phyllis, who had been waiting patiently to speak with Mike, talked with him for ten minutes before she said goodbye. "Nice of him to call."

"Didn't he want to talk to me?" Dan said.

"He had to run and didn't want to be late for practice. If it makes you feel better, he went four for four yesterday."

"Watch out Yankees, here comes Mike Shields."

"Is that your dream, or his?"

"Both."

After dinner, Kate and Josh went out to play and Phyllis said to Dan. "I was thinking about getting someone to stay with the kids after school."

"I think we should. Who do you have in mind?"

"Actually, they can go to Terry's house and I can pick them up on my way home."

"Have you talked to her about it?"

"Not yet. I wanted to see what you think."

Dan rolled his eyes. "Wait a minute, she's perfect. I know who we can get. Remember Connie Castino from the diner? I bet she'd do it. She said she needed a hobby and she can probably use the extra money. I have her number. She gave it to me last time we were in the diner."

Dan found Connie's number and called her. "Hi Connie, This is Dan, you're favorite detective. How are you?"

"I'm fine. Miss the boys. How are you? Catch any hoodlums lately?"

"One, some wino tried to break into the diner."

"You mean the rubble, must have left some stale muffins behind."

"So, got any hobbies?"

"Puzzles, I'm into puzzles."

"So are my kids. Speaking of them, you know my mother died and the kids miss her. She used to sit for them after school."

"I was sorry to hear about her"

"Thanks. How would you like to hang around my house and watch Josh and Kate after school? We have a den and you can do puzzles anytime you want. We'll pay you."

"Pay me? I wouldn't think of it. Buy me puzzles and it's a deal."

Dan smiled into the phone, "Really, You'll love the kids and you'll love Phyllis too."

"I know she's a saint after everything you've told me about her. And I remember you showing me pictures of Josh and Kate. How's Scotty, Bev and the babies?"

"They're all good. When can you start?"

"Next week. Forgot to tell you I bowl on Wednesdays."

"No problem. We'll work around it. Plan to stay for supper too. The kids get out of school at three and I'll get you a key"

Dan recited his address. "You know, I'm only twenty minutes from you, and traffic shouldn't be an issue."

"Fantastic. Can't wait to see you." Dan said before ending the call.

He smiled at Phyllis. "She's on board. You'll love her."

Chapter 52

Captain Syms had thrown Dan and Scotty out of his office after they dared to pose that hair-brained scheme to arrest Angel Salinas. The captain braced himself when he saw the two detectives coming toward him. "Don't bother to sit. You're not gonna be here long."

Dan and Scotty sat and Syms shook his head. "Where's my muffin?" he said.

"You almost broke my container," Scotty uttered.

"Okay, smart ass. I'm sorry, but one of you better have something good to say."

"It's like this." Dan said. We're all set for Salinas. Dixon's guys need to make that traffic stop."

"And why would Dixon have his guys hang around where Salinas works waiting for some truck with a broken taillight?"

"Because there's an outstanding warrant, we got lucky. Salinas failed to appear in court a few months ago."

Syms breathed a sigh of relief. "I thought you were going to tell me another crazy scheme."

Dan got up. "Let's go partner, we have to see Dixon."

They left the captain's office, and Scotty grabbed Dan's arm. "You didn't mention the gun."

"No kidding. As long as he didn't mention it, I didn't see a need to bring it up again. Let's get the ball rolling."

The detectives walked down to the traffic division and entered Dixon's office. "Don't see you boys here too often. How was the caf?"

"It was okay. No Connie's for sure,' Dan said "

"Seen the old lady?" Dixon asked.

"Actually, I spoke with her last night. She's gonna be taking care of my kids after school."

Scotty looked at Dan. "You didn't tell me that."

"I did now."

What's on your mind?" Dixon said.

"I want to give you a heads-up." Dan replied. "We need one of your units to stop a black Ford F-150 in the vicinity of Syracuse and Stetson, somewhere near Lenko roofing."

"What's so special about it?"

"The vehicle belongs to a known drug dealer named Angel Salinas and there's an outstanding warrant. You can look it up."

"Got a license number?"

"Connecticut plate KJ54339. We've been told it has a broken taillight, so that will give your guys cause to stop it."

Dixon turned to his computer. "I see the warrant. We'll put out a notice."

"How are you so sure he'll be in that area?"

"That's his main drop zone."

"Okay. We'll bring him in if you're right."

⅄

It was off to Lenko's in Dan's Accord. He parked across the street from the roofing company. "I see the truck," Dan said. "Time to do our thing, you go inside and distract the guy in the office, while I sneak into the lot and do what I have to do."

Both detectives got out of the car and Scotty opened Lenko's door as Dan casually strolled into the parking lot.

Roger Lenko, wearing an orange and black shirt with a rooftop logo above the pocket, was talking on his phone. Standing behind the counter he saw Scotty and said. 'I'll be right with you."

A German shepherd sat calmly next to the counter, and Lenko hung up the phone. "I'm Roger Lenko. How can I help you?"

Scotty cleared his throat. "I guess I need a new roof. Mine's been leaking and I was wondering if I could get an estimate?"

The dog began pacing and making noises. "Sit, and be quiet," Lenko said.

"Don't mind him. Stray cats are always rummaging around the yard and he gets a little antsy."

In the meantime, Dan got to Salinas's vehicle, and he opened the passenger side door slipping the Pico under the seat. Dan smelled marijuana inside the truck, so he opened the center console and confirmed his suspicions. A bong and several bags of pot were inside. He quickly went around to the back of the truck and smashed the passenger side tail light with his own gun, before walking back to the Accord. He called Scotty's cell.

Still inside the store, Scotty recognized Dan's call. "Hi hon," he said.

"It's done. Let's go." Dan said.

Scotty looked at Lenko. "Sorry, I have to run. My wife just got into an accident and I'll be back later."

He hurried out of the store and returned to Dan's car. "How'd it go?"

"Good. The truck was unlocked."

"You weren't so quiet. Roger Lenko, and his shepherd heard you. The dog started getting edgy, but Lenko told him to shut up. Apparently strays are always around and the dog reacts."

"Let's head back and wait until later. You call Sally last night?"

"Went over for coffee."

"Just coffee?"

Scotty smiled. "No. I brought some muffins."

"And some clean underwear, right?"

"Know what? You're a dirty old man. But I did remember them."

⅄

Around four fifty-five p.m., a roofing truck pulled into the rear of the Lenko's lot where the work crew got out, and went inside. About fifteen minutes later, Salinas walked to his vehicle and slowly pulled his F-150 out of the lot heading down Syracuse Street. Once he had driven a few blocks, he spotted a police cruiser in his rearview mirror; its flashing lights compelled him to pull over.

Officer Judy Jaworski approached the vehicle. "Good afternoon sir, may I see your driver's license, registration, and insurance card?"

"What did I do officer?"

"You have a broken taillight."

Salinas was surprised. "What? I don't have a broken light."

"Yes sir, you sure do. Just hand me your information please."

Salinas reached into his glove box, pulled out his registration and insurance card and handed them to the officer. He opened his wallet, took out his license and presented it to her.

He started to get out of the vehicle, but she instructed him to stay in the truck until she returned. Upon checking Salinas's data, a red flag popped up showing the outstanding warrant. She called for back-up, and a few minutes later a second black and white appeared. A burly officer named Blake approached her.

"He's got a warrant, and priors." Judy said.

Blake took the license, registration, and insurance card and he handed them back to Salinas. "Mind stepping out of the vehicle?" the officer said.

Salinas saw the female officer's gun drawn. "What's going on?"

"Put your hands behind your back, sir. Blake said."

The patrolman cuffed Salinas. "You *are* Angel Salinas, right?"

Salinas nodded.

"Seems you have an outstanding warrant," Blake said.

"What are you talking about? I don't have any warrants. I'm clean."

"You also have a suspended driver's license. You failed to appear in court on a previous charge of possession and intent to sell sir. Eight months ago. You don't remember that?"

An agitated Salinas said, "Hell no. I never skipped court. I never got no notice. My attorney, Sasser got those charges dropped."

"Is that what he told you?" Apparently he didn't. Mind if we search the vehicle, sir?" Blake said.

"For what? This is a traffic stop."

"Yes sir, but that warrant gives us some concern, and if you have nothing to hide then it should be fast and easy."

"There's nothing in there."

"Then do we have your consent?"

Salinas hesitated, knowing he had bags of pot inside the console.

"We can get the dogs." Blake said.

Salinas nodded his approval.

The female officer looked under the passenger seat and saw a handgun. She calmly pulled out the Pico. Upon opening the center console, she found several bags of marijuana, removed them and placed the pot alongside the Pico on top of the truck's hood.

"What the fuck?" Salinas shouted. "I don't have a gun. I don't know how it got there."

"Are you admitting the marijuana is yours?" the female officer said.

"I ain't saying nothing until I see my lawyer."

"This is your truck?" she asked.

"Yes."

"Then you're under arrest for having a concealed weapon and marijuana in your possession, a suspended license and an outstanding warrant. "Blake said. "Read him his rights."

Salinas was red with anger. "Are you kidding me? I never saw that gun before."

"You'll have to tell it to the judge," Blake said.

CHAPTER 53

Dan knew it could be a long night, so he phoned Phyllis and let her know he'd be late, maybe very late.

He and Scotty were waiting in the booking area when Blake escorted Salinas in.

"Angel, we meet again. What have you done this time?" Dan said.

"You son of a bitch, I know you set me up. Wait until Sasser hears about this."

"Not before you talk to us. You want to do that now, or after they throw you into a cell?"

"What's there to talk about?"

"Oh, I think we have plenty to discuss."

Dan turned to the booking officer. "After you mug him, I want him brought upstairs to the interrogation room, third floor."

⅄

Scotty and Dan entered the brightly lit room. A white table and four chairs were in the center. The false window on the back wall was a standard two-way mirror setup. Dan filled a pitcher with water and placed cups on the table, along with his notes.

They heard footsteps, and a uniform ushered Salinas into the room. "Have a seat, Angel," Dan said. "You eaten yet?"

"Get on with it, motherfucker."

Dan peered at his captive. "You remember Scotty?"

"So?"

"So don't make him mad."

"Yeah, what's this bullshit all about? I know my truck was clean, except for my pot. So what the fuck are you guys up to?"

Dan quickly went into grill mode, pointing at his detainee. "Let me explain some things to you. We know you have information that we want."

"Like what?"

"Like, let's start with your buddy Cecil Flores. Why did he kill Gomes and Davis?"

"You know she was a whore, right?"

"We do, but why were she and her boyfriend killed?"

"Boyfriend? You got it all wrong. Davis wasn't her boyfriend. He was gay. Look, you guys let this bullshit charge go, and I'll let you in on a secret."

Dan peered into his eyes. "Now you're talking my language. Let's hear the secret first, before we make any commitment."

"How about some water?"

Dan poured a glass and Angel gulped it down. "Here it is. You know they both worked at the airport, right?"

Salinas for the first time showed a little ediginess as he tapped his left foot on the floor. "Davis stole a couple of suitcases and he told Yolanda there was money in them. That's why she hung around with him. Only thing was, when he got the suitcases home, he claims they were filled with rags. She made the mistake of telling Flores about it. That's why he killed them: he thought they were hiding the money and they wouldn't tell him."

"You were there, though, so level with us. Did you help kill them? We know you walked Flores's dog earlier, and your vehicle was seen there."

"I already told you about that. Cecil showed up after I went home, and so did Yolanda and Davis. That's when Flores drugged them and set up the carbon monoxide poisoning."

"He told you all that?"

"Yeah,"

"What about you?"

"I'm straight. I don't want no part of that shit."

Dan placed his foot on the chair next to Angel and he leaned in, peering into his captive's eyes. "You telling us the truth? You got anything else to say?"

Angel's demeanor changed and he squirmed in the chair. "I might be in deep shit. It's Martinez. His guys are in town snooping around. They killed Flores, and lit Lucky's place."

"Who are they?"

"Martinez's goons Mo and Frankie. They came to see me, and I told them everything I told you. They also wanted to know how Davis's body ended up on Martinez's property."

Dan stopped and shook his head. "What did you say? Whose property?"

"Martinez—he owned that place."

Dan looked at Scotty. "Damn Colton had to know that." He looked back at Angel. "Back up a minute, all the way to the drug bust. You knew it was going down, didn't you."

"Hey, I quit that gang. Split ways with Vegas before it happened."

"Yeah, but you knew it was going to happen."

"I was nowhere near it. I was in Puerto Rico with my lady."

"Where are Martinez's thugs now?"

"I don't know, but they were heading to Samuel's."

Dan stared hard at Angel. "I believe you. Tell us about Jenkins."

"All I know is, everyone's looking for him. He drove the U-Haul, and from what I was told, he did put the money in the truck, probably in those suitcases."

Instantly, Dan made a connection. "Brenda Simmons," he said, turning to Scotty.

"Brenda who?" Angel said.

"No one you know. She was Davis's boss."

"And me? You wanna let me out of these cuffs now?"

The uniformed escort was standing by the door. "Take him downstairs," Dan said to him.

Angel stood. "I know Sasser will be here to get that warrant lifted." Dan said. "You'll be out of here tomorrow by noon."

"What about my truck? It's impounded."

"We'll get it back to you. Get out of here."

Dan pulled Angel's arm back. "If anything you told us is bullshit, I'm gonna be on you like white on rice. Got it?"

Dan eyed the big clock on the wall. "It's almost seven-thirty. Let's get out of here."

Chapter 54

Salinas had given the detectives an earful, and Dan was hyped to drop the news on Syms. He marched into the captain's office with the much more sedated Scotty.

"We got Salinas and he sang like a bird," Dan said. "But we've been thrown a new twist. Vinnie Martinez's guys killed Flores, and lit up Lucky's. According to Salinas, they're in town and they went to talk with Samuel about Cosby Davis."

"Slow down, and sit. You're on high octane today."

Syms looked at Scotty. "You spike his muffin?"

Scotty shook his head as Dan interjected. "All we know is their first names: Mo and Frankie." Dan leaned forward. "Get this. The property belonging to the Merlines was owned by Vinnie Martinez."

"I thought you said some other name?"

"We did. Manny Vinton was the seller, according to the Merlines and Jessie Colton. The Merlines may not have known Martinez's identity, but Colton had to. He's going to have to tell us a story." Dan looked into the captain's eyes. "I'm sure Willingham has another story to tell."

Dan could see that Syms knew he was right. "If we could find him," the captain replied.

Dan nudged Scotty, and they got up to leave. "We need to get Salinas's truck out of impound first. You know Sasser will be at this morning's arraignment and I want the F-150 out before Angel is released."

Syms nodded at Dan and pointed to the door. "Go, and take Sarah Lee with you."

"I see he appreciates me." Scotty said.

"Let's go down to get the truck. You can drive it back and call Angel once we have it here," Dan said.

"Which impound are we going to?"

"I'll call Dixon and find out.".

⋏

After learning where Salinas's vehicle was, Dan drove his car inside the Jackson Street impound lot's fenced yard, and he pulled up to the small brick building located to the right of the gate. Inside, a young man with braided hair, and pants hanging below his waist was trying to get his car back. He insisted he had insurance, but had no proof. He continued arguing with the cashier until Sergeant Cane intervened.

Cane, a hefty, balding cop stood in front of the man. "Just calm down sir, call your insurance company. They can fax a copy of your card over here."

The man turned around without saying another word, but he was clearly muttering four letter words as he hastily left the building.

Cane saw Dan. "If it isn't Mr. Shields," he said.

"Hey, Candy. Still got the muttons and fuzzy hair lip I see. That shiny top must have made that guy run out of here." Dan replied. "You know Scotty?"

"Hey, didn't know you two were chumming these days."

"Yep, me and Dan. Like the Lone Ranger and Tonto."

"Listen," Dan said. "Dixon had a black Ford F-150 towed here yesterday. We need to get it out."

"What's the name?"

"Salinas, Angel."

Cane looked it up "Got it. Second row. Space twenty-seven."

"Got the keys?"

"Sure do. Got the cash? One-fifty, and we don't take credit cards or checks. There's an ATM over there though."

Dan cringed. "Really? You gonna make us pay?"

Cane smiled. "You got a release order from Dixon?"

"No. How about calling him?"

"You call him. Let me know what he says."

"Got his number?"

Cane recited Dixon's number. Dan picked up the phone on Cane's desk and made the call. Dixon's phone rang. "Sergeant Gagliardi, traffic,"

"This is Dan Shields. Is Dixon around?"

"He's out. What did you want?"

"I need to get a vehicle out of Jackson Street and Cane won't release it without Dixon's consent."

"When was it brought down?"

"Yesterday, but we need it out now, and Cane wants cash. Look it's important that we get it right now or the owner is going to sue the shit out of us for a false arrest."

"Hold on. What's the vehicle?"

"It's a Ford-F150, belongs to Angel Salinas."

"Put Cane on."

Dan pointed at Cane, and handed the receiver to him. "It's Gagliardi."

Cane listened and he quickly hung up. He retrieved the keys and handed them to Dan. "It's all yours."

The detectives started to walk toward Salinas's truck. "Look to your left, about two rows down," Scotty said. "It's the U-Haul."

"Stay here. I'll drive the F-150 up to my car, and I'll be right back."

Dan parked Salinas's vehicle beside his Accord and he went back to talk to Candy. "Tell me something. The U-Haul in the back row, you know anything about it?"

"It's dinged up. Been here a while. It's from that big drug bust."

"Mind if we poke around? We're still on that case."

"Be my guest, but you realize you'll need a warrant to take anything you find."

"We're just eyeing it inside and out. I'm sure it's empty anyway."

Dan walked down the hill and caught up with Scotty. They approached the U-Haul. "Candy was right," Dan said. "It's dinged up, bullet holes and all."

They went to the rear of the vehicle and had barely enough room between the truck and fence to open the back and hop in. The compartment was empty. "Not much to see," Scotty said.

"There's something strange about this truck. It feels weird, Dan said. "Let's step out and look around this rig."

They stepped down and walked slowly around the vehicle. "I don't see anything," Scotty said.

"I'm telling you. It's not right. Something's off. Let's walk around again."

They got halfway around the truck and Dan stopped. "Step back a second, and tell me what you see?"

Scotty stared. "It looks like a bullet-riddled U-Haul to me."

Dan pointed from the front to the back of the vehicle. "Tell you what I see. It's a truck with a storage area on the outside that looks bigger than the storage area inside."

"Yeah, it does appear a little strange."

"Let's hop in again."

They stepped inside. "I see what you mean," Scotty said.

"The front seems closer than it should be."

Dan banged on the front wall near the cab. It sounded hollow. "Look at these rivets, top and bottom. Son of a bitch, that's a false front. Let's see if we can break it down."

"It's pretty strong," Scotty said.

"Damn it. That's got to be where the money was."

"But how could they get the money out of there?"

"Good question—let's take another walk around this thing." As they inspected the outside, Scotty stopped. "Come here. Look at the driver's side up there, in back of the cab. Don't those letters look a little funny?"

"You bet they do. The U and H are out of line."

Dan slid his hand along the side panel. "Well holy shit, this whole panel slides right out and opens up into that extra storage space. Two suitcases could easily slide in there. That's where they were, but how the hell did the suitcases end up at the airport? Jenkins is the key. Where the hell did he go? What happened to the money, and where the hell did Willingham go?"

Chapter 55

Dan was right. Hancock Sasser appeared with Angel Salinas at this morning's arraignment.

Always glib, the influential attorney was as sharp as ever. He managed to get Salinas's warrant tossed, and the new charges dropped. By eleven a.m. Salinas was free.

Upon returning to headquarters from the adjoining courthouse with Sasser, Salinas spotted his vehicle in the police parking lot.

"Shields did me ok. He got my truck,"

Sasser, dressed in a gray three-piece suit, went inside with Salinas and had the desk sergeant call Dan. The cagy detective knew he couldn't avoid the slick attorney. The last time he'd seen Sasser was two years ago. The fast-talking mouthpiece did his magic that day too, convincing the judge to let Vegas go with a slap on the hand.

Minutes later carrying Salinas's keys in his hand, Dan walked downstairs to see the two visitors. "Angel, we got your truck. Here's the keys," Dan said. "Morning Hancock"

Sasser nodded. "So whose gun was that?"

Dan grinned. "That's not important? I apologize for the inconvenience."

Sasser, holding his black leather suitcase smiled. "You know I could have you up on false arrest charges?"

"You don't mean false arrest. You mean planting evidence. The arrest was legit. There was an outstanding warrant."

"Right smart ass, next time it will be your ass."

Salinas twirled his keys. "I'm ready to get out of here."

He headed for his truck and stopped. "Wait. What about the taillight?"

Sasser looked at Dan. "Nice job. We'll send you the bill, right?"

"No problem. We'll take care of it."

Sasser extended his hand and shook Dan's. "Nice to see you again," the lawyer said.

Salinas got into his truck and Sasser walked back to the courthouse for another arraignment.

Scotty, waiting for his partner's return, heard Dan's phone ring and he picked it up. It was Brenda Simmons. "Hi, Brenda."

She sighed. "I need to come see you."

"What is it?"

"Something you need to know, but I can't talk about it here. I'm coming to see you now. I have a part-timer to cover me."

"Okay. You know where we are?"

"Downtown, I've been by the new building."

"Pull into the parking lot out back and ask for me or Dan when you enter the building."

Dan got back from his meeting with Salinas and Hancock, and Scotty said. "Guess who's coming in?"

"Willingham?"

Scotty pointed to the suitcases in his cubicle. "Brenda Simmons. She has something to tell us. She's on her way"

Dan shook his head. "I told you she would finally come clean, can't wait to hear what she has to tell us."

"So how'd it go with Salinas?"

"Great. Sasser was with him. He's sly, and for some reason he's letting the planted gun slide. Oh. We'll be getting a bill for the taillight repair."

"We?"

Dan smiled. "I thought we were partners. You know fifty-fifty."

"You'll have to take me to dinner first. You break it, you bought it."

The detectives waited for Brenda and forty minutes later Dan got the call that she'd arrived and had asked for him. He went down to meet her and escorted the edgy baggage supervisor up to the conference room where Scotty waited.

Wearing her work shirt with the lanyard still around her neck, she placed her purse on the table. "Have a seat. Let me close the door," Dan said.

Sitting across from the detectives, she took out a pouch of Kleenex. "Look, I'm scared. There's something I haven't told you."

Dan saw the angst on her face as her head bowed. "It's okay, Brenda. You're here now. No need to worry."

She looked up at Dan. Her palms were sweaty. Those suitcases were switched. I think Cosby did think there was money in them, but there wasn't; at least not in the American Flyers."

"What are you saying? Cosby stole the money and replaced the bags?"

She closed her eyes, wiping a tear with a tissue. "No. I think when the American Tourister bags arrived, they had money in them, and Cosby somehow knew it. He must have peeked inside them. He did steal the Flyers, but I'm sure he thought the money was in them. Someone else switched the bags."

"Who would that be?" Dan asked.

She was perspiring and wiped her forehead. Dan poured a cup of water and handed it to her. Brenda drank it and continued talking. "A federal agent came in the day after the bags arrived and he told me the suitcases were part of a federal case, and that I had to give them to him." She paused. "He walked out with the Tourister's, and told me he'd return them the next day. He came back with those two Flyer suitcases with the yellow tags attached. He told me not to tell anyone or he would have me fired, and possibly arrested for tampering in a federal case."

Dan walked around the table in disbelief. "So Cosby never knew this, and thought he was stealing the money. He never noticed the brand names either."

"Do you remember the agent's name?" Dan asked.

"It was Dobbs. He was short, fiftyish, dark suit, glasses, and thinning gray hair."

Dan and Scotty looked at each other. "The Feds, should have known it," Dan said. "Syms was right." He turned to Brenda. "I don't think Dobbs will be visiting you again. You're safe. Don't worry about your job."

Brenda smiled, looking relieved she'd told the whole story. Scotty escorted her out while Dan went back to see Syms, but his office was empty.

Dan was at his desk when Scotty returned. "Syms is gone. Something must have come up. We can see him later. I think we owe Jessie Colton another visit. We're going for a ride. I'm sure he'll be happy to see us."

❁

When Dan and Scotty burst into Jessie Colton's office before the businessman's secretary could warn him, He jumped up from his chair. "What the hell are you doing barging in like this?" he said.

"Sit down," Dan said as Scotty shut the door. "You have a story to tell us and you better not leave anything out."

Jessie sat in his leather chair. "What are you getting at?"

Dan pounded his fist on the desk. "Everything! Flores, Gomes, Manny Vinton, and one you forgot to mention: Vinnie Martinez."

Cornered, he turned to his liquor. "Mind if I have a drink?"

Dan sat in the chair next to Scotty. "If it helps you remember, better go for it."

Jessie poured the drink and sat back. "Look, what I tell you, you have to believe."

Dan had heard that line a million times. It always meant the guy wasn't leveling.

"Damn it," Jessie said, pointing to the photo on his credenza. "See that picture of my wife? That's how it all started."

He took a drink of his scotch. "Her name is Lily, and her father worked at a hotel in Colombia. Martinez got to know him. One day her father called and said he and Lily's mother were coming to America, said they'd won a trip to New York." Jessie closed his eyes. "I thought it sounded fishy, but before I could convince them not to come, it happened."

He paused. "Martinez set them up, and when they got to New York, their bags were searched. That bastard used them as mules. The dogs snuffed out cocaine. The inner linings were full of the stuff. Lily's parents were arrested and I had to go to New York with her to testify for them. That's one hell of an ordeal, and thank God her parents checked out, but they were sent back to Colombia. Then part two hit us: Martinez showed up here, threatening to kill us and her parents if I ever mentioned his name."

Dan's head was spinning, and Scotty was listening as if he were watching a soap opera on TV. "Hell of a story," Scotty said.

Dan shook his head. "Tell us about the house and the Merlines."

"Long story. Martinez was looking for a house somewhere out of the way where he could set up shop and do business here. That place in Tolland was perfect. Very secluded, and he used it for a couple of years. Then something happened and he told me he had to move to Florida."

"Do you know what that something was?"

"He never told me, and I never asked."

"Was he still Martinez then?"

"Good question. He used Manny Vinton here. Anyway he wanted to hang onto the house and rent it out, so he asked…Jessie paused, told me to manage the property. After it was vacant, the Merlines contacted me. I convinced Vinnie that maintaining, and paying taxes on an empty house was a losing proposition, and renting can get ugly, so he agreed to sell it."

"The Merline's had to come up with a lot of cash." Dan said.

Jessie drank again. "Tell me about it. I was as surprised as you, but they did it."

"Now let's hear about Flores, and Yolanda Gomes."

The businessman fidgeted and finished his drink. "Flores worked for Martinez at the Hi-Hat, and you know what that joint is."

"We do. We also know Yolanda was a prostitute by night and weekends."

"Yeah. Martinez gave me a pile of cash to set them up at Landon Place. Flores was already there, and Gomes came later. Coincidentally, they ended up side-by-side."

"You know he killed her and Cosby Davis, right?"

Dan stared at Jessie, who turned around, refilled his glass and said nothing.

"You never kept files on them, did you?"

"I did at first, but Martinez didn't want any way to trace them back to him, so I wiped them clean."

"So Sally never knew anything," Scotty said. "She gave us was what she thought was the truth."

"That file was real. It only had an ID and a few pieces of info."

"You realize we can arrest you for obstruction of justice, don't you?" Dan said.

"Listen. Think about it. If you were in my position, with Vinnie Martinez hanging over you, you'd do the same thing."

"When was the last time you talked to him?"

Dan saw the cold look in Jessie's eyes. "A couple of days ago," he replied.

"What was that conversation about?"

"He'd heard that you guys were asking questions, and he wanted to know what I told you."

"So he knows about us." Dan got up. "You familiar with a couple of his guys named Mo and Frankie?"

"Can't say that I am."

Scotty stood and opened the door. "If Martinez calls you again, I want to know about it. You have my card. Have a nice day," Dan said.

Jessie Colton hadn't lied about Mo and Frankie; he didn't know them, that was... until a few hours after the detectives had left his office. He saw a black Caddy in the parking lot and watched the Mutt and Jeff duo enter his building.

Seconds later Mo and Frankie sauntered into Colton's office. "You Jessie?" Mo asked.

Jessie stood. "Yes, who the hell are you?"

"Relax, just a couple of businessmen. I'm Mo and this here is my partner Frankie."

Jessie's heart began beating faster. Those were the names Dan had mentioned, and here they were, Martinez's goons. He tried to calmly sit, but his hands began to sweat. "What can I do for you? Have a seat."

Mo placed his fedora in his hand and Frankie immediately spotted Lily's picture. "That your wife?" the toothpick swirling gangster said.

Jessie turned. "Yes. She was a Miss America contestant."

"Nice, Mo said.

Jessie leaned forward. "So what do you want? I know Vinnie sent you."

"Relax," Mo said again. You got it wrong, he didn't send us, we came all by are lonesome."

Frankie gnawed on his toothpick.

"We know the whole story, and we know a couple of detectives have been here to talk to you. We want to make sure that you know whose team you're on."

Jessie breathed hard. "I'm not stupid. Vinnie talked to me and I told him I gave the detectives nothing." He glanced back at Lily's photo. "You touch her, and I'll have the police and an army on your asses."

Mo raised his brows. "Pretty strong words from a dip like you. If you play the cards you've been dealt then you have nothing to worry about."

Jessie looked at Frankie. "Stop staring at that picture, you pervert."

Frankie removed the toothpick from his mouth and pointed it at Jessie. "Yeah, I'd fuck her, and you couldn't do anything about it."

Mo put his arm on Frankie. "Shut up and don't open your mouth again. Show some respect."

Mo looked at Jessie. "Now, what was I saying?"

"I think you reminded me to keep my mouth shut too."

"Yeah, that's it."

"Don't worry. I get the message. Vinnie knows I wouldn't cross him."

Mo stood and pulled Frankie up. "Thanks," the big goon said. "I knew you'd appreciate our visit."

Jessie watched the henchmen leave his office, opened his credenza, pulled out the Dewar's, and drank a double shot.

He knew Dan had told him to call if he heard from Vinnie again, but technically he hadn't heard from the drug lord himself, so Jessie had no need to inform the detectives of Mo and Frankie's visit.

Chapter 56

"Traffic," Scotty said. "I didn't know it was so bad on I-91 north."

Dan looked at his smiling partner. "What the hell were you on that side for?"

"That's where Sally lives."

"You slept there again?"

"Who slept? I'm tired."

"I saw Syms, but Hardison was in with him. We can see the captain later. Come on. We're wasting time here. You remember Salinas telling us about the two thugs, Mo and Frankie?" Dan paused. "He said they visited Samuel, and I want to find out about their visit."

⅄

There were few cars at the funeral parlor; nothing scheduled until late afternoon. Dan and Scotty entered the quiet building and headed to Grayson Samuel's office. A man with gray hair, wearing a dark suit, and a woman in a black dress sat with their backs to the detectives. Samuel had a brochure with pictures of caskets in his hand, and he appeared to be having a discussion with the couple concerning the wooden boxes.

The detectives patiently waited, sitting in chairs outside the office, until the pair exited the mortician's chambers.

Grayson Samuel saw the detectives and he invited them in. "Thank you for waiting," he said. "Are we ready to exhume Cosby Davis?"

"Mind if we sit? Dan said. "We haven't got the paperwork yet, but I think the court order will be issued soon. I understand you had a couple of visitors."

"You mean those FBI men?"

Dan looked at Scotty. "Yes them. Do you remember their names?"

Samuel opened his desk draw and pulled out Dan's card. "The tall one wrote his name and number of the back of your card. Maurice Harris."

"Can I see that card? Tell us about them. Why were they here?"

"They said they had taken over the investigation and told me to call them when we're going to exhume Cosby. Is something wrong?"

Dan leaned forward. "Did they ever show you an ID?"

Samuel sat back and scratched his head. "Now that you mention it, they didn't. And they didn't even have cards."

"It's okay," Dan said. "Those guys were imposters, and we're onto them."

Dan handed his card back. "Please hang onto this."

"I don't understand. What's this all about?"

"It's about Cosby Davis. When we get the exhumation orders, we'll let you know." Dan paused. "We'll likely be asking you to call Mr. Harris to do as he asked when the time comes."

Samuel's face was nearly as pale as the body he'd embalmed for that afternoon's wake.

The detectives got up. "Try to remain calm," Dan added. "This will all be over soon."

Samuel stood and he watched Dan and Scotty walk out of his office.

Scotty whispered, "He turned white as a ghost."

"He did. I hope he doesn't panic when we ask him to make the call."

⅄

Syms's was alone in his office, but not for long as Dan and Scotty walked in. "We were here earlier. Hardison was in here, so we went to see Grayson Samuel." Dan said.

Syms clutched his Advil. "Save the Samuel story. Hardison knows about the shit you pulled with Salinas. Sasser knows, and that bastard attorney contacted the DA. So where'd you get the gun?"

Dan was stunned. He had a feeling Sasser wasn't really going to let that incident slide. "Lying son of a bitch," he uttered.

"It wasn't from the evidence room, if that's what you're getting at. I bought the Pico from Dewey. Besides the DA can't track the weapon, we sorta bought if off the books." Dan smirked as he looked at Syms. "I don't suppose you can expense the one-fifty I paid for it, and pay me back?"

Syms held up the ibuprofen bottle "Good thing I knew nothing about it."

He put the bottle down. "Hardison's pissed. You better get the drift. One more antic and you're gone. I can't save your asses."

"We've got a trail, and Willingham can help us put this puzzle together."

"Well, he's still hiding somewhere. No one can find his ass."

"Maybe so, but a couple of Vinnie Martinez's boys aren't hiding. They're posing as FBI agents, and they've visited Salinas as well as Samuel. They want to know when Cosby Davis's grave is going to be dug up."

Syms raised his head and peered out his window, as Dan uttered "That's where the money is. Someone, somehow, removed Davis's body and stashed the money inside his casket."

"Who the hell would do that?" Syms replied.

"Beats me, but they did. We also know that Davis stole the suitcases and thought he had the money, but the bags were switched before he grabbed them, and he was left with old rags."

Syms listened intently as Dan continued. "It was a federal agent named Dobbs who switched the suitcases. Brenda Simmons was told to keep quiet or she could lose her job and get arrested."

"I knew it reeked Feds," Syms said. "But why would they be playing games? If they already had the money, then what gives?'

"Willingham would know."

Syms gazed out his window. "Maybe Ted knew too much."

PART FOUR

Chapter 57

Marshall Dobbs had directed The Washington Division of the DEA for the past two decades. The fifty-four-year-old government employee had fought the never-ending battle against drugs since becoming a federal officer at age twenty-six.

Dobbs knew everything there was to know about seizing narcotics, carrying out raids, and even using a rapid-fire rifle.

Vinnie Martinez, the east coast kingpin was the one guy he'd been trying to take down for years, but Martinez was sly and he never wandered too far from home, except for trips to Cali.

The federal officer had never gotten close to capturing Martinez. This time when Dobb's informant had told the director about the huge deal that was planned, he was sure Martinez would show to collect ten million dollars, but the cagey drug lord never appeared. Dobbs had tipped Commander Ted Willingham, whose well-trained force crashed the deal, but they were left with several captives, a ton of drugs, a dead officer, no money, and no Martinez..

The back wall of the director's office looked like the post office's 'Most Wanted' board with names and pictures of dozens of drug cartel members. Vinnie Martinez's was at the top of the pyramid, with a dart aimed at it.

Several files were arranged neatly on top of Dobbs's desk. Pictures of his family lined the back wall credenza. A tall American flag stood in one corner, and two black leather chairs were opposite his desk. Dobbs placed his glasses on his desk, and turned to the man sitting in one of the chairs. "Ted, I think it's time to move on Martinez. My guys have been watching him and his boys, Mo Harris and Frankie Cruz. We know those two have been creating mayhem and lurking around as FBI agents. I know Martinez will show to get his money when Cosby Davis's grave is opened."

"Where's Jenkins?" Willingham asked.

Dobbs rubbed his hands together. "He's safe. I had to get him out of that jail fast, making sure they couldn't find him. It took him two years to gain Vegas's trust, but he did. I knew storing the ambulance in that warehouse would be a place Vegas would look."

"So what happened to the money?"

"We knew it was in the truck, so before Jenkins disappeared we broke into the impound lot and got the suitcases. Jenkins took them to the airport and handed them off to Yolanda Gomes."

"Her? She was in on it?"

"Jesus, Ted. She was nothing but a hooker working at one of Martinez's clubs in New Orleans. Dabney's. We offered her a way out of that life by getting her a job with the TSA, then transferring her to Hartford. We knew Martinez wouldn't mind as long as she went to work for Flores at the Hi-Hat."

"What did you need her for, anyway?"

"I had to have a TSA agent bring the suitcases to the lost baggage office. The plan was to leave the bags in storage until we were ready to bring Martinez down."

Dobbs turned to look out his window at the Potomac. "The problem was; it seems Cosby Davis had a habit of peeking into luggage, and he saw the money. He'd become friends with Yolanda and he told her he'd seen money inside those suitcases, and he intended to steal the bags. I had no choice, so I visited Brenda Simmons and got the bags out. I came back the next day and told her to put the bags back. They were matching cases stuffed with rags."

Dobbs turned back and looked at Willingham. "You know as well as I do, our jobs are dangerous, and sometimes there are casualties."

Willingham bowed his head. "All I think about is my guy Jimmy Calero. Losing him in the drug bust was bad."

"Well, in my case, it was Yolanda Gomes."

"So, where's the money?"

"I'm getting to that."

Dobbs filled a glass with water and took a drink. "That's where, maybe, we got a break with Davis being killed. After he was buried, I thought it would be risky, but brilliant, to heat up the money search by digging him up, placing the money inside his casket and planting his body on property that Martinez once owned. He thought he was sly, putting the property in the name of Vinton. We knew it was him, and I knew Martinez would freak when he found out about Davis's body being found there."

"So what the hell did you have Shields, Scott, and Syms going around in circles for?"

Dobbs sat, rocking back in his chair. "I had to let them go as far as they could. I wanted Flores, Vegas, and Biggie out of the way, and Martinez's guys jumped in at the right time. The others were collateral damage."

Dobbs was silent for a few moments. "What have you told those detectives?"

"Nothing, they think I'm dirty, but they're putting the pieces together, and Syms is on the fence. I think he still trusts me. I hear he's been looking for me. My guys are playing dumb. I told them I had to go to a top secret conference, and they couldn't tell anyone where I was," Willingham got up and poured himself water. "What about the exhumation?"

"I'm going have the injunction lifted as soon as you leave. It's all going to come down soon."

Willingham drank the water as Dobbs continued. "I'm going to tell you my plan. When I'm done explaining, I want you to meet with Syms and tell him what we intend to do."

The Special Forces Commander sat and listened to every word Dobbs was speaking, and after hearing it all, Willingham stood, picked up his hat and shook the DEA director's hand. "I'll see you back in Hartford."

"Go do your job," Dobbs replied.

Chapter 58

Captain Syms wasn't expecting the phone call from Willingham. "Where the hell have you been? We thought you were dead."

"I know. I had to go out of town on a top-secret mission. I need to come down to see you. We have a lot to discuss."

"Bet your ass we do. My guys are hot on Martinez. We know his boys are here."

"That's what I need to talk to you about."

"You gonna level with me this time?"

"Yes, but you better stock up on headache pills. I'll be there in an hour."

Syms took a deep breath and walked out to Dan's cube. "We gotta talk."

He rapped on Scotty's cube. "You too, down to my office."

Syms closed the door behind his detectives and he stood at his window. "Guess who called me?"

Dan and Scotty looked at each other. "Not the DA," Dan said.

"No." Syms said, plopping down into his chair, "Ted Willingham. He's coming down, says he has to tell us something." "Where the hell was he?" Dan said.

"Away, secret mission. That's all he'd say. Speaking of the DA, you idiots are lucky bastards. For some reason Sasser pulled his complaint for the planted gun. This is your lucky day. Go back to work until Willingham gets here."

λ

The detectives headed back to their desks. "Hey," Dan said. "Let's go for a walk. It'll only take fifteen minutes."

"Where are we going?"

"Follow me."

As they headed downstairs, Scotty saw where his partner was going. Dan stood at the desk outside the holding tank.

"Hi Dan," Dom said. "Showing Scotty what he's been missing?"

"Yeah, buzz us in."

They stepped inside the galley and slowly walked through the noisy lock-up. "What's your point?" Scotty said.

They stopped in the middle of the room. "Look around. Lucky we're not in the old place, because it was cold and stunk. These animals have it good."

The detectives continued walking. "Any one of these thugs could—and would—shoot, stab, or knock you unconscious for two bucks," Dan said.

"Hey Danny."

"Fuck you Dan."

"Eat my shit," was all they heard as they reached the exit door at the end of the corridor. "Same bunch of fuck-ups," Dan said. "I used to do this every morning to keep me juiced. This new place is too good for those criminals, but most of them will get a hand slap and be bailed out. They'll be back. Makes you think about what we do. The system is really fucked-up. How many times do I have to see the same faces before they go to jail for good, or get killed before they have a chance to go to prison."

Dan shook his head. "This shit ever get to you?"

"I don't think about it much."

"You might, if you ever get shot. I'm thinking about taking some time soon."

⅄

It wasn't long after they returned to the squad room that Dan and Scotty saw the Special Forces commander walking down the corridor and entering Syms's office. Willingham and the captain exchanged a few words; Dan couldn't hear what was said, but he could see that neither man inside that office looked happy.

Moments later Dan's desk phone rang, and he scooped up the receiver. "Shields."

"Come on down," came Syms's voice. "Grab Scotty."

The detectives entered Syms's office and sat to Willingham's left. "Good to see you," Dan said.

"You too. Sit and listen," Willingham replied. "We're lifting the injunction on the exhumation. It's going to happen soon. I've been in Washington with Marshall Dobbs. His plan is to let Vinnie Martinez know about the dig. He's sure the drug dealer will come for his money this time."

"So it *is* in Davis's grave," Dan said.

"Yes. It was the only way Dobbs could figure out how to nab the drug kingpin. Martinez is smart, and almost never leaves his home."

Willingham explained the links between Martinez, Flores, Davis, and Gomes. The revelation about her stunned the detectives, as did Jenkin's role, and the jail break. Willingham also explained why The DEA director had to show up at the airport, switch the bags, and lie to Brenda Simmons.

"My God," Dan said. "So he set this whole thing in motion just to capture Martinez. We almost got ourselves killed! Those big ass thugs at Lucky's were scary dudes. And fucking Biggie was no pushover."

"About the exhumation," Willingham said. "Mr. Samuel has to be informed."

"So does 'FBI agent' Mo Harris," Dan said. "Samuel needs to call him with the details."

"Precisely, Dobbs knows all about those imposters. He's still working out the details and wants to come here to discuss the capture with everyone—my team included, because we'll be taking Martinez down. We expect he'll have armed company."

"When's the briefing?" Syms asked.

"Monday morning."

CHAPTER 59

Monday morning at 9 a.m. Syms, Hardison and the detectives waited in the auditorium for their guests to arrive.

Dan and Scotty sat in the front row while Syms got the podium ready, and checked the microphone. Hardison, waiting at the door, saw his expected visitors coming toward him "Here they come," he shouted.

Willingham led his men into the large room. Marshall Dobbs, in a navy blue three-piece suit, followed. In his left hand was a soft briefcase with an eagle imprinted in the leather; government issue for sure. The DEA director introduced himself as he placed the portfolio on the podium. Willingham stood by him. His Special Forces unit sat behind the detectives.

Dobbs adjusted his glasses and opened the pouch, pulling out a few papers. He held up the court order for Cosby Davis's exhumation, and opened his notepad. He looked at the Hartford officers. "My friend, Ted, advised you that this exhumation will take place this coming Friday morning. In reality, I'm sure the actual digging will take place Thursday evening, sometime after dark." He looked at the four men seated in the front row. "This is when I expect Vinnie Martinez and his armed crew to arrive at the cemetery to dig up their money."

Dobbs stared at Dan and Scotty. "You two gentlemen have done terrific work. As soon as this meeting is over, I need you to take these papers to Grayson Samuel and have him ready to excavate. He is to call Mo Harris to tell him we'll be digging at six a.m. on Friday morning. That will give Martinez time to get up here. I'm sure he'll have armed company."

Willingham took the mic. "We need to make sure the backhoe is positioned at the grave Thursday afternoon. My guys will be hidden when Martinez and his gang attempt to dig up the grave sometime that night. Samuel doesn't have to know. He only has to be told when to get the digging equipment out there,"

"What time should we be there?" Dan said.

Dobbs, standing beside Willingham, placed his elbows on the podium and leaned forward. "That's the part that you may not like. This could erupt into another shootout. Ted's guys will do their best to make it quick and uneventful, but I can't jeopardize your lives. You won't be there."

Dan looked at Syms. "We gotta be there, with all the work we've done!"

Syms eyed his angry detective. "Calm down. It's their game now. We're all on the same team."

Dobbs addressed Dan. "I'm only protecting you. It's time for you to visit Mr. Samuel and put the plan in motion."

The meeting was over. Dan and Scotty had their orders and didn't waste time.

"We're going to the funeral parlor." Dan said to Syms.

"Good. See me when you get back."

⅄

"Gentlemen," Grayson Samuel said as the detectives entered his office. "Are we going to be exhuming Cosby Davis soon?"

Dan showed Samuel the court order.

"When are we doing this?" he asked.

"Friday morning. Do you still have my card with Mo Harris's number on the back?"

"It's here in my desk drawer."

"Good," Dan said. "You need to call him now and tell him the dig will take place Friday morning at six a.m. Also, tell him your equipment will be in place Thursday afternoon so the digging can be done on time, before visitors enter the cemetery."

The director picked up the phone, but put it back down. "My equipment? You mean a hearse?"

Dan cringed. "A backhoe."

Samuel smirked. "Then you'd better see Marvin Faulkner. He's the grave-digger. It's his backhoe."

Dan wasn't smiling. "What do you mean?"

"I mean we need to have him there."

"You don't do the earth-moving?"

"He digs, and we lower the casket. His place is on Riley Road. Want me to call him?"

Dan tapped Scotty on the arm. "We have to step out to talk."

"What the hell do we do now?" Scotty said.

"I don't want anyone else involved. Let's think about this."

"We better think fast. Maybe we should call Syms."

They stepped back into the office. "Is there any way you can have Faulkner drop off his backhoe Thursday afternoon? Dan asked."

"I suppose he'd do it. He can be an ornery old coot. He'll want to know why and he'll probably ask for more money too."

"You can tell him there's a court order to exhume a body, and the back-hoe has to be there no later than two p.m. Thursday afternoon."

"What about his men? They do the digging."

"Tell him it's a police matter and we'll be guarding the machine until his guys get there to operate it Friday morning. We'll pay any extra charges."

Samuel placed a call to Faulkner, and explained the circumstance. The mortician hung up and smiled at Dan. "He said he'll do it, but he wants an extra two hundred."

Dan gave the mortician a thumbs up. "It's time to call Mo Harris."

The director made the call. "Hello. Mr. Harris, this is Grayson Samuel."

The detectives listened intently as Samuel spoke. "I have the news you're waiting for. Cosby Davis's body will be exhumed Friday morning at six a.m. It shouldn't take long, and since we have an interment Thursday at noon, our backhoe will already be in place. We'll position it at Cosby Davis's grave, so that we can start right on time."

There was a pause. Mo said. "You're going to have a backhoe at Cosby Davis's grave Thursday afternoon, so that the digging can take place promptly at six a.m., Friday morning. Have I got that right?"

"That's correct."

"Thank you, I'll make sure a couple of agents will be there."

"You're welcome. I'm happy to help the FBI."

Samuel hung up and he let out a sigh of relief.

"That was great," Dan said. "We'll see you Friday morning."

No sooner had Samuel hung up than Mo called his boss.

"Vin, we're in," Mo shouted. "It's happening. You gotta get up here. Davis's grave is being dug up Friday morning, and here's the good part: the backhoe is going to be at the cemetery Thursday afternoon. We can get in there that night and do the job ourselves."

"Shit, Mo. You *do* have a head on those big-ass shoulders. What's that music? You at the Hi-Hat?"

"Been here the past couple of days, gotta tell you, the chicks here are better than the ones in New Orleans. Boozer hooked us up with Jasmine and Cookie."

"Damn, who said you could sample the merchandise? You pay up?"

"Gotta go Vin, see you soon."

"Hold on, you baboon, where you stayin' at?"

"Hotel Weaver, we have a suite."

"All right, so listen. I'm comin' up. I'm gonna get Johnny, Queeno, and Sanch. We'll be up Thursday morning."

"Bring heat, just in case. We gotta go shoppin. I ain't getting the Calvin's dirty."

"Get some shovels, too."

"Okay, Vin. Gotta go now, Jasmine's doing a show."

Willingham was in Syms's office as Dan and Scotty returned from their mission. "Done," Dan said. "The backhoe will be dropped off at the cemetery early Thursday afternoon, but Samuel hasn't a clue that he won't be needed Friday morning."

"Good work." Willingham said as he got up to leave. "I have to get back with Dobbs, Thanks again boys."

Dan shut Sym's door after Willingham departed. "Boy's?" Dan said. "So now we're boys. I still think he's dirty."

"Right," Syms replied. "I suppose Dobbs is dirty too."

The captain looked at Scotty. "Getting a little paunchy, you eating all your muffins? I know I haven't seen any lately."

Scotty laughed. "Hey. Sally uses up a lot of my energy, makes me weak at the knees and I don't have the strength to bake anymore."

"Maybe you can crawl on your knees to unemployment then."

"That reminds me" Dan said as he leaned on Scotty. "You lovebirds have a good time at the museum?"

"It was okay. Had a better time back at her place, she showed me her paintings. She's working on a horse picture."

Dan grinned. "I told you there was another stud in her life."

"Cut the small talk," Syms said as he gave Dan a scornful look. "Get the dig out of your head. You ain't going."

Dan slammed his hand on Sym's desk. "We have to be there. Dobbs can't do this to us," he said.

"Yes, he can," Syms replied.

"Bull. He can't stop us from going. It's a public cemetery, isn't it?"

"You're talking crazy Dan. Now drop it."

Scotty said, "Dan's right. He can't stop us from being there. We can be nearby and observe."

Syms reached for his tablets and stared at Scotty. "I thought you were the level-headed one, but I can see that you've been around him too long. He's got you fucked up too."

The captain pointed at Dan. "I'm telling you: you're not going. As a matter of fact, I don't want to see your faces until it's over. Take the rest of the week off. You get your asses out of my sight. I don't care if you stay around here sweeping floors or if you go home. Just you don't pull any horseshit, or I'm promising that neither one of you will be working here next week."

"Okay. You win," Dan replied.

The detectives left the room. "We're going pal. We're going," Dan said. "Be here Thursday around seven p.m. It won't be dark yet, but I'm sure Martinez won't be coming until nine or later. Meet me across the street. We're taking a cab to the cemetery."

"What about Syms? He will fire us."

Dan placed his hands on Scotty's shoulder. "Don't worry about him. If you didn't know by now, he's more smoke than fire, and he would have fired me long before now, if he had any intention to do so."

Chapter 60

Vinnie Martinez and three of his gang members had arrived and they were ready to get their money. They waited in Mo's suite at the Weaver hotel. "Been to that fucking cemetery before. Santiago, and a few other bro's are there." Vinnie said.

"Should be dark enough after nine," Mo said.

"Yeah, let's chill," Vinnie said. "Keep off the booze."

Frankie held a toothpick in his hand. "How bout hangin at the Hi-Hat?"

Mo laughed. "Man you are a pervert. Jasmine and Cookie didn't show you enough of a good time?"

"Hey, just thinkin about Johnny, Queeno, and Sanch."

"Know what?" Vinnie said. "You idiots stay here, me and Mo are going to pay Boozer a visit."

Boozer jumped out from behind the bar when he saw Vinnie and Mo. "How's it going here, since Flores got whacked?" Vinnie said.

"Good. I think business is up. I hired a couple of new girls"

Vinnie looked at the stage. "Wow, who the hell is that fine ass?"

"Sasha. Hell of an employee," Boozer said with a smile.

"Jasmine and Cookie ain't no slouches either," Mo said.

"So, I know you ain't here for the show," Boozer said. "What's happening?"

"Thanks for tipping me about Flores. We had to take him out." Mo said. "You understand right?"

"Shit. This place runs like a charm without him. He was getting worse every day" Boozer laughed. "Sure made a mess of the alley."

"Hey, we can't stay, just wanted to check out things. We'll be leaving tonight. You stay in touch." Vinnie said.

Vinnie and Mo headed back to the hotel to wait until it was time to strike it rich. "How about that Boozer? I may have to give him a bonus."

"Wait until he sees Honey."

Vinnie looked at Mo as the chauffer drove the caddy. "What makes you think I'm sending Honey up here? Best piece I ever had. She's livin with me."

⅄

Dobbs's plan began to unfold as the backhoe had been delivered on time, and it was placed to the left of Cosby Davis's marker.

The heavily treed cemetery at the end of a dead-end street gave Willingham's unit plenty of hiding places. The Special Forces team arrived in three vehicles, parking them all inside the red barn across the street. Two of his men set up lights between trees on opposite sides of the grave while the rest of the crew carried their weapons and took up positions all around the burial grounds. Willingham played lookout at the entrance.

Halfway down the street, a note in the window of a Chevy Malibu read :*Transmission Broken. Will be back tomorrow with tow.*

Dan and Scotty showed up at the cab company. Dan had on jeans, a blue Giants sweat, and a Yankees cap. Scotty wore Levi's, a black jacket and his Red Sox cap.

"Hard to believe we're on the same team," Dan said. He walked over to the dispatcher. "We need a ride to City Cemetery."

"Gotcha, Go outside to number 516; Malik will take you."

They entered the cab. "Where to?" the driver said in a Middle Eastern accent.

"City Cemetery," Dan replied.

"You been there before?" Scotty asked Dan.

"I had to attend a funeral there once, how about you?"

"Many times, I grew up a couple of miles away."

When Malik got within two blocks of the cemetery, Scotty said. "Stop. Let us off here."

The cab pulled over to the curb and the detectives got out. "How much?" Dan asked.

"Eight sixty-five."

Dan looked at Scotty. "Pay the man."

"Me?" All I have is my emergency twenty."

"That will cover it, He deserves a hefty tip."

"We can walk down this side street and cut through a backyard. There's a red barn across from the cemetery. I think we can hide there." Scotty said.

Dan balked. "What if Willingham's guys are in there?"

"Then I guess we're dead meat. I'm game if you are?"

"Come on pal. Show me the way."

They walked down the adjacent street to the cemetery as dusk was setting in. Looking like anything but police, the detectives casually strolled down the sidewalk. Several cars drove past them and a couple of strangers walking their dogs said hello as the two men in baseball caps passed by. Midway down the street Scotty saw an alley and they headed down a path that brought them to a fence that bordered the cemetery.

"There's the barn to our left. Let's hop this fence." Dan said.

Quietly, in the near darkness, they went over the short fence, and snuck to the back of the barn. They peeked inside the red building and both men breathed a sigh of relief. "Willingham's vehicles are in here. You can bet his guys are across the street hiding in those bushes, and up the hill behind the trees," Dan said.

"Let's stay here, out of sight, until it's time."

Daylight had vanished. Around nine-fifty, two sets of headlights appeared. The vehicles came slowly down the street and pulled into the cemetery. Willingham saw the cars from his spotter's position and he radioed his men. "They're here."

Both sets of headlights illuminated the area as the vehicles neared the target. "I see the digger," Mo said. He pulled up as close to the grave as he could get, Martinez's vehicle right behind, veered to the left so that both sets of lights were on the grave. All the men exited the vehicles. Martinez pointed to the digger. "Johnny, get on that thing and let's get going."

"Vin, the keys are in it. This should be a piece of cake."

Martinez watched as Johnny cranked up the machine and lowered the scooper into the ground. It removed a few piles of dirt, and Johnny scattered the loose clay around the grave. It only took a few minutes before the casket was in sight. He shut down the backhoe, hopped out and picked up a shovel, joining Queeno, and Sanch. They cleared the dirt from the sides and began lifting the heavy box out of the hole. Mo, and Frankie, sans the Calvin Klein's, grabbed the handles and they set the casket down beside the open trench.

"Damn, never knew ten million could be so heavy," Frankie said.

Eager to open the pine box, Martinez lifted the top.

Suddenly, floodlights shone upon the criminals. "Get down on the ground now!" Willingham shouted.

Martinez, Queeno, Johnny, and Sanch all hit the turf, but Mo and Frankie had other plans. Mo took a few steps toward his Caddy, reached in and grabbed his gun. "Fuck, I'm never going back to prison. I'd rather hang."

Before he could fire his weapon, a shot rang out from a sniper's rifle, and Mo dropped to the ground, dead as a doornail.

Frankie took his gun from his overalls and fired a couple of shots blankly into the bushes before he was hit right between the eyes, a toothpick dangling from his lips.

Martinez, Queeno, Johnny, and Sanch stayed on the ground as Willingham's men rushed them and placed the captives in cuffs.

Martinez watched as Willingham approached the casket. At that moment Dan and Scotty appeared, and the commander saw them. "Damn you guys, I told you to stay away from here!"

"Hey it's a public cemetery," Dan remarked "We came to pay respects."

"You clowns stay back." Willinngham barked.

Willingham peered into the open pine box and he gasped. "What the fuck? Who the hell is this? "

Dan eyed the body. "Holy Jesus, that's Cosby Davis!"

"Davis? How can that be?" a clearly ruffled Willingham said. "Then who the hell was the dead guy we found at Merline's?"

While Willingham and Dan wondered who that man was, the Chevy Malibu that had been parked down the road, now flashing red and blue lights entered the cemetery. Marshall Dobbs hurriedly got out and opened the car's trunk. He unloaded two American Tourister suitcases, one green, the other blue, and placed them on the ground. Dobbs opened the green bag, pulled out a wad of cash, and held it in the air. "Vinnie, is this what you were looking for?"

"You go to hell, you fucking bastard."

Dan turned to Scotty. "I knew the money wasn't in there."

Willingham's men lowered the casket back into the ground and covered it with dirt. "Samuel can finish the job in the morning," he said.

Dobbs gave the suitcases to Willingham to be held for evidence, and the cuffed renegades were ready to be taken to the Hartford jail. "Take care of these suitcases Ted. I have to catch a flight back to D.C."

"Wait," Willingham said. "So you knew Cosby Davis was in this casket?"

"I did."

"So who the hell was that dead guy at the Merline's?"

"Just some homeless guy. It was the only way to bait Martinez into coming for the money. You guys take care of the cash."

Dan, Scotty and Willingham were all caught off-guard by Dobbs.

"Hey," Dan said to Willingham. "Can Scotty and I hitch a ride back with you?"

"We gotta get these bodies out of here. My guys can wrap up here and clear the area. Follow me. My van is in that red barn across the street. Take those suitcases," Willingham said. "If you touch that money, I'll shoot you both. Martinez and the other gangsters will be in the vehicle right behind us."

⅄

Several police officers were at the jailhouse to process the captives. Captain Syms was there, too. Willingham escorted Martinez, and the three other detainees to the booking area. Not far behind were Dan and Scotty, each lugging a suitcase. Willingham pointed to the detectives. "Captain, I think these last two belong to you."

"What the fuck? You former employees, drop the luggage and get up to my office now!"

They all marched down the hallway and upstairs while Syms started his tirade. "God damn it Dan. If Hardison hears about this, we're all fired. And Scotty, you would jump off the Brooklyn Bridge if Dan told you to. We're all gonna be canned."

⊁

They reached the captain's office. "Close the fucking door. I don't want the walls to cave in."

"Captain."

"What is it, Dan? You want your pink slip now?"

"We still have unfinished business."

The captain was fuming. "You bet we do!"

"No, Harold, you don't understand."

Syms put his face close to Dan's "Don't you call me Harold! It's 'Captain' to you!"

The captain retreated to his chair, and picked up his giant bottle of pills. "See these? You're the damn reason I have them."

"Captain, listen! We have Martinez and the money. Dobbs had the cash all along inside those suitcases."

Syms downed a few tablets and took a deep breath. "So what's in the casket?"

Still standing Dan said. "Not what, sir. Who."

"So, who's in the casket?"

"Cosby Davis."

Syms jaw dropped, and he uttered "What? How can that be?"

"That's what we wanna know."

Syms stood and his fist once again pounded his bruised desk. "*Bullshit!* Who's that chief medical examiner?

"Max Arnstein," Dan replied.

"Get that son of a bitch out of bed if you have to. He told us the body he identified was Cosby Davis, and I want that coroner's ass down here *now!*"

Scotty called the University Medical Center, and obtained Arnstein's home phone number.

"Let me have that," Syms said.

He dialed the number and Arnstein picked up his phone. "Hello."

"Arnstein, this is Captain Syms"

"Is this an emergency?"

"You bet your ass it's an emergency. Explain to me how you could identify a body as Cosby Davis and it wasn't Cosby Davis. Get your fucking behind down here right now."

"Captain, it's after midnight."

"You bet it is, and I can have a squad car there in ten minutes to pick you up."

"I'm on my way."

"Damn right! You better speed your god-damned butt down here."

The rudely wakened, mussy haired coroner, barreled into the livid Syms's office about half an hour later. Stress written all over his tired face, and his shirt pulled out of his pants, Arnstein faced the captain. "Have a seat," Syms ordered. "I'm going to try to restrain myself."

The medical examiner nervously tapped his sneakers on the floor, while Dan and Joe sat back to listen. With fire in his eyes Syms peered at Arnstein "Not to be disrespectful, but how the hell do you tell us that you identified a body as Cosby Davis, when you know damn well it wasn't him! What the fuck is going on?"

The coroner clenched his sweating hands, and he looked pleadingly at Syms. "It's true, I told you and the press it was Cosby Davis's corpse. It goes against every moral principle I have, but just after the body got to the lab, a federal agent named Dobbs called me. He came to the morgue later that day and said the body was part of a federal investigation, and that the true identity had to be kept secret. He ordered me to tell you that the victim's name was Cosby Davis."

"So you made up that story about the wallet and DNA?"

"I had to."

"So who's the dead guy?"

"His name is Armando Jenkins."

The air went out of the room as Dan, Joe and Syms couldn't believe what they'd just heard. "Jenkins?" Dan said. "Son of a bitch, that's why we couldn't locate him. He was dead."

"God damn it Arnstein, Do you realize the shit we've been through?" Syms said.

The coroner was speechless.

"I think we've all had a long night. Let's get out of here." Syms said." I have to get back with Willingham."

"We have to," Dan said.

"Come on."

The captain turned to Arnstein. "Go home. You can't help us now."

Dan, Scotty, and their beloved captain trooped downstairs to see Willingham.

⋏

"Where's Dobbs?" Syms asked. "I want to talk to that bastard."

"He said he had to catch a flight back to D.C." Willingham replied. "He's gone."

"Gone? Don't you find that a little strange? He's been after Martinez all this time and he just takes off after he finally nabs him?"

"Maybe, but the money is in a couple of suitcases we took to the evidence room."

At that moment, a frenzied uniformed officer burst into the booking area. "Captain, you have to get down to the evidence room right away!"

"What for?"

"Burgess said it's urgent."

Syms turned to Dan and Scotty "Go see what he wants."

The detectives ran down the hall, a flight of stairs, and entered the evidence room. What's wrong?" Dan asked Burgess.

The frenzied evidence room custodian looked up in disbelief. "It's the money... It's counterfeit!"

"That's impossible!" Dan said.

"I don't think so. Look at these serial numbers. They're all the same."

"God damn it!" Dan said "It's Dobbs. Let's go."

He and Scotty ran back to Syms. "Dobbs is a crooked bastard, "a slightly winded Dan yelled. "The money he handed over is counterfeit. He has the ten million."

Syms stared at Willingham. "How the hell do you think he got fake money?"

Instantly, Dan remembered seeing that framed hundred dollar bill. "Holy shit. Now it all fits! It's Merline," Dan said. "He's in on it. He wasn't kidding—that framed hundred dollar bill hanging over his fireplace was literally the first one he ever made. He's a printer, prints forms and stuff—stuff like money! Son of a bitch, we've all been had."

Syms picked up a phone. "I'm calling Rich Carroll to tell him to head up to Merline's, and that we'll be there as soon as we can."

Willingham called Dobbs's cell number. "He's not answering. Son of a bitch. His voice mail says he's on vacation. Leave a message."

"God damn it!" Syms barked.

"Jesus," Dan said. "What are the odds that Merline went on vacation, too?"

State Trooper Carroll sped to the Merlines' house. When he arrived, the place was quiet, dark, and he saw no one. He rushed to the front door with his flashlight in hand and knocked, but there was no answer. No Buster, no movement at all. Carroll went to the rear door and shined his light. There he found a note: *Gone to Disneyland.*

CHAPTER 61

M arshall Dobbs had tired of a job that paid him several times less than the CEO of a business conglomerate. Now he was set to retire comfortably. The resourceful DEA director had skillfully carried out his plan, killing two birds with one stone.

Dobb's informant Armando Jenkins had driven the U-Haul and planted the suitcases at the airport. Jenkins also had driven Dobbs to the Merlines' in a rented SUV the night Will said he was in Maine. It was true Amanda and the kids were in Boothbay Harbor, but Will and Buster stayed home. Preacher Ferguson had indeed heard Buster.

Jenkins had been fully expecting his fair share of the ten million-dollar reward for his work, but Dobbs had other plans for him.

After Dobbs and Will had strangled Jenkins, they carried his body up the hill and placed him face down in the swampy grave. Dobbs drove the rented vehicle away, and later that night Amanda and the kids returned home. Covertly, Dobbs had watched the detectives' and Martinez's every step. His most brilliant move was instructing Max Arnstein to release the name of the corpse as Cosby Davis, not revealing the true identity...Armando Jenkins.

λ

Dobbs enjoyed his overnight Alitalia flight from LaGuardia to his new home in Florence. He stopped in the concourse to grab a cappuccino, and proceeded to the baggage area, where he retrieved his two new suitcases. He spotted a taxi driver holding up a sign with his name, and he knew his ride had arrived.

This beautiful sunny day was everything that Dobbs could have hoped for. As the overloaded Fiat headed for the serene hills of Tuscany, he viewed the landscape and knew it wouldn't be long before he reached his recently purchased villa.

The Fiat pulled into the long winding driveway, and Dobbs had finally arrived at his retirement home. An orchard, a vineyard, and ten million dollars: what more could anyone want? He had left his pension behind, but he didn't care; with enough money to last a lifetime, he looked forward to living the easy life.

The rest of the Dobbs family had flown in a couple of days ago. As he exited the vehicle, the family dog, carrying a red ball in his mouth, welcomed him. "Hey Buster. Good boy."

Next to greet him were his grandchildren, Alex and Zack. "Hi, grandpa," they said.

"Tomorrow, I'm going to buy you boy's new bikes."

Lastly, standing in the driveway were Will and Amanda Dobbs Merline.

"Dad, how was your trip? Are you hungry?"

"The flight was wonderful, and if you wouldn't mind, I could use some vino, bread, and cheese. Will, would you bring in my bags?"

The always-loyal coworker and son-in-law brought the luggage inside. Dobbs pointed to the blue, government issued suitcases. "Amanda, the one on the left is yours. It's the rest of your inheritance."

EPILOGUE

Dan had taken a year off to spend time with his family, and he planned to go back to work after Labor Day. The Shields house was ready for their holiday barbecue.

Guests began to arrive. A healed Kim Patton, her divorce finalized from Marty a couple of months ago, and Harold Syms arrived with Chief Hardison. Bev, her husband, and the twins were there. Connie, Phyllis, and Kate were bringing food out, while Josh showed his karate moves to Captain Syms.

They were all gathered out back by the pool when the final guests made their way to the festivities: Joe Scott, Eli Scott, Sally Grennon Scott, and the youngest invitee, a baby girl with soft red hair named Brianna.

Scotty and Dan settled into chairs by the pool. They each had a Heineken in their hand.

"How's married life?" Dan asked. "Sally looks good."

"Everything's great."

Dan opened his beer. "I see you've been eating well. Looks like you've put on about ten pounds."

"That's what I like about you. You have a keen eye for the obvious, and if you didn't notice, there's a Tupperware full of muffins on the table."

"Eli's getting big," Dan said.

Scotty beamed, grabbed a few chips, and took a gulp of beer. "He lives with us now."

Dan smiled. "Nice. One big happy family."

"How's everyone doing here?"

"Terrific. Phyllis loves her job, but unfortunately you'll be seeing my face at headquarters soon."

Scotty spotted Kate. "Look at that little girl."

Dan smiled again. "Kate's been invited to the Junior Olympic gymnastics trials. She's some competitor."

"What about Mike? Where is he?"

Dan nearly choked on a chip. "He's sort of good news and bad news."

"What's that mean?"

Dan had a strange look on his face as he turned to Scotty. "Are you ready for this? He was All-American at ASU, and was selected in the second round of the baseball draft."

"That's great isn't it?"

"Not around here it isn't. . . he was taken by the *Red Sox*!

THE END